HIS CURVY DISTRACTION

A SMALL TOWN CURVY GIRL ROMANCE

BOOK BOYFRIENDS WANTED
BOOK 17

MARY E THOMPSON

BOOK BOYFRIENDS WANTED

Come in and visit MacKellar Cove. You will get to see all the things that make this small town a truly special place to be. There's the bookstore and the local bar. There's the bakery and town square. And there's love all around. Grab a drink, a slice of cake, and get to know your next book boyfriend and book best friend! Never miss a thing when you sign up for Mary's newsletter.

Romancing the Curves comes with subscriber exclusive freebies, sneak peeks, and a first look at everything Mary has to offer. Be the first to know about new releases and sales and all the curves ahead!

SUBSCRIBE NOW AT MARYETHOMPSON.COM

Happy reading!

For L...

1

OMAR

Do. Not. Get. Hard. Do not. Keep it together, Omar. Do not thrust yourself against her hand. Bad idea.

The flash of the camera just behind Natalie Edwards, on her knees in front of me as I tried to pull up my pants, was the reminder I needed that I was the damn mayor of MacKellar Cove.

I looked up at the photographer, a man I didn't recognize, but he clearly knew who I was. The smirk on his face when he looked at his phone said the picture looked so much worse than the reality of the situation.

"Hey," I barked, drawing the man's attention.

He jerked his head in my direction, smirked at Natalie, then turned to go back into the crowd.

I started to follow him, then remembered the beautiful woman on her knees. I saw when she walked out of the bathroom and the guy rushing by slammed into her. When I reached for her, she fell, and she grabbed on to me. But she still hit the ground, hard.

"Are you okay?" I asked, my need to find the asshole who

took our picture warring with my need to make sure she wasn't hurt.

Her hazel eyes widened under that curtain of bangs I wanted to brush out of her face so I could get a good look at her. She cradled her hand to her chest and looked up at me, those doe eyes doing almost as much to my dick as her hand did.

Although her eyes hurt a lot less than her fist.

"I'm so sorry."

I shook my head. "It's fine. You couldn't help it. But I need to find whoever took that picture and make sure it doesn't end up ruining my re-election. Are you going to be okay?"

She nodded, reaching for the wall to brace herself as she stood.

I took her other hand and helped her up. Those bangs slid back, revealing more of her face when she looked up at me.

For a minute, we were alone. The bar vanished, the outside world melted away. It was just the two of us in that hallway, her beautiful eyes staring up at me and my brain telling me kissing her was a very, very good idea.

"You're huge." The way her eyes widened before she slammed them shut said she didn't mean to say that. "I meant tall. You're tall. I'm used to looking at kids, not adults, and you're really big. Tall. I need to go."

Before I could reply, she was gone, disappearing into the crowd just like the photographer.

Dammit. I needed to find him.

I dove into the crowd, searching for the man with the picture of Natalie and me. Hudson Grant, the owner of O'Kelley's and a good man, was behind the bar. I approached.

"Mr. Mayor," Hudson said when he saw me. He didn't let anyone else serve me if he was there.

"I told you to call me Omar."

"We'll see. What can I get for you?"

"I'm looking for a man. About my height, brown hair, maybe late twenties. Flannel shirt and jeans. Have you seen him?"

Hudson's brows climbed higher with each word of my description. "Uh, I saw a guy matching that very detailed description walk out a few seconds ago. Do you—?"

"Thanks!" I rushed toward the door, not listening for the rest of Hudson's question.

I sidestepped around people and waved to a few who tried to stop me, then burst out into the cool evening. I looked left and right and saw a man strolling toward Catherine Park.

I instantly regretted my choice of shoes, but I had no choice. I took off after the guy, hoping I could catch up to him and talk him into deleting that photo.

He stopped to cross the street, then jogged across to the park.

I was a few steps behind him when he stepped off the curb. I hurried across with him, then spoke. "I need you to get rid of that picture."

He startled, spinning to me with his hands up to defend himself.

I took a step back and held my hands up. "Whoa. I know you know who I am. I just want to talk to you."

The guy looked around, realizing how alone we were. "What do you want?" His voice cracked with the question, the bravado from the bar gone.

"I just want you to delete that picture."

"Why should I?"

My mind raced with reasons, but if he was willing to take the picture in the first place, it was unlikely those reasons would convince him to delete it. "I can pay you."

His brows went up, and the smirk came back.

Fuck. Wrong answer.

"If you'll pay me, someone else probably will, too."

"That picture... What you think you saw wasn't what you saw."

He smiled and crossed his arms. "What do you think I think I saw?"

I opened my mouth to argue but quickly shut it. Admitting anything would only give him more fuel.

A different tactic might work.

"The woman runs a summer camp program. Something like that could ruin her."

The guy shook his head. "You can't tell who she is. The only face visible is yours, Mr. Mayor."

"I don't believe you."

The guy started to reach into his pocket, but he stopped.

Dammit.

"I'm not going to fall for that. But I will keep your offer in mind."

"That picture isn't going to be good for anyone."

"It'll be good for me. Think of how much I can make with it. A nice night out with my girl. Good Christmas present for her. I think I'm going to hang on to this picture for a little while."

"That's a bad idea."

He smirked and shook his head. "I don't think it is. But you have a good night, Mr. Mayor."

I wanted to throttle the little dipshit, but that would only make things worse. Instead, I stood there while he walked away and took my hopes of getting elected mayor with him.

Explaining something like that to the residents of MacKellar Cove was going to be nearly impossible. I was the interim mayor. Temporary. Only there because the last mayor was a misogynistic jackass who tried to fire the woman who ran the tourism department.

And now someone had a picture of me in a public place with a woman on her knees in front of me. I didn't look any better than the last guy.

Which meant I was going to lose the election. Unless I got that picture back.

Because I wanted to be mayor. I wanted to be elected. I was good at my job. And keeping it meant continuing to serve my adopted hometown and the people who lived there.

Including the woman who put me in that position.

I scoured social media and the local paper for weeks, past Thanksgiving and into December, and saw absolutely no sign of the picture. I met with the town's legal counsel and was told there was nothing they could do since it was a personal matter and not a town matter. I considered calling Ramsey Holland, who was an acquaintance and a local lawyer, but decided against it. Ramsey was well-connected and could easily become as much of a risk. I didn't expect it from him, but I also didn't know him well enough to be sure.

A knock on my office door brought me out of the latest attempt to find the man who took the picture. I called out for Jane, my assistant, to enter.

"Mr. Mayor, you have a visitor. Ms. Rucker from the community center asked if you're available."

I nodded and waved for Jane to let Amelia in. Amelia

and I had worked together on a few projects and I found her to be friendly and as much of an advocate for the center as she was the kids it served.

"Good morning, Amelia. How are you?" I asked, standing and extending my hand to her. A man I didn't recognize followed her into my office.

"I apologize for barging in, Omar, but Harry stopped by this morning and I wanted to make sure we spoke to you about his proposal."

I smiled at Amelia and Harry, curious about what the man had to say. He appeared close to sixty with a sprinkle of gray hair at his temples that circled the back of his head. He wore faded jeans and a flannel shirt, a nod to the chilly winter that sank into the area over the last few weeks.

"Nice to meet you, Harry. What can I do for you?"

"You, too, Mr. Mayor. Um, so I went to see Amelia, and she insisted we come straight here. I didn't realize this was such a big deal." Harry glanced at Amelia, who grinned widely at him.

"Tell Omar what you told me. About the campground."

Campground? They definitely had my curiosity piqued.

"I own the property where Mountain View Campground used to be. It hasn't been open in a while, a decade maybe?" Harry looked at Amelia to confirm, and she nodded. "Anyway, my wife and I held on to the property, trying to decide what to do with it. We had plans, but we're getting older, and now we're moving away, leaving the cold behind and heading out west to where our kids live, but we love MacKellar Cove. We loved having kids up at the campground, and families, and we hate the idea of it just being destroyed and sold to some developer who will ruin everything the place used to be. You know?"

I nodded. It didn't happen as often in MacKellar Cove,

but it still happened. The area was beautiful, but relatively untouched. Perfect for the right developer, and keeping them out of the area and maintaining the quaint, small-town feel was important.

"My wife and I want to donate the campground. Thought it would be a great place for the community center to use. I suggested summer camp, and Amelia got really excited."

My brows shot up. A former campground as a summer camp? It definitely sounded perfect.

"What I was thinking," Amelia said, "was we could relocate the new program that Natalie Edwards started up last summer. She did all the outdoor stuff, and her camp was massively popular with the older kids. She wanted to expand, but she's at the community center, so there's not a lot of space. But if she took over the campground, she could take a lot more kids, and we could expand what we do at the community center."

My mind stalled on Natalie's name, and it took me a minute to catch the rest of what Amelia said. "Is there a need for that?"

Amelia nodded, her smile fading. "We've already had some families reach out. It's more than six months to summer, but the parents who work full-time need options. We had to turn some away last year, and a lot of them had to find spots in other programs out of town."

"That's not what we want."

Amelia shook her head. "No, it's not. But there's only so much we can do. With this property, we can do more."

"Have you spoken to Ms. Edwards about it?"

Amelia shook her head again. "No. I wanted to speak to you first. Make sure you were okay with it. It's a big plan, and since Natalie's camp is under our umbrella, it's a town program. She has her own budget under the community center since she's fulfilling a part of our need, but she falls under my cost center. There's no way we can afford all the work Harry said it needs."

And there it was. The reason they came to me. Money.

"I know, I know," Amelia said. "There's no budget. I get it. But this will pay for itself. And since Harry wants to donate the property, all we need to pay for are the repairs and updates."

I nodded. It was the best deal around. Free land. But if it cost more to update it than we had available, and more than we could get back out of it, did it make sense? "What does the property look like?" I asked Harry.

"It's just over five acres. There were hookups for thirty campers, but they're all disconnected. Need to be removed, though. There's an old camper we used as an office that's in okay shape. It's not pretty, but it's functional. Needs to be cleaned probably since no one's been there in a long time. There's a lot of recreation space. A pool that hasn't been open in a while but was okay when it was last used, sand volleyball court, and basketball court and whatever other games. A few other things you might want to remove."

"Like?"

"Fire pits, driving paths, picnic tables. There's no water access, which is why the pool is there. It was fenced, but the fence is not up to code and needs to be replaced. The road in and out is gravel. It's... The land is the value, Mr. Mayor. I'm not going to stand here and tell you I'm giving you a prime piece of real estate. It's in rough shape. But I think it could be great. I think it will be great."

The smile on Amelia's face told me she agreed. It was going to be a big job, and one that had the potential to cost more than it was worth. If I agreed, it was something that could define my campaign. Something that could win me the election, or something that could sink my chances faster than a failing pool.

But without risk, there was no reward. And this risk was almost as big as the reward had the potential to be.

"I think it can be great, too."

Amelia squealed.

"But." I met her gaze. "We need to keep an eye on the budget. We need to figure out what it really needs and be smart about what we do."

"I agree. But this is going to be great. Thank you, Omar."

"Yes, thank you, Mr. Mayor. I really appreciate your time and the chance to do this for the town."

"Thank you, Harry. It's very generous of you, and it's a huge thing to give back this way to the town."

"I love this place. I hate to leave it, but I know we'll be back to visit. My oldest just had a baby, and my wife is itching to be out there with their family. Our first grandchild." Harry puffed up like a proud grandfather.

I couldn't help but smile. Even without my own kids, I knew the pride people felt when their family grew. I'd hoped to feel that one day, but it wasn't meant to be for me. Not yet, anyway.

"This will help so many local grandchildren. You'll be like their honorary grandparents," Amelia said. She was good. She knew the right thing to say.

Harry dabbed at his eyes and swallowed hard. "Thank you, Amelia. Thank you so much."

Amelia hugged Harry. "You and Sue make sure you call me before you head out west, okay?"

Harry nodded and moved toward the door. Amelia followed him, then stopped and said she needed another minute with me but would see Harry soon.

"Thanks again, Mr. Mayor."

"Thank you, Harry. Enjoy that grandchild."

"I will. Thanks."

Harry stopped outside my office and spoke to Jane while Amelia approached my desk again.

"The campground is in rough shape. I know that. And I know this is going to be tough, but if anyone can make this happen, it's Natalie. She's amazing, Omar. I don't think you know each other, but she's really passionate about helping kids, and she's a special person. Leaving this in her hands is the right move."

"I've met her a few times, but I don't know her well." My dick still twitched when I thought about her fist wrapped around it. "But if you think she's the right one to lead this, I'm not going to tell you no. I will tell you I meant it when I said we need to watch the budget. No going overboard."

"When have you known me to go overboard?" Amelia asked. She was right.

"You don't, but that doesn't mean Natalie won't. Give me a few days to look at what we have available and what we can spare. We might be operating on credit for some of this until we get the income from the summer camp in."

"We can also do fundraisers and ask the community to help out. There are a lot of people who would be willing to do things like that. We organized a big event in my neighborhood a few years ago. Helped fix up the community center. And every week there's a group that comes and does little projects at the center, even now. This is a great town, Omar, and we can take advantage of it."

I nodded. "Let's see what Natalie comes up with, and we'll go from there. I'll be in touch early next week with a budget, and the three of us can meet to make a plan."

"Sounds great. Thanks, Omar. I'm really excited about this."

"I'm glad it's going to work out."

Amelia shook my hand, then let herself out of my office, stopping to speak to Jane for a few minutes and gush over pictures of Jane's eleven-month-old.

I turned to my computer to come up with a budget for Natalie's new project. Yet again, Natalie Edwards had the potential to make or break the election for me. And she didn't even know it.

2

NATALIE

"Natalie!" Amelia called across the community center. "I need to talk to you!"

I hurried out of the storage room at the back of the basketball court. The panic in her voice put me on edge as I rushed to find her, with a tennis racket in my hand.

"Whoa!" Amelia said, holding her hands up and coming to a halt.

"You scared me. What's wrong?"

"Are you going to hit me with that?" Amelia asked, a smirk telling me she was not worried.

"I was trying to see what we have for activities. I was thinking of a new game I could teach the kids at summer camp. Something that doesn't take up a lot of space since we're limited outside."

"That's what I want to talk to you about. I have a new property for you. A huge one. Where you could do anything you want."

My heart raced as she spoke. I could feel her excitement pulsing through me. "What are you talking about?"

"The meeting I had earlier? A local couple is moving

and wants to donate their campground. To us for use as a summer camp."

"Are you serious?" A campground? That would be a ton of space.

"Yes!" Amelia squealed. "It's perfect. You can do everything you've ever dreamed about doing. You can expand. You can take more kids. There's so much that can be done."

"Wow. That's..." My mind raced with the possibilities. A campground would mean so many options. So many kids we could take. More than I ever thought possible. We could play games and be outside and spread out and—

"Natalie!"

I shook my head, realizing Amelia was talking to me. "Sorry." My cheeks warmed. Amelia knew me well, and she was used to my awkwardness, but I still hated when I went off into my world.

"You don't have to apologize to me, Natalie. I know you're thinking about all the things you can do. But before you get ahead of yourself, it's not perfect."

"Nothing's perfect."

"True, but this place is probably even less perfect. It's five acres, but that's about the only good thing about it from what Harry said. It will need some work to get it into shape for camp, but I think it's possible."

"I don't have the money to do a lot of upgrades." My anxiety ramped up, making the dreams I let filter in slip away just as quickly as I conjured them up.

"Don't worry about that yet. Omar is going to look at the budget and see what the town can afford."

"Omar?" I squeaked. Oh, no. It was bad enough that the man was my boss's boss and could fire me whenever he felt like it, but after the way I manhandled him just a few weeks earlier, there was no way he was going to be on my side for the summer camp.

"I took Harry to meet with Omar earlier. Omar agreed that it's a great option for summer camp, and he's going to come up with a budget for us. Something the town will support since the camp will be under the community center umbrella. It wouldn't be on you to come up with the budget."

"Okay. But if there's that much work, do you think I can actually do it?"

Amelia grabbed my hands and held them together, hers on the outside of mine. She waited until I looked up at her. "Honey, listen, it's a lot. I know it's a lot. But I know you are only thinking about the kids. It's worth it for the kids. It's worth it to go to Omar and hear what he has to say. And if he doesn't have enough of a budget for us, we will figure out the rest."

"How will we do that?"

"Fundraisers, community events. We can have some of our repair nights out there, too. You know people will help out."

"I don't want charity, Amelia."

"It's not charity, Natalie. It's why we live in a place like MacKellar Cove. We all look out for each other. We are all here for each other. You know this."

"I guess, but I don't like taking from others."

"Let's talk to Omar first, and we'll go from there. But for now, let's just enjoy that you don't have to worry about creating games you can play in small areas. You're going to have five acres to use, Natalie. Including a pool."

"A pool?"

Amelia nodded, her smile growing.

"Okay. I will stay open-minded. It might be worth it to have everyone help out."

"Yes, it will. You're providing a service for the town, Natalie. People appreciate that."

I nodded. She was right. I was told so many times by parents how much their kids loved camp last summer. So much so that they were already trying to sign up for this summer, months before registration was open.

But if I had five acres of space, I could take on three or four times as many kids. I could offer so much more. And I could hire more teenagers to help out and run things.

It was a dream. As long as it was in the budget.

It would be. It had to be. It was for the kids. There was no way even a scrooge like Mayor Knight would say no to something for the kids of MacKellar Cove.

My best friend and roommate, Daisy Lincoln, was just as excited as I was about the campground. We spent the entire weekend dreaming about things we could do to the property.

"Ooh, look at this," Daisy said, turning her computer toward me. She looked up the site online and was pulling up satellite pictures and old photographs of the place. "The pool is nice."

I nodded, staring at the screen. The old pictures of Mountain View Campground were stunning. It was a campground, sure, but it was beautiful. Wide open spaces with lots of room for activities. Volleyball and basketball. The pool was ideal.

I just wondered what it looked like now. "It was great."

Daisy laughed. "Oh, just wait. It'll be amazing."

"You can't possibly think that. Why would someone give this place away if it was in amazing condition? Amelia said it's in rough shape. I'm sure it's horrible."

"And if it is, we'll fix it up. We'll make it perfect."

"There's no such thing as perfect," I told her.

Daisy waved her hand, always dismissing my pessimistic attitude. I wasn't sure why we worked, but she adopted me as her best friend the day we moved into our college dorm. Daisy was happy and bright and optimistic about everything. She dated constantly and was the happiest person I knew.

As opposed to me, where I was anxious, tense, and expected the worst in every situation. Daisy made me believe not everyone was bad, but it was not a lesson I had an easy time learning.

One I still wasn't sure I learned when it came to men.

"When is your meeting with the mayor?" Daisy asked, bringing the one man I had the hardest time with to the front of my mind.

"Tuesday. Amelia said he was coming up with a budget, and we needed to see what we could do after that."

"So, come up with a plan. Figure out what you can do, what you want to do. The pool is a must. It'll be amazing for the kids. And you need to have clear space for the activities. The basketball and volleyball courts will be great. And parking for employees and parents. Ooh, what about a tennis court or a soccer field? I mean, with five acres, you could do just about anything. A huge sheltered area would be great to get the kids out of the sun, too. Picnic tables and a grill, so you can do lunch for the campers once a week or something. There are so many things you could do."

I nodded, imagining all of it. It would be amazing. I

couldn't wait to get out there and see what the place looked like and jump in and make it exactly what I wanted.

"I might not be able to do all of it, but it would be amazing. Eventually."

"Of course. Eventually." Daisy flipped through more pictures and dreamed with me until my phone dinged with a message. "Is that him?"

My cheeks warmed with her teasing tone. I'd been talking to a guy online. I never thought I'd be one for online dating, but it gave me a chance to slow down and gather my thoughts before I replied.

Not that it led to an instant connection. I'd met a few of the guys I spoke to online and it did not work out, but the latest match made me feel like I wasn't such an oddity.

I grabbed my phone from the coffee table and smiled.

"What did he say?" Daisy asked. She was happy for me, even though there was nothing to be happy about. We were talking, not engaged.

I read the message and shook my head. "He asked what my favorite time of day is."

"He has a weird way of flirting," Daisy said, scrunching her nose. She was cute, blonde and curvy and always smiling and laughing. She drew the attention of men wherever we went.

"We're getting to know each other."

"As long as you like him, that's what matters."

I got up from the couch so I could talk to him without feeling like Daisy was hovering. "I'm going to go talk to him."

"Have fun." Daisy grabbed the remote and turned on the TV.

I went to my room and closed the door, crawling under the blankets to talk to him.

THISISAWKWARD

I love late at night. I have a roommate, and she's my best friend, but she's a morning person. I'm more quiet than she is, and at night when she slows down, I feel like I can breathe a little better.

BIGCITYCONVERT

Same. Not the roommate part, but the slowing down and able to breathe part.

THISISAWKWARD

What do you like to do in the evenings?

BIGCITYCONVERT

Go for a drive. I love to get out and clear my head. What about you?

THISISAWKWARD

I'm not a car person. I prefer to sit and read a book. Something quiet. Something alone. I spend a lot of time with people during the day and like to have time alone at night.

BIGCITYCONVERT

Me, too. I work in a busy place, but driving has always been a way for me to clear my head. Head up the river and find a small place for something to eat.

THISISAWKWARD

Favorite food?

BIGCITYCONVERT

Tough question. There's not much I don't like, but I think favorite is anything on the grill. It's a treat I don't get to enjoy often.

THISISAWKWARD

We don't ever grill. I like it. Reminds me of my childhood. My dad loved to grill in the summer.

BIGCITYCONVERT

Did you grow up in the area?

I hesitated. We hadn't shared a lot of personal information. We'd been talking for a month, and it made sense he was pushing to learn more.

I drew a breath and answered.

THISISAWKWARD

A little north, but yeah, in the Thousand Islands. You?

BIGCITYCONVERT

No, not even close. Down state, closer to NYC.

THISISAWKWARD

What brought you up here?

BIGCITYCONVERT

Vacation with my ex-wife. When we split, I moved up here. I loved it and wanted to come back. Small town feel was exactly what I was looking for.

Ex. Wife. I was not expecting that. I also wasn't sure how I felt about it. He was honest, but was it something I was okay with? Did it mean he had kids? Did it mean he wanted kids?

That was why I didn't date. My brain ran away on me, spiraling without knowing anything.

BIGCITYCONVERT

Did I scare you off with that admission?

THISISAWKWARD

I'm trying to decide.

BIGCITYCONVERT

Thanks for that honesty. Full truth, it's been years. There were a lot of reasons, but at the end of the day, it was not a good marriage. No kids, and no regrets about my marriage ending.

THISISAWKWARD

Thank you for telling me.

BIGCITYCONVERT

Does it give you a little less anxiety about me?

THISISAWKWARD

If you only knew how funny that question was. But yes.

BIGCITYCONVERT

Maybe one day you can tell me.

THISISAWKWARD

Maybe one day.

When I didn't hear from him for a few minutes, I plugged my phone in and got ready for bed, dreaming about all the things I wanted to do for the summer camp.

AMELIA and I met at the community center on Tuesday morning. She was excited about our budget meeting with Mayor Knight, but I was just hoping I didn't throw up.

"Since the snow has stopped, I think we should go out and look at the campground today. I haven't been there in years, but I would love to get a look at it."

"Sounds good," I told her. I was curious about the place, too. I was ready to get started on cleaning it up and making it work for the summer.

Amelia insisted I didn't need to bring anything, so we climbed into her SUV and headed toward town hall. She parked in a visitor space and we hurried inside to beat the chill soaking in through our coats.

Amelia knew everyone. She stopped and talked to half the people we passed, asking how their families were and details about their lives.

I didn't know who any of them were. I smiled awkwardly, not saying anything while she talked. I hated being in social situations. I never knew what to say, and I always felt like I was interrupting, even though I had every reason to be there.

We finally continued to the mayor's office, and Amelia warmly greeted the woman sitting outside the office.

"Jane, how are you? Is your son sleeping better?"

"Oh, Amelia, thank you. You saved us with your tips. I don't know how we can thank you."

"No thanks necessary. It's not easy being a first-time parent. It's been a while, but I remember those days." Amelia smiled.

I stood there, again feeling out of place.

"Jane, is— Oh, Amelia. You're here. Ms. Edwards," the mayor said, appearing out of nowhere.

Mayor Omar Knight was the kind of man that was impossible to ignore. And impossible to relax around.

Amelia didn't seem to feel the same.

"Omar, so good to see you again. Thank you for making time to speak to us." Amelia smiled and winked at Jane, then followed Mayor Knight into his office.

I followed behind them like a child going to work with her parents.

Amelia took a seat and wasted no time asking Mayor

Knight about the budget. "What are we working with, Omar?"

Omar drew a breath and gave her a number that made Amelia suck in a breath.

"I know it's not as much as you were likely hoping, but it's the best we can do right now."

"Omar, you know that's barely going to be enough to do the minimum. We need more money," Amelia argued.

"I told you I wasn't sure we could afford much."

"You and I both know we can do better. This is for the residents of MacKellar Cove. The summer camp helps out the working families with kids in school. The families that need kids somewhere safe."

"Amelia, I don't really know what else to say."

"Say you'll do better."

He groaned softly. His gaze cut to mine and held. "What plans do you have for the campground? I understand you'll be the one running it."

I opened and closed my mouth and looked at Amelia. I wasn't prepared with a proposal. I didn't have any idea of what I wanted to do.

But Amelia nodded, silently telling me to speak.

I thought back to the things Daisy and I spoke about and channeled my best friend.

"The pool needs to be repaired so we can use it. The kids will love it. And the courts fixed up. A large covered area with picnic tables for a place to sit out of the sun during lunch, and for when the weather isn't so great. And a paved lot for cars would be ideal. Maybe a soccer field, tennis courts. Lots of space for the kids to run around and play and enjoy their summer."

Mayor Knight stared at me like I was out of my mind.

His gaze hardened with every suggestion I made. "There's no way all of that is in the budget."

"She's talking big picture, Omar. Not right now. We know it'll take time to get to that point."

"But it's for the kids. This is going to help the town and give the kids a safe place to be. We have to do whatever it takes."

"No," he said.

Well, crap.

3

———————

WHAT A HEARTLESS JERK! HE HAD NO COMPASSION. NO vision. No sympathy. Did he think all kids were given these opportunities? I knew from personal experience they were not. There were tons of kids in MacKellar Cove who only went outside during recess at school. Kids who only ate when they were at school. Kids who didn't have someone at home looking out for them.

Amelia and I created a place for those kids. We gave them the kind of summer kids should have. And now we were being given the opportunity to do that for more kids, and the big stuffy jerk of a mayor was saying no.

Not even maybe, just no.

I sat there with my arms crossed, trying not to fidget, while Amelia did her best to talk him down.

"Omar, you know what a huge opportunity this is for the community. What this can do for the families here."

"We can't afford all of that, Amelia. It's not possible. We're not talking some huge budget. We're barely able to scrape by enough to pay for the required repairs to the property to make it functional for the kids. And this?" He gestured toward me, his glare following his tossed aside hand. "This isn't realistic. It's just not going to happen."

"Give us a few days, Omar. A week. Natalie hasn't even been out to the site yet. With the weather, we couldn't get over there. We're going right after this meeting. We'll come back in a week with a plan."

He shook his head before she even finished speaking.

My heart raced. My palms were soaked. Sweat pooled under my boobs and saturated my bra. My throat was tight. I wanted this. I hated how badly I wanted this, but as I sat there and listened to him take it all away, rip my dream right out from my fingers, I wanted to cry. And scream. And tell him where he could shove his expensive outfits and classic car.

Yeah, I knew all about his car. Everything about the man screamed high class and fancy. He had no idea what life was like without the privilege of money.

"I don't see any of this happening, Amelia. I really don't."

"I understand, but we do. We know what it could do for this town. We know the need is there. And once we get out there and see the place and get a better idea of what we're facing, we can come up with a more concrete plan. You said yourself we might be operating on credit. Give us a chance, Omar. Let us have another week to see what we can do in the budget you have available, and we'll go from there."

Mayor Knight let out a long breath, one that did not ease any of the anxiety racing through my bloodstream. He was ready to say no, and I was ready for it, but I was holding on to that tiny piece of hope I felt coming from Amelia.

She was not going to accept no.

"Fine—"

Amelia squealed.

"But!"

She fell silent, but her smile didn't slip.

"But if you don't have a more solid plan, one that more closely fits into this budget, we're going to have to delay all of this. And the only way it can go into the budget for next year is if we cut other things. You know how this works, Amelia."

"I do know, Omar. And I appreciate you giving us the chance to figure this out. We will not disappoint you."

"I hope not." He slid a glare in my direction, the jerk. "Talk to Jane about getting on my calendar again, and dial back your list of demands to something more realistic."

"We will. I promise." Amelia stood and grabbed my arm, tugging me from my chair. "Thanks, Omar."

Amelia practically dragged me out of the office, not giving me a chance to say anything else. She kept her arm looped through mine like I was a toddler about to run off at any moment.

"Jane, Mr. Mayor agreed to meet with us again next week. Does he have an opening on his calendar?" Amelia smiled at Jane, holding me tight to her side.

Jane clicked a few buttons and stared at the computer screen. "Um, it looks like he's available on Wednesday next week. Morning or afternoon?"

"Morning is usually better for me. No kids in the building," Amelia said.

Jane nodded, smiling at Amelia. "How about ten?"

"Perfect. Thank you so much, Jane. We will see you then." Amelia dragged me out of the building, only letting go when we made it to her car.

I climbed in and buckled my seatbelt, grumbling as Amelia walked around the car. When she slid behind the wheel and turned the car on, she finally turned to me.

"We have to be reasonable about what we can do. I love your ideas, but there was no way he would go for all of that."

"I... He put me on the spot."

"I know. And I know you were only sharing things that would be amazing, but he doesn't see the same thing we see. He doesn't know how hard things are for these kids."

I nodded. Amelia wasn't mad at me. She was capable of seeing both sides. Of understanding what everyone needed in a situation.

"Let's go look at the place, then we can start to make a plan. Maybe get in touch with some contractors who can help out. If it's for the summer camp, there might be companies who will do the work for free. A lot of them like to do volunteer work, and having a project for them is a benefit."

I nodded, wondering how she did it. How did she figure out how to talk to people and make them want to help her bring her vision to life? I could barely string a sentence together most of the time, when talking to adults, and Amelia was already thinking ten steps ahead.

She pulled out of the parking lot and turned toward the edge of town, heading east to the campground. She drove in silence for a few minutes, letting me gather my thoughts.

"What would you have said when Mayor Knight asked what you wanted to do?"

Amelia glanced at me.

I chewed my lip and wrung my hands. I knew I said the wrong thing, and I wanted to understand why.

"Omar is worried about the expense. He's going to be up for election in the fall, which means he's thinking about what he needs to do to maintain the support of the people of MacKellar Cove. Spending a ton of money on a site for a summer camp is not going to win over the residents who are going to elect him."

"But this is for kids. How can people say it's not okay to do it?"

"Because not everyone who lives here has kids. You and I aren't getting any benefit from having the summer camp open, besides employment. Neither of us have kids who would be helped by it."

"But we know it will make a difference."

"Yes, it will. I know that. And I support it. But if you're a retired couple living on social security and your taxes go up to pay for a summer camp, your perspective is different. That couple might say they want a new mayor. One who isn't going to spend a bunch of the town's money on something that's only going to benefit a small group of locals."

"I just..." I let her words sink in and really listened to them. "Okay, you're right. I only see where it'll help, but yeah, I understand what you're saying."

"That's why Omar pushed back." Amelia turned off the main road onto a dirt path that was barely wide enough for her car. "He has to think of everyone. So if the town has ten thousand dollars, for example, he has to decide if it would be better to spend that money on this camp or if it would be better to use it on something like repairs to the River Walk or upgrades to Catherine Park or saving that money and cutting taxes a tiny bit for everyone."

I got what she was saying, but I stopped listening when the road opened up to a clearing and I got my first look at the campground.

It was... Not what I was hoping. "Wow."

"Holy crap," Amelia breathed, putting the car in park.

We got out and stared.

A large tree laid across the basketball court. The surface looked okay, but until the tree was moved, we couldn't be sure. The nets were missing. Weeds had taken over the edges of the court and made it impossible to see where the court stopped.

We walked closer and found what was supposed to be beach volleyball. There were more weeds than sand there, and again, the net was gone. One of the poles was bent, meaning it would need to be replaced.

The pool was covered but the amount of leaves on top of the cover told me more than I needed to know about the condition of the pool. The cover was definitely in water, but I didn't want to think about the color of the water. And there was no fence around the pool. One old panel stood at the end, but the rest were completely gone.

Wires and old hookups stuck up all over the cleared area of the property. Thirty campsites. All in need of work. Conduit and connections had to be removed, and the entire property dug up from each site to wherever they went to the road.

"Well, the camper looks okay," Amelia said. Her hands were on her hips, her focus on the camper parked not far from the pool. "Want to look at it?"

I shrugged. No words formed. I wasn't sure whether I was excited or terrified. The space was beautiful. The Adirondack Mountains rose up in the distance. Trees swayed in the breeze. It was quiet and peaceful and a true gift.

But holy crap, it was a disaster. I couldn't even begin to think about where to start. The pictures Daisy found online felt like a different property than the one Amelia and I were looking at.

Amelia opened the door to the camper and immediately stepped back. "Oh, God. It smells horrible in there." She gagged and moved farther away, leaving the door open to air the place out.

The smell reached me, and I fought the urge to vomit. It was old food and possibly a dead animal mixed together. "There's no way we can do this."

"Yes, we can. The smell is already getting better," Amelia said.

I shook my head. "I'm not just talking about that. The whole thing. How can you stand there and think there's any way this is possible? All this work, all this property. It's too much. It's too big. What was I thinking when I imagined this? Why did I think this was possible?"

Amelia stepped in front of me, blocking my view of the camper. She grabbed my hands. "Natalie, stop. Listen to me. Are you listening?"

I nodded.

"Don't panic. We take this on one thing at a time. It's not going to be easy."

"Not easy?" I laughed like a maniac. "Not easy would be one of these things. We have a tree on the basketball court. There's no way the pool is functional. The volleyball court might as well not exist. And that driveway? Your car barely made it back here. What are we going to do if it rains? Or if someone has a big vehicle? This isn't possible. This is just not going to work. The mayor was right."

"No, he was not. Close your eyes."

I scowled at her.

"Humor me." She squeezed my hands. "Please?"

I drew a breath, then regretted it when I smelled the horrible scent from the trailer. I blew out my breath, then inhaled through my mouth and closed my eyes.

"Okay, first, all those campsites are gone. The property is clear and wide open. Can you see it?"

I tried to push aside the vision I knew was reality. Get rid of the connections and wires. It took me a minute, but I managed. "Okay, I see it. But—"

"Nope, don't get ahead of me. Focus on the wide open property. Without all those hookups, we can build that big structure you mentioned. Something that will hold a hundred kids or more."

"Two hundred," I said, my lips lifting in a smile. "The elementary school has a thousand kids, and if we can have a hundred at the community center and four hundred here, two groups of two hundred, we should be able to take all the kids who need it."

"Okay, two hundred kids. Picnic tables?"

"Yeah. Rows and rows of them. With open space in the middle. For games and stuff when the weather doesn't cooperate."

"People could get married here. Another way to pay for the location."

"That could help."

"Okay, good. Keep your eyes closed. What else do you see?"

I let my imagination take over. "The pool is fully fenced in, so it's safe. It's bright and blue and full of kids."

"I can hear them laughing," Amelia said.

I breathed a laugh, thankful she was working with me. "The basketball court just needs to be cleaned up. The volleyball court can be fixed or moved. And we can relocate the fire pits. Maybe consolidate them so there aren't as many and they're bigger, with grates over the top so we can use them to grill one day a week. Maybe s'mores. This place could be used in the winter for a holiday drive-thru light display or a winter wonderland kind of thing."

"I like that idea. You're coming up with ways for it to pay for itself."

I sighed heavily and opened my eyes. "But it's never going to happen."

"Why not?"

"Because all of that income is after we spend the money to make this place into that. We can't afford it."

"Maybe not all of it, not right now, but if we come up with a plan, I think it'll be something Omar approves."

"How in the world are we going to do that?"

"Natalie, you've done more with less. The yard outside the community center has none of the things you just mentioned. Yet, you still made it into something fun for the kids. A place where they're already begging to come back to. We take all of this one project at a time."

I looked around the campground and realized she was right. It was a ton more space, and even though it was in rough shape, it was bigger and better than what we already had.

"There's that look," Amelia said.

I tilted my head. "What look?"

"The one that says you're getting it. You will figure out a plan. And Omar will approve it."

I drew a breath and looked around. It was too perfect to not try. To let it all sit there. "It's not going to be easy."

"Don't they say nothing worth having ever is?"

I pursed my lips and shook my head. "Yeah, well, it would be really nice if it was easy."

"This town will help. You know they will. I'll talk to my son, and we can find people willing to pitch in. The clean up will make a huge difference. Just getting the trees around the driveway trimmed back, the tree off the basketball court, and this grass cut, it'll be a different place."

"What are we going to do about this camper?"

Amelia looked at it. She rested her hands on her hips and shrugged. "Burn it?"

I snorted a laugh. "As much as I love the idea, I'm not sure we can afford that. Think any of those volunteers would be willing to help clean it out?"

"Maybe there's someone with zero sense of smell."

"Lucky person," I said.

"Yeah, because that's horrible."

I nodded. "It's so horrible."

Amelia chuckled. "Let's look at more of the property. Then we can start making a plan."

"Sounds good."

BY THE TIME we got back in the car, I wanted the camp so badly I was ready to start the work myself. It was going to be a lot, but I could see it. I could imagine where everything would go. It was going to be perfect.

If there was such a thing as perfect. It would be damn close, though.

We got back to the community center, and Amelia went to her office. I retreated to mine and started dreaming about what we could do.

On my whiteboard, I drew a map of the campground. I added the current structures, including the hookups and the camper, then I made a list of all the things that needed to be done.

- *Remove hookups*
- *Clear and pave road*
- *Clean up volleyball court*
- *Remove tree and repair basketball court*

- *Clean pool*
- *Fence in pool*
- *Exterminate camper*

Those were the bare minimum tasks to open the camp and know it was safe. If we couldn't open the pool, we would have to put barricades around it. The volleyball and basketball courts were not bare minimum, but they would make the camp more fun and hopefully wouldn't take much work or money.

The only part I really wanted to add in was shade. But there was no way that was in the budget.

Maybe someone had an old circus tent they didn't want. And by some miracle wouldn't be opposed to donating it to the summer camp.

I shook my head and pinned my list next to the drawing on my whiteboard. Even if Amelia managed to get people to help, there was no way we would be able to do all of it in time. But I refused to give up. Even getting halfway there meant we were closer for the following summer.

I just had to put aside my impatience and accept that *some people* weren't as concerned with the welfare of children.

And then change his mind.

4

OMAR

I straightened my tie as I walked into the kitchen, the coffee just finishing brewing. I grabbed a mug, then retrieved eggs and butter from the fridge and a loaf of sourdough bread from the pantry. It was going to be a good day.

I sipped my coffee while I cooked eggs. The sourdough went into the toaster, coming out a perfectly light golden color at the same time the eggs were done. I sat at the table and read the local newspaper on my phone.

Dirty dishes went into the dishwasher, which I made a mental note to run after dinner, then I headed to the garage.

"Hello, beautiful," I said to my pride and joy. The electric blue Camaro was new-to-me and still something that made me smile whenever I walked into the garage. I hesitated to drive her to work, but I made sure I walked by her every day. If my day went as planned, I hoped to take her out for a drive since I only had one meeting.

I passed my baby and went to the black SUV I drove every day. It was still a good vehicle, but it was more utility than anything else.

Town hall was still quiet when I arrived, so I was able to

go through emails and get my mind organized for the day ahead. It shouldn't require that, but when Natalie Edwards was going to be in my office again, I needed it. The woman dominated my thoughts, and I could not let her do it again. I had to be clear-headed when she arrived. Rational.

Open-minded.

Just because she walked in last time with a bunch of overpriced ideas that she didn't have the budget for and then tried to get me to agree just because *it's for the kids* didn't mean she would do it again.

But if she did, she'd get the same answer as last time.

I drew a breath and let it out slowly. The woman either made me angry or made me horny. I couldn't let her have either emotion.

My morning was uneventful, which was a good thing. When Jane knocked on my door at two minutes to ten, I expected her to bring Natalie and Amelia in, but instead, she was alone.

"I just spoke to Natalie Edwards, and they're not coming."

"What do you mean, they're not coming?" I barked.

Jane flinched.

"I apologize. I did not mean to direct my anger toward you."

"It's okay." Jane twisted her ring around her finger. "I don't know what happened. Natalie just called and said something came up and Amelia wasn't available."

"So where is Ms. Edwards?"

Jane shook her head. "I don't know."

I locked my computer and closed the file I was working on. "We agreed to this time, did we not?"

"Yes, sir."

"And she calls at the last minute to say she can't be here?

What could she be doing that's more important than this? She's the one who said this is for the kids. All her big dreams need to happen because of the kids. And now she can't be bothered to show up? Does she think she's going to get any money from this office if she doesn't have a plan for it?"

"I... I don't know."

I sighed heavily and shook my head, letting out my breath slowly. "Will you please call Ms. Edwards back?"

"Um, okay. What do you want me to tell her?"

"Tell her I'm on my way to the community center to see her. That I expected an update today, and that if she expects the town to support her cause, she will be there to see me." I stomped to the door, then paused. "Actually, don't call her. I'll just show up."

I left a fumbling Jane standing in the middle of my office as I stormed out.

What was wrong with this woman? Did she not remember the meeting we had a week ago? Where I told her no when she made all her demands? Now she wanted to cancel our meeting instead of showing up and asking for what she needed.

Not happening. Her budget could be zero, and her job could be gone if she was going to be that disrespectful.

I slammed the door on my SUV and stalked into the community center ten minutes later. The place was quiet, like a school after hours. I was ashamed to admit I had never been inside the building, so I had no idea where anyone was.

"Hello?" I called out, hoping someone would appear and direct me to Ms. Edwards. Preferably in a public setting where we would not be alone.

"Hello?" a woman replied. The woman I was looking for.

And dammit, going there was a bad idea.

Natalie had her brown hair pulled up high on her head, loose tendrils falling around her shoulders like she'd been messing with her hair and tugged pieces out without realizing it. Her hazel eyes were wide, even wider when she saw me.

"Mr. Mayor," she blurted. She looked back into the room she came from, like she was going to go back into it and ignore me.

I walked toward her, not giving her the chance to hide. "We had a meeting."

"Yes, and I called to cancel it. Did you not get my message?"

"I got your message. But I had this time blocked off on my calendar to meet with you. So, we're going to meet."

"Now?" she squeaked.

"Yes, now. Is that your office?"

She looked back at the room again, and my gaze followed hers.

The room was barely a closet, and definitely not an office, but there was a tiny desk shoved in with a chair wedged into the corner. A file cabinet took up the majority of the space with a whiteboard above it on the wall with a drawing of the campground.

"You won't fit in there," she said.

"It looks like you barely fit in there."

She jerked back like I offended her, then rolled her lips in. "I'm aware of my size, Mr. Mayor."

"Your size?"

"I assure you, my weight has nothing to do with my ability to run this summer camp."

"Why the hell would it?"

"You..."

"I what?"

"Nothing. We can go up on the stage. There's space up there." She nodded toward the elevated platform at the far end of the gym.

I moved toward it, but she went into the office. "Are you coming?"

"If you insist on meeting now, then I need to get my things. If that's okay."

I nodded and stared after her as she stepped into her office. She turned sideways to make it between the desk and the file cabinet, then sat down in the chair. She swiveled her seat until she was facing the other wall, then opened a drawer hidden beneath the desk and pulled out a file. She reversed the steps and caught me watching her when she walked into the gym.

"I thought you were going to go to the stage."

"You also thought I was making a comment about your weight. When I said you barely fit in your office, it was a comment about the size of the office, not you. That's not a place anyone could work comfortably."

"Forgive me, Mr. Mayor, but we don't have space here like you have at town hall. Our time is better spent with the kids, and every office is small to make sure the common areas are as big as possible."

I nodded, seeing that same spark she had when she spoke about the kids before. The spark that said she was as passionate as Amelia about the kids she worked with, and not just trying to manipulate me to get what she wanted by pretending she cared. She meant what she said.

She gestured toward the stage, then followed me. I sat at one of the tables and tried not to breathe in her scent when she sat across from me.

I failed.

She smelled like markers and strawberries. A strange combination, but one I didn't hate. Oddly.

"Amelia had an appointment this morning she'd forgotten about and wasn't available for the meeting. She's the one who, um, puts things together and makes it sound right."

"I thought this was your project."

"It is. But Amelia is better with people than I am."

"Okay, well, I'm not here to judge your speaking skills. I need to know what you're planning to do with the budget for the campground."

She drew a breath, her chest rising with the move. She bit her bottom lip, and dammit, I had to shift in my seat.

"The campground needs work. A lot of work. The bare minimum we need to do is remove the wiring and connections for all the old campsites. Unfortunately, that could mean a lot of landscaping afterward. There is a tree down on the basketball court, and the volleyball court has more weeds than sand, but the bigger concern for me is the pool."

I opened my mouth to argue with her about it, but she rolled right on as though she didn't notice me.

"It'll take a lot to get the pool functional, I'm guessing, but whether we do that now or later, the pool needs a fence. As it is now, the department of health is not going to give us an operating permit. It's unsafe to leave it open like it is."

I nodded slowly. I hadn't been to the location, but she was right. Any pool had to have a way of stopping people from wandering into it. And a camp full of kids was going to have even tighter rules than anywhere else. "Do you think all of that will fit into the budget?"

She shook her head. "No. I know it won't. We've been talking to contractors about what it would take to get everything done. We don't have official quotes, more ideas, but I have a plan. It's not simple."

"Okay, let me hear it."

She looked up at me as if she was seeing me for the first time. The light in her eyes made me wonder what she expected from our meeting.

Was I really that big of an asshole?

"Everything I mentioned is phase one. It's the bare minimum for a functional space. Ideally, we would also have a structure for the kids to get out of the sun and weather, if there's rain during the day, but that's more of a nice to have thing."

"Is it, though? What happens if there's a thunderstorm?"

"There is a small camper on the site. It wouldn't hold a lot of people, so we would be limited to the number of kids we can safely have inside the camper."

"I thought the whole point was to expand the programs."

"It is, but if we don't have the budget to make these things happen, I can't pull it out of my ass."

I snorted at her vehement response.

She clapped a hand over her mouth. "I'm so sorry, Mr. Mayor. Please don't fire me for that."

"Fire you? Why am I going to fire you?"

"Because you don't like me. And I... grabbed..." She glanced down. "You. And Amelia isn't here to make sure I don't say things like that to you, so I'm sure you're just going to fire me and I'll have to go back to teaching, which I hated, but I'll do it because I love this town and I love the kids here and—"

"Natalie! Stop. Please. I'm not going to fire you. Just take a minute."

She closed her mouth. Her face was red, her eyes wild and bouncing all over the place, except at me. She ran her hands through her hair, stopping when she reached the ponytail that contained most of her hair. She removed her hands, then yanked the band from her hair and let the strands fall loose down her back.

Fuck me, the woman was a temptress. And she didn't even know it. She wasn't doing it to tease me, she was just flustered.

She fluffed her hair, then wrapped it in her hand, spearing her fingers through it until she contained all of it in one hand. She wrapped the band around the ponytail and tied all her hair back up into a sexy knot on top of her head once more.

A knot I desperately wanted to untie. A knot I wanted to loosen with my fingers.

I cleared my throat to eliminate the tightness that took over my whole body.

"I'm sorry," she said, still looking away from me. "I did not mean to make this so uncomfortable. I seem to do that all the time, which is why I canceled the meeting. Amelia is better than me."

"You're fine," I grunted. Could she hear the desire in my voice? Dammit. I needed to get a handle on myself. "What is phase two?"

"Phase two would be the structure. Amelia suggested using it for weddings, and I thought we could use the property for a winter wonderland kind of thing. We're trying to come up with other ways the property could bring in money for the town so it's not a drain."

"Those are good ideas," I said.

Her gaze snapped to mine again. "Thank you."

"Do you have other ideas? Other phases?"

She nodded. "I... There's a lot of space at the property. Almost too much for summer camp. It would be easy to have the kids get lost out there, so I would consider multiple structures to hold different types of camps. Maybe a science camp, a camp that focuses on sports, one for theater, and a general one that does all of it. We could build a bigger pool. Possibly even move the entire community center out there. But all of that is way long term. Phase three would be fencing in the property."

As she spoke, and her excitement grew, I hesitated to agree, but I loved to watch her talk. She loved the whole thing. She lit up as she spoke about the options and ideas she had. It was infectious and drew me in.

By the time she finished her thoughts, I was leaning toward her, the distance between us shrinking. My gaze dropped to her lips.

They parted, a tiny inhale making me freeze.

Dammit. I forgot where I was. What I was doing. I had to get the hell out of there. "Maybe we should finish this another time."

"I thought... Yeah, that's a good idea," she agreed slowly.

I stood, turning away from her so she didn't see the effect she had on me. "I'll have Jane reach out to reschedule our meeting for another day."

"Okay." Natalie's voice was soft, timid.

I made my way down the stairs onto the gym floor, giving me space from her, and turned to look up at her. The jeans she wore were loose around her legs but hugged her hips. Her top was a simple tee, an old band tee that was well worn and soft looking. She was in her element, ready for anything the kids threw at her when they showed up in a few hours.

"Is Amelia going to be here later, or are you on your own with the kids?"

She startled at my question and shook her head. "I won't be alone. We have staff that comes in for the afternoon."

I nodded, unsure why I asked the question. "Good." I took a few steps away, then stopped again. "We will have another meeting, Ms. Edwards. You have some great ideas. I think some fundraising options will be good, too. As far as what you told me today, I agree with your current assessment and what has to happen before you can open."

A smile tempted her lips, but she stifled it with her teeth. "Thank you, Mr. Mayor."

"I do expect that you'll keep me informed of what you're doing, though. And no more canceling meetings. It's not a good look, Ms. Edwards."

Her throat worked as she swallowed. Her nod was one of a reprimanded child instead of an adult taking responsibility for her actions.

I didn't want her to feel like either.

"This project is important. I know that. But that means I need to know everything that's going on. I need to be kept informed every step of the way. I can help get things done, but only if I know what needs to be done."

"Thank you."

I nodded. She hadn't moved off the stage with me, which meant every step I took carried me farther from her. That was a good thing. I needed space from her.

But I didn't want space from her. I wanted to sit at that table and learn everything there was to know about her.

I wouldn't, though. Once burned and all that. I wasn't meant to share my life with someone, and getting close meant sharing things. Casual dates and even more casual sex were better for me.

And neither of those applied to a woman like Natalie Edwards.

It was best for me to go.

"Thank you for your time today, Ms. Edwards."

"Thank you, Mr. Mayor."

I nodded once more, then turned and left the building.

When I made it outside, I drew a full breath of cold air, letting it sink in and fill me up. It wasn't a cold shower, but it would have to do until I finished my day and could go for a drive and put all thoughts of Natalie Edwards far behind me.

Where they needed to stay.

NATALIE

I LISTENED AS THE DOOR CLOSED BEHIND THE MAYOR AND nearly fell over. I could finally breathe with him gone.

I could not be attracted to the mayor. I couldn't. It was a bad idea. It was the worst idea. He was not in my league. Not even close. Those looks he gave me...

I misread those. He wasn't attracted to me either. It was just an emotional time and...

Crap, I didn't know. But there was no way Mayor Omar Knight actually wanted me. No matter what the look in his eyes made me think. I had misread far too many looks from men in my life and knew trying to guess what he was thinking was an even bigger disaster than the last time I thought a man was looking at me with desire.

Oh, no. That time was embarrassing. After a few weeks talking to a guy on Book Boyfriends Wanted, we met in person. We danced and kissed, only to find out he was using me to make his ex jealous. It worked, and she stole him right out from under me. Not that it was really stealing when he wanted it to happen.

I wasn't attached, so it wasn't a big deal, but this time?

No. Mayor Knight was someone I had to work with. I could not get sucked into a fantasy of my own making. I had to be real.

"Did I see Omar leaving?" Amelia asked, startling me out of my daydream about the man in question.

"Yeah." I cleared my throat, gathering the papers all over the table. "He came by for that meeting."

"I thought you were going to his office." Amelia gave me her stern mom look, with one raised eyebrow, a hand on her hip, and her lips pursed disapprovingly. "Did you make him come here?"

I shook my head. "No. I didn't."

"Then why was he here?"

"Because I canceled the meeting," I confessed softly.

"Natalie. I thought you were fine with it."

"I thought so, too! Then I came in this morning and knew I couldn't do it."

"Yes, you can. I know you can. You are so passionate about the summer camp, and when you show that, it's infectious. But you have to be willing to show it."

"I did. I think. He said he agreed with what I said about getting things done before camp opens."

Amelia grinned. "That's great news! Did you talk about the phases?"

I nodded. He prompted me, giving me a chance to formulate my thoughts without feeling like I was rushing through things. "We did. I think he agreed with everything, but I'm not entirely sure."

"What do you mean?"

"He wants to meet again next week. With both of us."

"That's not bad. It means he's on board with everything. He's not giving up."

"He ended our meeting kind of abruptly," I said, biting

my lip to keep in the way his looks made me feel before Mayor Knight got the hell out of there.

Maybe he saw how I felt on my face, and it scared him off. Crap. I was trying not to let him know I was drawn to him. I hadn't meant to lean in when we were talking, but it must have bothered him.

"He probably had other meetings. He's busy, especially with Christmas in ten days and people taking time off for the holiday. Jane said today was the only day he had available to meet, so he probably had somewhere else to be."

"Yeah, I'm sure you're right."

Amelia nodded. "Don't worry. We'll meet with him next week and go from there. Speaking of the holiday, we have a full group for the break. What are you thinking for activities?"

I jumped into plans for the winter break and let my thoughts of Mayor Knight drift away.

THE ONLY DAY Mayor Knight had available for a meeting the following week was two days before Christmas. It was the last day of school before winter break, and the last day of afterschool care for the year.

It was a busy damn day. A day Amelia couldn't get away to meet with the mayor. No matter how important it was.

"I'm sorry, Natalie, I really am, but you can handle this. You already had a meeting with him."

"And it was not good."

"What? I thought it was fine. You said he agreed with you about the proposal and the phases. What happened?"

Crap, crap, crap. I could not tell my boss that I was

thinking about kissing her boss during the meeting. That would not be okay. "It was fine. Sorry. I'm just awkward. I didn't feel like I explained everything well, and I—"

"Natalie, you are fine. You need to stop doubting yourself. I mean, really, I don't know why he wants me there at all. I'm not involved in the project aside from being your boss. I trust you completely."

"Yeah, but you run the community center."

"And one day you will, Natalie. If you want. I have no doubt you could do this."

"Where are you going?" I asked, panic rising up.

Amelia laughed. "Nowhere. But one day I might retire and enjoy my old age with less activity. Every morning when I roll out of bed, I find a new pain."

"You're still young," I said.

Amelia laughed even louder. "You're too sweet. I have no problem with my age. I know the alternative to growing old is dying young, and that's not what I want either. But I feel the need to slow down coming. Not yet, but one day. And I have to think about who will take over. I'm hoping it'll be you."

I wasn't sure what to say. I saw the way Amelia operated, the way she talked to people and made everything look so easy. She was an amazing boss, fair and kind and creative, and I was positive I couldn't do all the things she did.

"You don't have to decide anything right now. But what I want you to do is go to that meeting with Omar and channel me. Push back on him if he's asking too much. And weekly meetings are too much. I don't really know what the point of today's meeting is. We haven't been able to make any progress with the busy time of year and the weather."

Amelia's tone made me question the meeting, too. I

didn't think about it when Mayor Knight asked for it the week before, but I was flustered and anxious with him showing up at the community center.

Why did we need to meet?

The question ran around in my mind as I returned to my office to gather my things. But what things? I had no new information. I hadn't scheduled anything. No one was doing much until the holidays were over. I'd asked.

I walked out of my office with nothing in my hands because I had nothing new to show the mayor. I thought about canceling the meeting, but after the way he behaved last time I did that, I knew I had to show up, even though I had nothing to show him.

I said goodbye to Amelia and left for the meeting with Mayor Knight. Town Hall was quiet when I got there, many people either gone for the holidays or out for other meetings. My guess was the first one.

Jane was sitting behind her desk when I arrived and told me I could go in. The door to Mayor Knight's office was open, so I stepped inside, feeling like I was walking into the lair of a beast.

His head was down, focused on a stack of papers in front of him. He looked tired, like he was worn out by the job.

I took a second to appreciate the man, the curve of his fingers, the bunch of his muscular shoulders, even the beard that covered his jaw. I wondered what it would feel like against my skin. My pulse jumped at the thought, and I must have made a noise because he looked up at me.

His gaze locked on mine, something intense and intimate passing between us. I was frozen, locked in place like he'd cast a spell on me that limited my movements.

What would he do to me if that were the case?

I shook my head, breaking the contact and snapping the tension in the room.

"Is Amelia with you?" he asked.

"She wasn't available. Today is our last day of afterschool care before the winter break, and she has a lot to have ready since tomorrow we have kids all day."

"Why didn't you reschedule this meeting?" he barked, as though angry at me for showing up.

His frustration spun me up. "I wasn't the one who asked for this meeting, Mr. Mayor. You are. And last week you had a fit when I canceled a meeting at the last minute because Amelia wasn't available."

He drew a breath and nodded. "You're right. I apologize."

"Thank you."

He nodded.

I took a seat across the desk from him, thankful for the large barrier between us. It was twice the size of the tiny table we sat at a week ago, and would be a much bigger divide to cross.

Not that I was going to. I couldn't. I wouldn't. I had to keep things professional.

"So, what updates do you have for me?" he asked after a minute of silence.

"None."

"None?"

I shook my head. "Every contractor we've spoken to in the last week said they aren't booking into the spring yet and to be in touch after the holidays. They have projects to finish up through the winter, and their schedules can be highly dependent on the weather, so everything is up in the air right now."

"You're telling me you have no new information. Amelia couldn't be here. And you haven't made any progress?"

I resisted the urge to growl at the man. How dare he question me? I wasn't the one who wanted the meeting. I wasn't the one who needed to micromanage everything. "That's exactly what I'm telling you. I'd love to have more news, but we're not doing anything at the site right now. Not with winter break next week. Amelia would be telling you the same thing if she were here right now, but she's not because she's working on stuff for break."

"Two weeks," he barked. "I want you back here in two weeks, and I want an update."

"And then what? Are you going to give us more money?"

"We don't have more money."

"Then why do I have to be back here in two weeks? Why do I have to be back here at all? Are you like this with all your departments? Do you micromanage everyone? Do you make everyone answer to your unrealistic demands? How in the world do you get anything done if you're meeting with every single town employee who has a project happening every two weeks?"

He rose from his seat, leaning toward me like he did the week before, but this time in a less than friendly way. "You're untested. You're getting a huge bonus with this gifted property. You have never run a project like this, and I don't know if I can trust you to do what's best for the town."

I matched his stance, rising up from my seat and leaning forward. "You can't trust me? Are you kidding me? No. That's not the truth."

"Then what is? If you know me so well?"

"You don't like me, Mr. Mayor. You've made that clear. You have something against me. I don't know what it is, but you've decided I'm the problem and that you don't want me taking control of anything. You just want to shut me up and—"

He kissed me. Holy crap, he kissed me.

His lips slammed against mine, a sharp inhale on his side saying it was as much of a shock to him as it was to me.

I should pull back. I should stop it. I should resist.

But I couldn't.

My hands went to his shirt and pulled him closer. I parted my lips under his and licked his lips.

He growled and reached for me. His hands went into my hair, tilting my head to the side and devouring me like he'd been starving for me the same way I was starving for him.

My thighs hit his desk and reminded me we were in his office. I wanted to say I didn't care, that kissing him made everything else disappear and not matter, but we were in his office.

Anyone could walk in and see us. Take another picture of us.

"Dammit," I breathed, breaking our kiss and releasing him.

He let go of me immediately, his eyes remaining closed as he fisted his hands at his sides.

"Mr. Mayor…"

"Please don't call me that." He opened his eyes and captured me with the need reflected back at me. "Please."

"Omar, I…"

"And don't tell me that was a mistake. Just… you can go. I'll see you in two weeks."

I nodded, unsure what I wanted to say anyway. It was better if I put space between us. Better for everyone.

I forced a smile for Jane, then got the hell out of the building. I told Amelia we had another meeting in two weeks, and put my head down and worked the rest of the day, definitely not obsessing about Mayor Omar Knight kissing the absolute hell out of me.

I woke up the next morning with the sheets twisted around my ankles and my body flushed and aroused from the dreams I had about Omar all night long.

That was not okay. I was tired, and I was turned on, and I was going to be surrounded by children all day.

At least I didn't have to worry about the parents.

I dragged myself to the shower and cleaned up quickly before going to the kitchen. Daisy didn't open the store until ten, so she was still asleep. I fixed coffee quietly, leaving some for her, and grabbed a banana and a bagel, then left for the day.

Amelia was already inside and setting up games when I arrived. We had a sheet on the front table for parents and guardians to sign kids in and out. I shoved Omar even further out of my mind and helped Amelia get ready for the arrival.

At six on the dot, the first parents dragged their bleary-eyed kids inside, some helping them take off jackets and boots before stashing their outdoor gear in a cubby for later.

It wasn't long before the sounds of basketballs bouncing, kids laughing, and sneakers squeaking were the only thing I could pay attention to.

That was what I needed. Not Omar Knight and his far-too-tempting kisses. Not thoughts of him that kept me up half the night. No, I just needed to remember who I was and why I was in his office in the first place.

It was for the kids. Always for the kids. So we could put the smiles on their faces all summer when they came to summer camp. So we knew they were safe and cared for all summer.

Mayor Knight was going to help make it happen, but

that was all he was going to do. He would help. It was his job as mayor.

And it was my job to stay away from him and not lose my mind with a man who would never work with someone like me. He needed to stay a fantasy. For good.

6

—————

THE FIRST DAY OF WINTER BREAK WAS A SUCCESS, BUT I WAS tired when I got home. Not nearly as tired as Daisy, though. My always cheerful best friend was working long hours leading up to the Christmas holiday and looked exhausted when she made it home from work on Christmas Eve.

"Are you okay?" I asked, alarmed at the dark circles under her eyes and the hollow look in the blue.

She collapsed onto the couch next to me. "I'm so tired. I did not anticipate the need in this town for a toy store at Christmas."

"I thought that was one of the things you looked at before you opened Lincoln Toys."

She nodded, her head falling to the back of the couch. "Yeah, but it's so much busier than I thought it would be. Inventory is almost gone, and some people were not happy when what they wanted wasn't available."

"You're closed until next year. And people who wait until the last minute have to accept that it's their fault. Plus, that tells me you did amazing for your first holiday season."

She smiled and nodded. "You're right. It's a good thing

that I'm doing this well. It's silly to complain about my business being successful six months after I opened the place. I've met so many people, too. And I'm learning that next year, I need to hire more help around the holidays so I don't wear myself out so much."

I grinned, amazed at the way she turned everything around so quickly. She impressed me on a daily basis, but pulling herself back from exhaustion was something I'd never seen her do. "Make notes now so you don't forget by next Christmas."

She got up and went to her handbag near the door, digging in the pocket where she kept her phone and bringing it back to sit on the couch again. "How was your day? How was the first day of the winter break rush?"

I shrugged. "It was good. Busy, but the kids had fun and are all excited to come back next week."

"You always have fun with the kids. You're so good with them. What activities do you have planned?"

She typed while I talked. "We have outdoor playtime, so all the kids brought snow gear. We had a lot of gym time. Trinity is doing crafting time two days next week, which will help break up some of the day."

"It'll be busy, but it's going to be fun. For the kids and you."

"I hope so. When do you leave to go see your parents?"

Daisy closed her store and took the entire week off between Christmas and New Year's so she could visit her parents. "I'm going to leave early in the morning. They wanted me to come tonight, but when I thought about it, I worried about driving so late."

"I don't blame you."

Daisy nodded, then set her phone on the table. "Did you eat yet?"

"I did not. I made lasagna."

She groaned. "You know how to spoil me."

I snorted and followed her to the kitchen. "Yeah, because it's not a mutual thing." Whoever was home first would cook. We shopped for certain meals every week, but neither of us was ever married to a plan. We liked to have an idea but be flexible about what we cooked and when.

"Yes, well, you could have waited to make lasagna until I was gone." Daisy sliced a large piece for herself before slicing an equally large one for me.

"I wouldn't do that. I should have made this yesterday so I would know you ate lunch."

Her cheeks reddened, telling me she skipped lunch, again.

"You need to take care of yourself."

"I know! I will do better after the holidays."

"New Year's resolution," I teased.

She laughed loudly and nodded. It had become a joke for us that next year we would do all the things we said we needed to do. Lose weight, date more, meet new people, drink more water. We never stuck to any of them, and by December, we were right back there, making the same promises we always made.

"Maybe one will stick next year."

"Maybe."

We ate in silence for a few minutes, the TV playing the movie I put on earlier. The lasagna was good. Very cheesy, but the addition of a layer of zucchini noodles and ground turkey gave it a different flavor compared to the traditional meat lasagna.

"This is really good," Daisy said. "We need to make it like this every time from now on."

"I was just thinking the same."

Daisy chuckled. "Maybe we should try to stick to some of those resolutions next year."

"Which ones?"

"Adding vegetables seems to be a good one."

I nodded and laughed with her.

She sighed. "I need to ask for help. Accept that I can't do everything."

"That's going to be hard for you. You never ask for help."

She laughed. "I know! That's why I need to do it. There was a kid in the store today with her mom, and I had to stop myself from yelling at her when she was messing with one of the toys."

"Seriously?" Daisy never lost her patience. I admired it, but hearing she was close today was cause for concern.

"I have never been this tired in my life. I love Lincoln Toys, and I love that I work for myself, and I am so happy I was able to move here with you, but it hasn't been easy. This last year has been both the best and worst of my life."

"I'm sorry, hun. Why didn't you tell me?"

She snickered. "See my resolution."

I snorted. "Touché."

"What about you? What's one you want to keep?"

"I want to keep all of them."

Daisy shook her head. "No, you don't. We both know that. We make those resolutions based on things we think we're supposed to want, not on what we actually want."

"I want to get better at talking to people."

"Maybe that should be your resolution."

"Getting better at talking to people isn't a resolution."

"You're right. It's a goal. So what should your resolution be? Talking to a stranger once a week? An adult stranger?"

I scowled at her, hating that she read my mind as quickly as I had the thought.

Daisy laughed. "You're so predictable."

"Yeah, yeah. Yours is easier."

"Says you. How many times have you asked for help recently?"

I wrinkled my nose and knew she was right. I wasn't good at it either. "This is why we don't stick to our resolutions."

Daisy laughed and leaned over, resting her head on my shoulder. "True, but it's also why we're in the same place year after year without changing things. I know you want more out of life."

Tears welled in my eyes as I nodded. "Yeah."

The whispered word was enough for Daisy. She didn't push, and she didn't have to. She made her point, for both of us.

We finished the movie and dragged ourselves to our rooms. I listened to her get ready for bed in her room and wondered what the next year would bring for both of us.

Everything with the campground was still up in the air until the weather improved and we could start working out there. I was determined to do whatever it took to have it ready for the summer, but unless I could make some progress on cleaning it up, it wouldn't happen in time for this summer.

Summer camp registration officially opened March first.

Dammit. I was starting to see why Omar wanted to meet in two weeks. He knew what I just realized. I needed to get things done. Fast.

Could I do it if I took Daisy's advice and talked to strangers? If I put myself out there? Or would I just make it worse because people didn't like me?

I didn't have Daisy's infectious nature or Amelia's

commanding presence. I was a wallflower, happy to be out of the spotlight and willing to let others lead.

But this camp was my baby. It was my dream. And no one else was going to make my dreams happen. If I wanted it, I had no choice but to go for it.

Which meant pushing my comfort zone, and yeah, asking for help from adult strangers.

God help me.

THE NEXT WEEK was gone in an instant, and the calendar flipped to the new year. Daisy returned from her visit with her family refreshed and happy and ready to tackle the new year with her resolution to ask for help already started.

"My dad packed the car for me, and my mom sent me back with food so I didn't have to worry about stopping for more than gas. My nieces and nephews were happy to play with the toys I brought them and gave me very honest opinions about what they liked about them." Daisy was proud of her accomplishments.

And they were accomplishments. Asking for help from family seemed easy to me, but Daisy never felt like she could. Her family was amazing, but they were all like her and did everything themselves, so asking others was a challenge from birth. Nature and nurture were ganging up on Daisy and telling her to do it all herself.

And she was bucking both to make herself better.

Dammit. But good for her.

"What are you up to today?" she asked. The Monday after New Year's Day, we were both back to work and happy to be diving into our normal routines again.

"I'm at the community center today. Amelia wanted to

talk about summer camp since we need to make some decisions."

"Do you think you're going to be able to make the campground work?"

I shrugged. "I don't know. When we were there, it was a lot of work."

"And you're going to ask for help, right?" Daisy said.

I snorted. "Yeah, yeah. When I figure out what I need to do."

"I thought you were going to do some fundraisers."

"That was Amelia's idea, but it feels like begging. Please come give me money, then give me more for camp."

"Yeah, but it's what you need to do in order to make it happen. You can't just ignore the budget."

"I'm not ignoring the budget. But I'm going to do what I can. I might spend some time there later today. The power company confirmed everything to the site is completely shut off, and with the ground a little warmer over the weekend, I want to see if I can dig out some of those lines."

"By yourself?"

I shrugged. "If it doesn't work, I'll figure something else out, but I have to try. It's a lot of work, Daisy."

"I know, but... I worry about you."

"I'll be fine. I won't do it if it's too hard. I promise."

"Just be careful. It's pretty isolated out there."

"I'm not worried. Plus, I won't be there for long."

"Please text me when you go. So I know if you don't come home that I need to worry."

"I will."

"Thank you."

"You're welcome."

Amelia was walking out of her office when I walked into the community center twenty minutes later.

"Oh, you're here! Good. Can we talk about summer camp?"

"Yeah, let me put my coat in my office."

"Good. I'll grab my notes."

I nodded, worried that she had notes. I didn't realize there was something for her to make notes about.

I picked up a notepad and a pen from my desk and met Amelia on the stage to talk about summer camp. And whatever else was on her mind.

"Last week was good, don't you think?"

I nodded. "It was. We had a full house, but it was a lot of fun for the kids. And a big help for the parents."

"I agree. Which is why I was thinking we have an opportunity to turn your summer camp into so much more than a summer camp."

"What do you mean?"

"Well, winter break, spring break, any of the conference days and stuff like that, parents are scrambling to find a place for their kids. Half days, early dismissal, everything adds up. What if we had a way to take all the kids for all the days?"

"All the days?" I asked.

Amelia grinned like it was the best idea ever. "Yes! I mean, we had to limit the number of kids we had in here because of space, but you and I both know more needed a place to go. The stay at home parents were taking in kids of working parents and some parents were just off. They can't do that all year. It's unreasonable. But we have the space now."

"But it's not indoor. The campground is... There's no way we can make that happen with the budget we have."

Amelia nodded. "I know. And I'm not trying to say we should change what you have planned, but I think there's a huge opportunity for us. A chance to make life better for so many parents."

"How? How in the world can we do any of this?"

"We do it in phases, like you told Omar. Phase One is all the requirements that will make it safe plus the structure to keep the kids out of the weather. But I think we make the structure something that can be used year-round. Something that can have all the windows open in the summer but closed up and heated in the winter."

My mind raced to catch up to what was clearly not a new idea for Amelia. When she first approached me about the summer camp, I was excited, but this... This was ten times what I imagined.

"I don't know if it's going to be possible."

"I know you need time to think about things, so I'm talking to you about it now. I really think this could be amazing for the community. And if we start having fundraisers now, it'll be easier to make this happen for the spring."

Fundraisers. I hated that word. Not just because I hated asking people for things, but because it usually meant talking to people. Sharing my vision and thoughts with dozens and dozens of strangers.

"It's an essential part of running a place like this, Natalie. I know you don't like fundraisers, but you have to get used to the idea if you're going to be in charge of this whole place one day."

"I still don't understand why in the world you would ever leave me in charge."

"Because you have a passion for this. You love what we do here. You love these kids, and you love this community.

You're the only one I have ever considered leaving this place to. Not that I get to decide, but no one else has ever loved it here the way you and I do."

My throat got tight. I swallowed around the lump. I did love it, but I couldn't imagine walking into the mayor's office and speaking to him the way she did, or speaking to anyone the way Amelia did. She was smart and strong. She could gather her words and make sense of her thoughts.

I was none of those things.

But I was passionate about the kids. And about the community center. Maybe that could be enough.

"Get out of here and think," Amelia said. "I see those wheels turning."

"I just got here."

"Yeah, and I know you have things running through your head. You'll figure them out faster if you can go where you need to go. Think about what I said, though. About not just having summer camp there but all the camps."

I nodded. "I will. And thank you, Amelia."

She winked. "We'll figure it all out."

She was right. I hoped. But she was definitely right about me getting out of there.

I grabbed my coat and knew the only place I wanted to be was at the campground.

The road was soft on my drive in, which gave me a little hope for the ground. I parked next to the camper and got out of my car, inhaling the fresh air and letting it clear my mind.

The area was more than big enough for a few buildings. We could do so many things at the site. Big things. A craft cabin. A sports arena. A tumbling gym. A games space.

With the idea of indoor camps in my head, I wanted all of it. Like everything else, we needed to figure out what the actual need was, but Amelia made it seem as though there were a lot more kids in need than we took. I had heard from a few that they were looking at other towns for camps. Some for the options, and some for the space.

The big ideas would have to wait, but what couldn't wait was cleaning up the campground.

I grabbed a shovel from the trunk of my car. I'd asked for the utility companies to mark where underground wiring was, and I was ready to start digging up the first of the wires.

The shovel sank into the dirt with very little resistance. It didn't go far, two inches or so, but it was enough for me to feel like it was something.

I started at one of the campsites. Digging down two feet to where the conduit ran through the ground, wires protected and safe. I tugged on one end, happy when the whole thing moved.

It was slow work to dig up the wires. Two feet didn't seem like much until it was over the entire site. I backfilled the holes as I dug out the next section of the conduit.

One came free, the entire path cleared from the old campsite to the junction where they all came together. I looked back and smiled. It wasn't easy, but it was possible.

Knowing I did that one made me feel like I could do anything. I could dig up wires and save the town some money so we could make the campground an amazing place for the kids. I could make this work. I could talk to people and raise money and watch my dreams come to life right there on that old campground.

I went to work on the second one, digging up the conduit for that one as easily as the first. I took my coat off halfway through digging, the exertion soaking my clothes with sweat and the need for cooling taking over.

I was halfway through the third one when I hit a rock

when I was digging. I dug around it, knowing it needed to come out. It wasn't huge, but it was bigger than I could easily move. I used the shovel as a lever and pried it up and out of the hole I created.

The conduit was exposed and I could yank it up, leaving the space free to backfill with the dirt I'd removed from the hole. I set the shovel down and laid the conduit to the side, then grabbed my shovel to get the dirt back in the hole.

I tripped on the rock. My ankle screamed with pain. I slid, my other foot falling into the hole I'd made. The shovel nearly whacked me in the head.

A ripping sound had me clutching my backside, praying it was my pants and not a muscle that tore. The cold breeze on my upper thighs confirmed it was my pants.

It was good news. I was okay. I just had to figure out how in the hell I was getting out of the hole I dug for myself.

Oh, the irony.

7

———

MY ASS WAS SOAKED. MY PANTS WERE SHREDDED. MY ANKLE was twisted. And I was stuck.

It didn't matter how hard I tugged, I couldn't get my uninjured foot out of the hole. It was wedged, and without the leverage of a good foot on solid ground, I was not going anywhere.

Of course, I left my phone in my car. So I wouldn't drop it anywhere. And of course, no one was going to just drive by. Which meant I either had to figure out how to get myself out of the mess I was in or hope Daisy came looking for me when I didn't come home.

In six hours or so.

"Argh!" I shouted at the sky.

My normal anxiety was a pain in the ass when I was around adults, especially strangers. It left me tripping over my words and fumbling with what I wanted to say and how I wanted to act, or just shutting down completely. What I was feeling, trapped in the hole I dug, literally, was an entirely different kind of anxiety.

This was a new fear. A true fear for my life. Was I going

to survive? I was already shivering since I discarded my jacket, again in my damn car. What the hell was I thinking?

I closed my eyes and drew a breath, remembering the years and years and years of therapy that helped me to function. First, box breathing to bring my racing heart down to a level where I could think.

Second, evaluate the situation.

"Really bad," I told myself. "But I can do this."

Hearing my own voice was better than feeling so alone.

"The mud is wet and cold. My ankle hurts a lot. I have one foot high and the other low. If I push my hands down to push myself up, it doesn't work. I have two choices, tuck and roll or risk getting more stuck by putting my injured foot in the same hole."

My pulse raced with the options, knowing neither was great. But I couldn't think of an option that didn't require me getting even dirtier than I was.

"I can do this. I will reward myself with a bubble bath and scrub every inch of my skin. Twice. No more mud baths ever in my life. Why would I want a repeat of this?"

Another deep breath.

"Okay, we're going to roll."

I stretched out in the mud, my too thin shirt instantly saturated by the squishy mud. It made the world's most disgusting sucking, wet, sloppy noise ever and soaked through my shirt and filled my bra.

"So gross," I groaned.

I'd cleaned up vomit and wiped noses. I'd dealt with spilled food and even the occasional bathroom accident. But none of that was on me.

"Roll, roll, roll," I whispered to myself as I tried to get myself out of the hole.

With zero success.

"Dammit!" I shouted, again to absolutely no one.

Panic was setting in, and exhaustion and fear were right there cheering the panic on. If I didn't get the hell out of there soon, I was going to go headfirst into a panic attack.

I had no choice. Rolling out of the hole wasn't an option with my foot wedged in. The mud at the bottom sucked my boot deeper with every move I made to pull it out.

Putting another boot down there wasn't appealing. But neither was staying there all afternoon and freezing to death.

I pushed myself upright again, trying to work my foot free. It moved a little, but not enough to get it out of the hole. The squishy sound told me I had to overpower the soft mud that I was so thankful for when I started digging because it was better than frozen ground.

"Fuck you, mud," I muttered.

Another deep breath. Ignore the tangy scent of dirt and the feel of mud caked onto every inch of my body. Ignore the panic clawing at my throat and desperate to come out. I was going to do this.

I pushed my free foot down into the hole, wedging it on the side instead of letting it go all the way to the bottom.

"Gah!" I shouted, the pain so much worse than I expected it to be.

"I got this. I have to. Okay. One. Two. Three!"

I pushed with my bad foot, using my arms and leg to pry my good foot out of the damn hole.

I rolled to the ground, laughing and relieved and covered in mud, but free from the ground.

There had to be some slap in the face lesson about falling into a hole of my own creation, but all I cared about at that moment was getting up and getting less frozen.

I moved to stand and collapsed to the ground again.

"Ow!" My ankle was not okay. I couldn't stand up. Which meant I could either crawl to my car or try to use the shovel as a crutch.

"This will be interesting." I used the shovel to help me stand, keeping my foot off the ground as much as possible. It hurt to even graze the ground, but I had to get out of there. I had to get back to my car.

Each step was slow. I stabbed the shovel in the ground, then hopped on my good foot, the one that was soaked all the way through and squished between my toes. One step. Then another. And another.

I finally made it to my car and realized I had a whole new problem. I was covered. Head to toe. There wasn't an inch of me that didn't have mud on it. And I had nothing to protect my car from myself.

Daisy and my mom and everyone I knew in the area said always keep a blanket in your car. Create an emergency kit. Be prepared.

I didn't go anywhere. Work and home. My parents' house sometimes. The grocery store and bookstore and out to eat. All local places. Nowhere I needed an emergency kit to get to.

I should have listened to them. And now my seats were going to be ruined because I hadn't.

I opened the door and debated. I shook my head and laid my coat over the seat, hating that I was going to destroy it but knowing it could be washed. Probably. Hopefully.

The drive home was not fun, but I made it. I parked in the driveway and was extremely grateful Daisy wasn't home to watch my hobble-stomp-grunt walk to the front door. I let myself in and pried my muddy boots off, wincing when I had to get it off my injured left foot. My socks were almost as muddy as my boots, and my clothes were no better.

"Daisy?" I called out, hoping my suspicions were correct and her car not in the driveway meant she was not home. "Are you here?"

Silence met my questions, and I chewed my lip for a minute. I checked outside again and decided it was for the best to strip to my underwear right there at the door and carry my clothes to the laundry room instead of risking getting the entire house muddy.

I scooped up all my clothes and cringed at the feel of the muddy fabric against my skin, but it was better. I hurried, as fast as my ankle would allow, to the laundry room next to the kitchen and stopped.

"Now what?" I asked no one.

Tossing the muddy clothes into the washing machine didn't seem like a great idea, but we didn't have a utility sink and I didn't have a better idea. I could wash them more than once if I needed to.

"Ugh."

My underwear needed to go into the laundry, too. I debated for a few seconds, then stripped my bra and panties off. Right there in the middle of the house I shared with my best friend.

"Please don't come home," I sang to myself, praying I wasn't about to bear it all to my bestie.

I dumped the detergent into the dispenser and started the machine. I covered myself with my muddy arms and hobbled to my room, closing the door with no incident.

At least something was going my way.

I turned on my shower and let the water warm up before I climbed in, wincing and cringing with every step on my left foot. The boot and the cold had kept the swelling down, but I knew it was going to blow up as soon as I was warm. Especially if I didn't get off my foot.

I washed my hair and body thoroughly, twice, then plugged the drain and added bubble bath to the tub as it filled. I sank into the warm water and sighed.

So much better.

I stayed in the bath until the water cooled and my ankle throbbed. I pulled the plug and pushed myself out of the tub, as awkward as a baby deer. I sat on the edge to dry myself off and watch my ankle swell.

Dammit.

I made my way back to my room and found my most comfortable clothes and got dressed. My bathroom was as stocked as a pharmacy for bandages, so I grabbed an elastic bandage that would stick to itself and hobbled to the kitchen.

Ice for my ankle, a sandwich for my belly, and water for my headache. Then I was on the couch with the remote and wrapping the ice around my ankle before the swelling got too bad.

That was how Daisy found me an hour later when she made it home, looking like her day was no better than mine.

"I'm so tired," she breathed, hanging her coat in the front closet. "How was your— What the hell happened to you?" She rushed to me, sitting next to me. Her eyes widened at the wrap around my ankle.

"I was trying to dig out the old connections for the campsites and fell."

"Are you okay? Do you need to go to the doctor? Why didn't you call me?"

I shrugged. She was my best friend in the world. The

only person who wasn't family that I felt like I could be my whole and true self around. She didn't judge me or criticize me. I loved her like the sister I never had, and I knew the feeling was mutual.

Which was why tears welled up when I heard the concern in her voice. I would have been equally upset if she was hurt.

"You're not okay," she said. "What do you need?"

I laid my head on her shoulder before she could get up. "I'll be okay. I probably need to burn my coat, and my clothes might have ruined the washing machine, but I'll survive."

"Okay, go back to the beginning and tell me what happened."

I took a breath and told Daisy about digging up the campground and how easy it started, then leaving my phone in the car and throwing my coat in there with it, and finally slipping on the mud and getting stuck in the hole.

"Do you think it's broken?"

I shook my head. "Sprained probably. I could have torn something, but I don't think it's that bad. I need to replace the ice and put my laundry in the dryer. If it's clean."

"Sit down," she said as I tried to get up. "I will take care of all of that. Did you eat?"

"I wasn't sitting here waiting for you to come home and take care of me."

She glared at me. "What would you say to me if I were the one with the ankle injury?"

"The same," I admitted.

She grinned. "Exactly. New ice? Do you want me to unwrap it, or are you going to?"

"I will. I need to take this ice off it and give it a little while. It's been on there almost an hour."

"Okay, so you unwrap while I put your clothes in the dryer. Food?"

"I had a sandwich."

"Meds?"

I shook my head. "I didn't take anything."

"Do you want something?"

"Not right now. I might before I go to bed."

"Okay."

Daisy left to take care of my laundry, then stayed in the kitchen while I unwrapped my ankle. It hurt, but the swelling was better and I could move it slowly.

It wasn't broken, but it was going to hurt for a week or two.

Daisy came back to the couch and sat next to me with a sandwich of her own and a container of ice cream with two spoons.

I smiled at her and took the offering. Whenever one of us was sick or hurt, we always got ice cream and shared it. Heartbroken? Ice cream. Walked into a pole? Ice cream. Cold or flu? Ice cream.

Daisy ate her sandwich and watched the end of the movie I had on. When it was over, she took the ice cream and her plate back to the kitchen, then brought back a new ice pack.

"I told you being out there alone wasn't a good idea," Daisy said.

"It's my responsibility. I'm the one who's going to run the camp."

"Amelia is your boss, though. Shouldn't she be involved?"

"She has enough to do with the community center. And she wants the campground to be more than just a summer camp. She has ideas about building a four-season building so we can have kids there for winter break and spring break and year-round."

"That's what sent you out there today."

I shook my head. "I was already planning to see what I could do, but I went earlier than I planned and got more done. I wanted to get it all done."

"To save money? I thought you had a budget."

"We do, but it's not enough for this building Amelia is talking about."

"So, she doesn't want to help, but she wants to expand your project and make it more complicated for you? I know you were talking about a structure, but I thought you wanted open-air."

I nodded. "That was the plan, but she's not wrong. There are a lot of kids who need a place to go during the year. We just finished up the holiday break and there were kids who didn't have a spot because there's only so many we can take."

"That's a lot more money than you were planning to spend. Is that why you were trying to get this done alone?"

I nodded. "I have to. The budget the mayor gave us is not enough to do the things that need to be done for us to open, let alone even more."

"But if Amelia wants to add on to your plan, shouldn't she be asking for more money?"

I shrugged. "I don't know. The mayor made it pretty clear that there was no more money and that he's not going to change his mind."

"There are always funds that they can use for things like this. There's a town need. Did you ask him?"

I pursed my lips and gave my best friend a look that clearly said she forgot who she was talking to.

Her laughter said she got it. "Okay, fine. You're not going to talk to him. But Amelia should."

"She might, but even if she does, we're still not going to have enough. The entire budget we have right now wouldn't cover the cost of a building. Or the other work. I know I can't make up for all of it, but anything I can do myself helps the budget."

"Unless you get yourself killed," Daisy said softly.

"I survived," I said, knowing that was a real possibility if I hadn't gotten out of that hole. I didn't text Daisy when I went out there because I was so flustered about the new building idea. If I hadn't gotten out of there, she would have been the only one who suspected where I was or knew I was missing. It could have been bad.

"I think you need to plan a fundraiser. Sooner rather than later."

"You know I'm no good at things like that."

"You're also no good at digging up the ground and not falling into the hole you made."

I scowled at her.

"You know I'm right. And you know everyone will help."

"And you know I suck at talking to people."

"You tell yourself that, but when you talk about these kids and this camp, it's different. People will see that. And you won't have to do it alone. I'll help, and Amelia will hopefully help. And this is important. It's not like you're trying to get people to give you money for the hell of it. You have a purpose, and you have a clear mission. We need to make this happen."

"I don't know, Daisy. I just—"

"Something small. We can ask Hudson if we can use his bar, and talk to Chelsea and Haley and all the women at book club. I'm sure there will be people willing to help."

"We should talk to Goldie. She's good at these things."

"Ooh, good idea. Yes. All right, we're going to book club on Sunday so we can get things moving on this."

I grumbled but knew she was right. I needed money to make the summer camp amazing. I couldn't do it all without some help.

Guess that resolution was going to happen after all.

8

OMAR

I wasn't a fan of mornings, but I knew getting to work early was for the best. Especially when I had a meeting scheduled with Amelia and Natalie. I refused to think about Natalie and that kiss. Two weeks and I was fooling myself if I thought I'd forgotten. But I couldn't think about it. I had to focus, do my job, and be objective.

Not only that, but now that it was the new calendar year, I had to start thinking about my election campaign.

First, the meeting.

My early morning was quiet with emails and a few phone calls, but nothing major. I signed off on two projects. One was to repair the gazebo at Catherine Park after an ice storm chipped away at the support structure. The other was to have the trees around the schools trimmed back so they didn't obstruct views from the schools to the parking lot.

I was ready when Jane said Amelia and Natalie had arrived. That's what I told myself.

Then they walked in. Amelia shook my hand and asked how I was doing. It was a challenge to answer her because I was focused on Natalie.

She wore a dark tee and jeans, but the way she moved said she was injured.

"What happened?" I asked her, needing to know she was okay.

Natalie looked at Amelia, her eyes wide and scared.

"I fell," Natalie whispered.

"Are you okay?"

Natalie nodded.

I wanted to ask more, to find out what happened and how she was hurt, and if I needed to kill someone for causing her harm, but before I could voice those inappropriate questions, Amelia kept going.

"That's part of what we need to talk about today," Amelia jumped in.

Natalie's eyes widened even more. She shook her head.

Amelia ignored her and focused on me.

I looked between them and waited for someone to tell me what was going on.

"Natalie was working at the campground alone on Monday and slipped. She sprained her ankle. She will be fine, but we need more money in order to make this project work."

"I told you, we don't have more money," I argued, even as I ached to do anything to stop her from getting hurt again.

"Which is why we're going to have a fundraiser. Many of them, I hope, but the first one is going to be in six weeks, right before mid-winter break. Because our plans have changed."

"Changed?" Every inch of me tightened with that news.

Amelia nodded, her eyes wide and excited. "Yes. We have a huge opportunity with this location. If we can build the structure like Natalie suggested, but we can close it in, we can use it for so much more. We can have kids there for breaks during the school year, not just summer camp. We can host functions there. We can use it for more than just a summer camp."

"And you think you can raise enough money to pay for it?"

"I do," Amelia said with confidence. "Maybe not with one fundraiser, but I think we can. But the most important thing for me is keeping my people safe. Natalie was out at the campground digging up conduit for the sites alone and fell. She could have been more seriously injured, or worse, and no one would have known. She was trying to save money because you won't give us more."

Amelia was a shark. I never saw it before, but the woman knew exactly what to say to prove her point. "No more. We can't risk that. No one is allowed out there without a plan. Whether that's another person or a scheduled check-in or something, but we can't risk people getting hurt."

"I'm happy to hear you say that, Omar."

I looked closely at her and knew I walked right into whatever she wanted.

"Natalie doesn't agree with me, but hearing it from you might change her mind."

Natalie scowled at Amelia, but schooled her features when she caught me looking at her.

"Ms. Edwards?" I asked.

"Fine," she grunted.

"Are you taking time off to recover from the injury?" I asked her.

"No. I... I'm fine."

"I thought your job was to chase after kids all afternoon."

"Amelia is working with me."

"So, your boss is making accommodations for your injury instead of insisting you take time off to recover?"

"Would you rather fire me, Mr. Mayor?"

That spark in her eyes and the way she said Mr. Mayor told me she hadn't forgotten that kiss we shared anymore than I had.

And dammit, that spark was why I kissed her in the first place. I wanted to see it again and again, but I couldn't act on that desire. I had to keep it together.

"No one is getting fired. Especially for doing something on town property with your boss's knowledge. If she's fired, she'll have grounds to sue the town, and I'll be the first one any lawyer worth a damn will name," Amelia told me.

"Sue us?" I asked.

"I'm not suing anyone," Natalie said softly. "I was the one who went out there alone. I won't do it again."

I got the feeling it was an argument they'd been having and that my presence was simply so Amelia had someone else on her side.

"Now that we have that settled," I said, attempting to bring the conversation back around, "what is your plan for the fundraiser?"

"We're going to hold it at O'Kelley's. Natalie has been in touch with some locals, including Goldie Spear, Hudson Grant, and Trent MacKellar. She's working with Daisy Lincoln to come up with some plans."

"What do you need from me?"

"More money?" Amelia suggested.

"I walked right into that one. Anything else?"

"If you were willing to put in an appearance at the fundraiser, I think it would help. Telling the town you support the efforts will help to make it a success."

"What is your goal with the fundraiser?"

"We have three goals. The first will be to bring in the rest of the money required to do phase one of the work on the campground. Natalie insists she's going to finish digging out the campsite connections, but I'm not sure it's possible. At some point, we will need a professional. The tree on the basketball court is something my son said he can take care of. Cleaning up the volleyball court is also easy. The pool is the big thing. The money from the town is going to go toward making the pool safe. The building will be phase one-point-five because we both feel it's necessary, but it's way outside the budget. Ideally, that's what the fundraiser will help with."

"That's two goals," I said. "The electric and pool, then the building. What's the third?"

Amelia looked at Natalie.

Natalie's eyes went big, but Amelia didn't back down. Finally, Natalie opened her mouth. "Scholarships."

"Excuse me? I thought this was going to make money for the town, not cost us money."

"Yes, but there are families who can't afford camp. Parents who have to work in order to pay for their kids to have food, which means the kids can't go to camp so they're home alone all day. Ten percent of the students in MacKellar Cove Central School District get free lunch from the state. Another ten percent get reduced price lunch. These families don't have the money to pay for camp, so the kids are slipping through the cracks. A scholarship would give some families the chance to have their kids at a safe place for the summer and know they are being fed and cared for."

"How many scholarships do you want to have?"

"I have a donor who agreed to three already. I'd like to

start with ten. I want more, eventually, but ten would be great."

"Done."

"Excuse me?" Natalie said. She looked at Amelia, then back at me. "What do you mean?"

"I will pay for the other seven scholarships personally. The only requirement is that no one knows they came from me."

"You can't... why... how... Mr. Mayor?"

"The money you raise needs to go toward getting the camp set up. We can set up a separate scholarship fund through the town and have people donate to that outside of the fundraiser."

"You would do that?" Natalie asked. She looked at me like she did the day I kissed her. Like I wasn't the man she thought I was. Like there was more to me.

I nodded. She worked for me, so I had to stop any hope that things between us could be different. "I would. And I will. We have a charitable contributions chairperson, and I will be in touch with her later today about what needs to be done. Having it go through here also means you won't have the task of choosing which students should get the scholarships."

The relief on her face with those words told me it was the biggest worry she had. "Thank you, Mr. Mayor."

"I think maybe it's time you called me Omar."

Her gaze snagged on mine and held. The way her chest rose and fell slowly said she was just as trapped in the moment as I was. "Omar," she whispered.

Amelia cleared her throat, and Natalie snapped out of the trance that held us both.

"Um, and you should call me Natalie."

"As you wish, Natalie."

Her eyes widened again, and she rolled her lower lip in, pinching it between her teeth.

I cleared my throat that time and moved away from the woman who was making me forget my place. "Please get me the information for the fundraiser, and I will make sure I am there. And don't go out to the campground alone again. Not without a plan to make sure you're safe. I don't want anything to happen to you, Natalie."

She nodded, staring at me.

"We will. Thank you, Omar," Amelia said, dragging Natalie from my office with hushed whispers I couldn't understand.

And probably didn't want to.

SOME OF THE local men had invited me to join them on Thursday nights at O'Kelley's, and I always said no. For some reason, after my meeting with Natalie, I decided to go.

The bar was not a place I'd been in many times. It had a good, casual feel, but I wasn't a big drinker and bars were never my favorite places to spend time. But if I was going to get reelected and if I was going to show my support for the fundraiser, I was going to need to get over going to a bar.

"Mayor Omar Knight. To what do we owe the honor?" Hudson Grant asked when he spotted me. Hudson always made sure to say hello when he saw me in his bar, but this was a different situation.

"Evening. I thought I'd see what this guys' night is all about. Derek and Patrick have both invited me, and I've always had other things going on."

Hudson nodded, letting the half-truth slide. "Well, glad you joined us. Can I get you something?"

"Anything local?"

Hudson nodded and grabbed a glass, filling it with precision before placing it in front of me. "Enjoy."

I nodded and took a sip. It was light and refreshing, with a hint of something deeper underneath. "Very good."

Hudson grinned. "It is. One of my favorites."

"Mr. Mayor! How are you?" Patrick Hill asked, taking the seat next to me. "Is it okay if I sit here?"

"Of course. Good to see you, Patrick. How's Goldie?"

"She's good." The man beamed at the mention of the woman he loved. "She's hoping you're running for reelection. Any decision on that?"

I looked at him, wondering why he didn't know. "Uh, yeah. I thought it was public knowledge that I was running."

"Great news. You'll make her very happy. She really likes working for you. We all do."

I appreciated Patrick's vote of confidence. "Thank you."

"Omar," another voice said. "I didn't know you were going to be here."

I turned and saw Amelia's son, James Rucker, approaching. James was a police officer but not someone I'd met more than a few times. He seemed to have a good sense of humor and a low tolerance for bullshit, but a huge heart for the underprivileged in our community. He definitely got that from his mother. "Nice to see you, James. How are you?"

"Good. Making plans to help my mom out with that tree. Have you seen that campground? It's going to make a beautiful summer camp."

"Did she tell you to tell me that?"

James blanched a bit. "No, sir. My mom is pretty straightforward with people. She doesn't do manipulation or coercion."

"I apologize. I didn't mean to imply anything. She definitely speaks her mind. Unlike Natalie Edwards. That woman has to get worked up before she says what she's thinking. She could take a few notes from your mother."

James smirked at me, clearly catching something I didn't want him to catch. "I'm sure she could. But Natalie isn't around a lot when I'm at the community center. The few times we've spoken, she's ducked out before I got her all worked up."

My cheeks warmed at the obvious implication. I nodded and sipped my beer, hoping James would let the subject drop before I confessed even more about how I wanted to get Natalie Edwards worked up.

"Another beer, Mr. Mayor?" Hudson asked, taking my attention from James.

I shook my head and realized the one I was drinking was almost gone. "Omar, please. And I'll switch to water. Thanks."

Hudson nodded and filled a glass with ice, then added water before setting it in front of me. He worked down the line of men who filtered in and joined me at the bar while I did what I could to calm my mind and panic.

Daniel Ryan, former front man of a massively successful band who gave it all up when he met the love of his life and moved to MacKellar Cove, slid onto the stool next to me and scowled at the mirror behind the bar. "Daisy Lincoln is going to destroy my peace and quiet in this town."

"Daisy's a firecracker. What is she talking you into?" Knox Randall asked. Knox owned Al's Hardware, and we hadn't had much contact, but I knew he was someone who was well respected in town.

"She's trying to get us to do a show for some fundraiser. She's relentless. Sofia is trying to talk me into it now." Sofia was Daniel's girlfriend and business partner. The two of them were creating their own version of success with songs they were writing together, but Daniel had mostly given up performing and the life of fame that kept him on the road and under the thumb of others.

"That's the fundraiser for the new summer camp," Ramsey Holland said, joining the conversation. "You should do it. Melody is helping Natalie and Daisy plan the whole thing. My daughter's best friend goes to the summer camp and loves it. Said Natalie is her favorite adult that isn't her mom or Melody. Daisy's hitting up everyone to make sure the fundraiser brings in what's needed. Natalie got hurt, and Daisy went a little nuts."

"Is Natalie okay?" Knox asked.

It was completely irrational that I was mad Knox was asking. The man was engaged and had a pregnant fiancée, but I didn't want him to be asking about Natalie.

"She's fine," I answered. "Her ankle is sprained, but she said she's okay."

"You're friends with Natalie?" Hudson asked.

I realized I had the attention of all the men gathered. James raised his brows and smirked at me, waiting with the rest of them for my confession.

"She works for me. I had a meeting with her and James's mother, Amelia, earlier. Amelia read Natalie the riot act and got me to agree that she can't be out there alone and risk getting hurt again," I said.

The others exchanged looks and nodded.

"Glad she's okay," Knox said. He looked past me to someone else. "Have you or Laura checked her out? Make sure she's good?"

I turned and found Doctor Nico Allison shaking his head.

"We don't usually deal with injuries like that, but I'll

make sure Laura knows. Daisy has been dragging Natalie to book club." Nico grinned wryly, and the other men chuckled.

"What's book club?" I asked.

"All the women get together Sunday night at Book Boyfriends Unlimited and talk about how amazing we are," Hudson said.

The others snorted their laughter.

"Something like that," James said. "Usually they're bitching about something one of us did."

"Speak for yourself," Ramsey said. "My wife doesn't complain about me."

"Anymore," James retorted.

Ramsey flipped him off, and James laughed.

"Children, we have a guest. Knock it off," Hudson told them. He jerked his head in my direction.

"Whoa, I'm a guest?" I asked.

Hudson raised one eyebrow. "You've never been here for guys' night, and you're kind of everyone's boss, so we need to be on our best behavior."

I shook my head. "No. I don't want that. I didn't come here tonight to make everyone uncomfortable. I just wanted to..."

"Not think about Natalie Edwards for a little while?" James said.

The others exchanged a look but didn't say anything.

I met James's gaze and shook my head. "You're not helping that, you know?"

James smirked. "That's not why we come here. We come here to figure out what to do about our women. Not forget them."

"She's not mine."

"Maybe not yet, but you clearly want her to be." Hudson crossed his arms and dared me to argue.

"Well, I guess my plan to get out and not think about her didn't really work." I grabbed my water and drank half of it, debating what to do.

"Don't worry, Mr. Mayor. What we say at the bar stays here. Now, tell us about Natalie and how she has you so wrapped up and crazy," Patrick said.

I looked at all of them. Could I trust them? Did it matter? It wasn't like things could get worse.

9

———————

"Natalie is... She's..."

"Infuriating?" James suggested.

"Intoxicating?" Knox added.

"Addictive?" Hudson said.

"Are you all looking to screw around on your women?" I snapped.

"No, sir. We just understand that look on your face," Patrick said.

I looked at the smirks of the other men and realized they were goading me. "I... You all suck."

They laughed at my expense, and I found myself chuckling with them.

"Listen, we know what it's like when you find a woman who turns you inside out and makes you want to punch walls and kiss her until you run out of breath, at the same time. We've all been there. And we've all helped each other through it," Hudson said.

"There's no shame here. Maybe some enjoyment of your discomfort, but we're on the other side, sir. We know how painful it is to be where you are," Patrick said.

"First, you need to quit calling me *sir*. Or *Mr. Mayor*. If I'm going to be here, I can't have that separation." I met the gazes of the men there and waited for each to nod. "Second, Natalie is not mine and isn't going to be. I just need to figure out how to get her out of my mind."

"Why isn't she going to be yours? I don't know of anyone she's dating," James said, picking up his beer to take a sip.

"She's an employee. It wouldn't be right." I shook my head, knowing the way it looked and the way people would talk.

"Goldie is my boss. It kept us apart for a long time because she was worried about the same thing, but one of the things I love about her is she would never compromise her integrity or what's right for the town because of my opinion. I'd venture to say you're the same," Patrick said, leveling me with a look that was as much questioning as it was assurance that he was right.

"I would never use my position—"

"Which is what he's saying," James interrupted me. "My mom is a huge fan of yours. She speaks very highly of you."

"So does Goldie," Patrick added.

"And everyone else who works with you," Knox added. "Or has had the pleasure of getting to know you. Derek tells me all the time how good of a person you are. Not mayor, person. You're more than your title. And you're allowed to have a personal life."

"Natalie is..." I couldn't find the words to describe her. And I wasn't sure they would understand if I did.

"When I met Anna, my wife," Hudson said, capturing my attention, "I hated the woman. She was obnoxious and loud and in my face all the damn time. She hated me, too. Thought I was going to fuck up her son by giving him a job. Fuck up their lives."

"But she married you."

Hudson nodded, the smile of a truly happy man lighting up his entire face. The stern, serious, intimidating bar owner was a softie for his family. "We learned to see beyond the mask. Anna was hiding a lot of distrust as a result of her ex-husband. I was hiding a lot of pain from losing my wife. Neither was recent, but neither of us had gotten over our pasts. It took her needing my help, and me proving I was not the same as her ex, for us to see each other differently."

"And you're saying I need to do that with Natalie?" I asked.

James shook his head. "No, what he's saying is every woman is different. I judged Trinity the day we met. Saw a stranger and thought she was stealing. Wasted a lot of time we could have been getting to know each other because I jumped to conclusions about her."

"I slept with Haley before I knew her name. Impossible to resist her, but not the way I intended to start a relationship," Knox confessed.

"You're engaged and have a kid on the way, right?" I asked.

Knox grinned proudly. "Best one-night stand of my life, and even better date the next night. But that didn't mean it was easy."

"The question is, do you want to forget Natalie, or are you wanting to get to know her better?" Ramsey asked.

I shook my head, not sure of the answer.

"There's this dating app," Daniel said. "Works wonders for finding someone."

The other men groaned.

"Book Boyfriends Wanted?" I asked.

Daniel nodded, and the others shook their heads.

"What's wrong?"

Daniel chuckled. "The app has a crazy way of pairing up people that are meant to be. We've all fallen victim to it."

"You all met your wives and girlfriends on there?" I asked them.

Every single one of them nodded.

"I thought you and Melody went to high school together," I asked Ramsey.

"We did. And we were separated and heading for divorce when we were paired on that app. Got us talking again and brought us back together," Ramsey said.

"Damn. I didn't know that."

Ramsey shrugged. "Not something I advertise that I fucked up my marriage and almost lost the woman I love."

"Understood," I said, seeing the pain in his gaze.

"If you want to forget Natalie, sign up for the app. It'll find you someone else. Maybe someone who doesn't have you so twisted up," James said.

I nodded, thinking about ThisIsAwkward. Maybe it was time to ask her to meet. To stop worrying about if she was someone I knew and take the leap.

After all, if she could get me to stop obsessing over Natalie Edwards, it was worth it to risk feeling foolish with another woman.

BY THE TIME I got home, I was talking myself out of reaching out to ThisIsAwkward. We'd been talking for a while, and if the guys were right, maybe she was the right one. The one who would put my focus back where it belonged on the campaign and not on the summer camp director who made my life and brain a scrambled mess.

BIGCITYCONVERT

How is your week?

Yeah, not a great opening, but it was better than blurting out that I wanted to meet her.

I put my phone away and got ready for bed, hoping I would get a message back and could work meeting in person into the conversation.

I crawled into bed and checked my phone and saw a reply.

THISISAWKWARD

Busy. A lot going on at work. How is yours?

BIGCITYCONVERT

Same. Work sometimes invades my personal time and makes things harder.

THISISAWKWARD

I know what you mean. My roommate works most weekends, and sometimes I help her out. During the week I have a fairly normal schedule, but there have been more times lately I've been doing things off-hours.

BIGCITYCONVERT

Maybe you could make time this weekend for us to get together. Actually meet in person.

I stared at the screen for an abnormally long time, waiting for her to reply. But she didn't.

I finally gave up and put my phone away, hoping she would answer eventually. In all our conversations, she came across as someone who didn't run away from their feelings, but someone who had big ones. And meeting in person could lead to some big feelings.

I was definitely feeling some.

But hopefully, she was open to the idea.

I waited over an hour for her to say something, but she never did. If I was going to get any sleep, I needed to turn my phone off and ignore the fears racing around that she had no interest in getting together. She was one woman. If it didn't work out, it was okay.

The next morning, after a crappy night of sleep, I forced myself not to check my phone before I was ready for the day. I was drinking my coffee when I finally gave in and looked at my phone. I had an answer.

THISISAWKWARD

My roommate told me this means it's time to put up or shut up. I guess I have to say yes.

BIGCITYCONVERT

You don't have to do anything. I didn't mean to make you feel that way.

THISISAWKWARD

I don't have a great track record with dating.

BIGCITYCONVERT

I'd argue no one does. Success means you don't do it anymore.

THISISAWKWARD

Well, can't argue with that.

BIGCITYCONVERT

I like talking to you. I think you're someone I would enjoy talking to in person, too. But if you're not interested, I understand.

THISISAWKWARD

It's not that. This is why I struggle. I don't express myself well. Especially when I have to say or do something quickly. I like this because I can slow down and think and delete messages a dozen times before I send them.

BIGCITYCONVERT

There's nothing wrong with that.

THISISAWKWARD

Until we're sitting across from each other and you expect me to keep up my side of the conversation and I say something stupid and you decide I'm not worth the effort.

BIGCITYCONVERT

That doesn't sound hypothetical.

THISISAWKWARD

It's not. It's happened. Nearly every time I've met someone.

BIGCITYCONVERT

What if I tell you something no one else knows? Something that might make you feel better?

THISISAWKWARD

It would have to be really good to make me think you're not going to walk out on me as soon as I sit down.

BIGCITYCONVERT

First, that's horrible. Second, trust me when I say I'm taking a risk, too.

THISISAWKWARD

Okay. Lay it on me.

BIGCITYCONVERT

I've never felt like I fit in wherever I am. As a kid, I was a nerd and spent all my time studying. When I got married, my ex was outgoing and flashy and dragged me along. After our divorce, I moved here and never made connections to a lot of people. Where I'm at now, I think that's going to end up hurting my future, but I don't like people who are fake. Who do things for the wrong reasons. I'm trying to get to know people, but I don't think people see me for me.

THISISAWKWARD

Well, damn. You went deep. Thank you. And I'm sorry. I understand, though. I have the same struggles. I think a lot more people do than you realize.

BIGCITYCONVERT

Maybe.

THISISAWKWARD

Do you still want to meet?

BIGCITYCONVERT

Are you saying that was a big enough confession to get you to agree?

THISISAWKWARD

Yes, it was.

BIGCITYCONVERT

How about tomorrow night? You pick the place. Wherever you would feel comfortable.

THISISAWKWARD

There's a bar in MacKellar Cove. O'Kelley's. Have you ever been?

BIGCITYCONVERT

Yeah, I know it.

THISISAWKWARD

What time?

BIGCITYCONVERT

Five?

THISISAWKWARD

I'll be there.

BIGCITYCONVERT

I'm looking forward to it.

THISISAWKWARD

I'll try. By then I might panic and not come.

BIGCITYCONVERT

Should we meet tonight?

THISISAWKWARD

Oh, I'm not sure I can do that.

BIGCITYCONVERT

When would be best for you?

THISISAWKWARD

Is this because you really want to meet me
or because you're trying to end things?

BIGCITYCONVERT

I really want to meet you.

THISISAWKWARD

Okay. Tomorrow at five.

BIGCITYCONVERT

See you then.

She signed off the app, and I smiled. I was meeting This-
IsAwkward in less than twenty-four hours.

And putting Natalie Edwards out of my mind.

I CHANGED my clothes three times before I walked out the door for my date. I debated what car to drive, but decided to take my Camaro, knowing if things didn't go well I'd want to take a drive.

O'Kelley's was busy but not crowded, which was good. It would get busier later, but for dinner it wasn't too bad. Even better, I didn't recognize anyone there except Hudson behind the bar.

"Omar," Hudson said as I approached him. "Nice to see you twice in less than a week."

"You, too."

"What can I get you?"

"A beer, please."

"Dinner?" He poured my beer, the same one he gave me two nights earlier, and set it in front of me.

I glanced at the door and down at my phone. "I'm not sure yet."

Hudson's brows jumped almost high enough to vanish under the snapback of his blue ball cap. "You're meeting someone."

It wasn't a question, but I nodded the confirmation anyway.

"You took our advice and signed up for Book Boyfriends Wanted."

I shook my head. "I signed up a while ago. But I did take your advice and asked the woman I've been talking to to meet me."

"And you chose here?"

"No, she did. Speaks volumes to who you are and the way people trust you."

Hudson chuckled. "I've accepted my position. It used to piss me off when the women would meet their dates here, but I realized the same thing you said and decided I'd rather have them come here than risk something happening because I ran them off."

"That's admirable of you."

He snorted. "Not really. Got my ass handed to me when Finley and Trent met up in here. She didn't know who he was, and when she got pregnant, she was pissed that I didn't give her a head's up."

"Ouch," I said with a wince.

"It all worked out in the end. She got her happily ever after."

"She's a close friend of yours?"

Hudson nodded, a smile softening his features. "She is. Has been forever. And my wife works for her now, so we spend a lot of time with them. Finley changed Trent in all the ways he needed to change."

"I can't say I've met him more than a handful of times."

"He'll be here this Thursday if you're available again. Although I imagine it depends on how tonight goes."

I laughed. "Doubtful about that one. At this point, I'm hoping she shows up." I checked my phone again. She was five minutes late.

"Did she give you any indication of what she'd be wearing so you would know who she is?"

"No. Should she have?"

Hudson shook his head at me like I was a fool. "Usually the guy does that. So she can duck out if she doesn't feel safe."

"Dammit. I suck at dating."

"We all do."

I unlocked my phone and opened the app while Hudson walked away to help another customer. I sent ThisIsAwkward a message telling her what I was wearing and that I was at the bar when she arrived.

I resisted the urge to ask if she was still coming. Something told me calling her out on being late would not go over well.

I sipped my beer slowly while I waited for someone to show up. A few times, the door opened, and I held my breath, but no one sat next to me. I refused to watch the door in case she walked in and decided to walk right back out again without approaching me.

After thirty minutes, I decided I'd give her another fifteen minutes, then I'd leave. If she changed her mind, I'd be upset, but she was allowed. If she didn't, and something happened, I had to be reasonable. I didn't know much about her, and she could have had an emergency.

The door opened at thirty-nine minutes late, and I took a sip of my beer. Hudson smiled at whoever walked in. He glanced my way, then smirked.

My entire body stiffened. She was there. And debating. But she showed.

For a minute, I waited, straining to hear anything in the bar. Pool balls clacked together, people talked, music played. And then I felt her behind me.

She slid onto the stool next to me, the scent of strawberries hitting me before I glanced over.

"Natalie?" I blurted.

"Oh, no."

"What are you doing here?"

She made a move to get off the stool. "This was a bad idea. I knew it was a bad idea. I never should have come here."

"Are you ThisIsAwkward?" I blurted.

She froze. Realization slammed her eyes closed. She shook her head, a breath of a laugh escaping from her nose. "Wow."

"Is that a yes?"

She opened her hazel eyes and looked straight at me. "Yeah. Which means you're..."

"BigCityConvert," I said, knowing the confirmation was easier with me revealing information.

"Of course you are."

"And you're not happy."

"Are you, Mr. Mayor?"

"I asked you to call me Omar."

"Why? We both know this isn't going to work. I never should have come here. I knew I shouldn't have come. Hell, that's why I'm late."

"You didn't want to come?"

"These things always go poorly for me. Men take one look at me and decide I'm not who they were hoping would show up. I'm..." She sucked in a sharp breath. "I'm not the same person."

"Someone else was messaging me?"

"No! That's not... That's not what I meant. I meant I'm not quick on my feet. I'm not beautiful and fun and outgoing and all the things men want in a woman. I'm... well, I'm awkward."

"And that means you can't date?"

"No, it means no one wants to date me. And you already know all those things about me, so I know you don't have to stick around and find them out. Have a good night, Mr. Mayor."

"Natalie, wait!"

"Isn't that interesting," a man said from not far away. "And here I thought that was a one-time thing between you two."

I looked at him and found the photographer from the night months ago. The man who refused to bury the picture he took of Natalie and I. "What the hell do you want?"

He smirked. "Not a thing. Have a good night, Mr. Mayor."

"That didn't go well," Hudson said, pulling my attention from the man.

I looked back, and the man was gone. "Do you know who that was?"

"Uh, Natalie?" Hudson said.

"No. The man..." I shook my head. "Never mind."

"You want that dinner now?"

"Yeah, I might as well. Since I don't have a date tonight."

"Sorry, man. I thought for sure when she walked in it was going to be a good thing."

"Wasn't meant to be."

10

NATALIE

I SWIPED AT MY CHEEKS AS I HURRIED AWAY FROM O'KELLEY'S. I knew meeting up with him was a bad idea, but Mayor Knight? Could it get any worse?

I got to my car and slipped, almost face-planting against the side of my vehicle. I caught myself at the last minute, but of course, my feet didn't stay put. I slipped, my ankle howling in pain.

No, wait. That was me howling. Like a wild animal on the street.

Ugh.

I pulled myself up and got into my car, starting it up and getting the hell out of there. No more dating. I couldn't do it. I was foolish to think it was an option for me. Why? Why did I try?

Because you want a family.

"I don't need it," I told the voice in my head. I convinced myself a long time ago that my anxiety was too much. It knocked me down too many times, and most people silently faded into the background, not bothering to understand or try to be there for me.

Daisy was the first and only person outside my family who accepted me for me and didn't judge me or try to change me or tell me I'd get over it. Daisy was family, as far as I was concerned. I didn't need anyone else. I was fine.

Instead of going home to the apartment I shared with Daisy, I drove a little out of town and pulled into the driveway of the house where I grew up. Daisy would want to know all about the date and how the new guy was, but I was too raw and overwhelmed to be able to share anything with her. Knowing how her face would fall and how she'd want to go after Mayor Knight was more than I could handle.

I would tell her. Just not right now.

I let myself into my childhood home and was not at all surprised to find my parents on the couch watching the evening news.

"Natalie! What are you doing here? Is everything okay?" Mom asked, getting up and hurrying over to me. She turned on the light, waking up my dad, who jumped before realizing I was there.

"Natalie. Good to see you. Forgot you were coming over tonight."

"That's because she wasn't supposed to be, Dean." Mom smacked the back of his chair.

"Oh. Well, good to see you, anyway."

"Thanks, Dad." My parents were an odd couple, although when I was little I didn't realize it. Dad was married before, and had two daughters from his first marriage. They lived with their mom when I was young, and I didn't realize most people didn't have siblings a decade older than them until I was in college. I also didn't realize it wasn't normal for your dad to be almost twenty years older than your mom.

But my parents loved each other. Dad said his first

marriage was a good one, but it wasn't the right one. My sisters spent time with us, but they were closer to their mom. It had been years since I'd seen either of them. They both left the area for college and never came back once their mom moved away.

"How are Renee and Eva?" I asked Dad, taking a seat on the couch where Mom had been.

Dad looked at Mom and sat up straight in his chair. "They're good. Renee is destroying the patriarchy, as she says, in LA and loving every minute of it. Eva is busy as all get-out with the kids keeping her running. But they're both good."

"That's good. I haven't seen them in a long time. Tell them I said hello."

Dad nodded. "I will."

"What's wrong, Natalie?" Mom asked.

I shook my head. "Just a bad date."

"Do I need to get my gun?" Dad said.

I chuckled and shook my head. Dad hadn't fired a gun in decades and would probably hurt himself if he tried to use the rusty old firearm at the back of the closet. Not to mention there hadn't been ammunition in the house since I was born, according to my mother, so the threat was an empty one.

"Nothing happened that requires violence, Dad."

"Then what did happen?" Mom asked.

I shrugged. "I'm me. And he's... He's too perfect for someone like me."

"Did he say that?" Dad barked.

"No. He wouldn't. But I know him, and I didn't realize it until I sat down. There's no way we would work."

"Why not?" Mom asked. "You don't give yourself nearly enough credit for the amazing woman you are."

I shook my head as she spoke. "It's just not going to happen. He's... He has to be in the public eye because of his job, and I'm no good at that. I'm definitely a behind-the-scenes person."

"You don't have to be."

"Oh, yes, I do. And I'm okay with that. I know who I am. And I know who I'm not. It's taken me a long time to accept that, and I'm not going to try to be someone else for anyone."

"What makes you think this man is looking for someone who is in the public eye? Did he say you're not good enough?" Dad asked.

"No. He's too diplomatic for that."

"You make it sound like you had a date with the mayor," Mom joked.

Dad laughed.

I stayed silent.

"Well, whoever it is, he's not worthy of you if he doesn't see how amazing you are."

"Thanks, Mom."

"But I do wish you'd give yourself more credit. Amelia has been keeping me up to date on all the things you're planning and doing with the new summer camp. It sounds like it's going to be amazing."

My lips lifted into a smile just thinking about it. "I'm really excited. It's going to be a lot of work, and it's going to take a long time to get it to where we really want it, but it's going to be amazing."

"Tell us about it. What are you planning? Where are you at right now?" Mom and Amelia had been friends forever. It was one of the many reasons I felt comfortable with Amelia. They were similar in a lot of ways, including the way they both encouraged me to be myself and not worry about people who didn't understand me.

"Still planning. We have a very small budget, so we're working on setting up a fundraiser. Daisy is helping me with that."

"She'll have everyone involved, without a doubt," Mom teased. She loved Daisy as much as I did, and she knew Daisy didn't let things go when she decided it was right.

"She will. She's been great. Especially since I know she's busy, too."

"But she loves you and will do anything to help you."

"I know. I've talked to a few contractors, but we're limited on what can be done right now because of the weather. As soon as spring is here, we're going to jump on everything and really get moving."

"That's a good idea. Is there anything we can help with? I can clean. Amelia mentioned a trailer?"

I gagged at the thought of the trailer.

Mom laughed. "That's pretty much what she said. Tell me about the rest of the site."

I jumped in, detailing everything we had, everything we planned, and all the ideas I hoped to get to one day. By the time I finished talking, Dad was asleep again, and I needed to get home if I was going to get any sleep.

But I left feeling better, and that was the whole reason I went home.

Daisy cornered me in the morning and asked how my date was. She assumed when I didn't come home until late that it had gone very well.

She was shocked to hear just how wrong she was.

"I walked out."

"You what?!?"

"I met him, and it wasn't right. There was no way it would work out. So I left."

"But you don't even know him. And you've been talking forever and really liked him. You can't possibly tell me in ten minutes you decided all the conversations you had were wrong. That he's that different from the man you were talking to."

"He's…" I wasn't sure if I wanted her to know who he was. I wasn't sure if I wanted anyone to know. It felt safer with that piece hidden. "He *was* different. Maybe I rushed my judgement, but it's not going to work. I was foolish to think dating was a good idea. It's easier online. It's easier to be able to stop and think about what I'm going to say."

"Did he say something? Dating is not foolish. You want a family, and unfortunately, the only way to find a person to create that family with is in person."

I shook my head. "He didn't say anything. It… It's not going to work with him."

"So where did you go after your date?"

"To my parents' house."

Daisy's face softened into a smile. "How are they?"

"They're good. It was nice to visit for a little while."

"And a good place to go to avoid me and my questions for the night?"

My cheeks burned with the truth as Daisy gave me a stink-eye. "Yeah, yeah."

She chuckled. "I understand. And I'm sorry. I was hoping things would work out with this guy."

I nodded, thinking back to when I walked into O'Kelley's and saw him sitting at the bar. He waited. He didn't run out when I wasn't there exactly on time. He always made it seem like he would be okay with my... quirks. Then he turned around, and I saw who he was and I knew there was no way.

Mayor Knight was polished perfection. He was pulled-together and on display all the time. He didn't have a single scandal and everyone in town loved him.

Perfect and awkward did not work. It never would. So I had to walk away and stop thinking about him. He wasn't who I thought, and I wasn't who he thought, and we weren't ever going to be more than we were online.

"I need to work on fundraiser stuff," I blurted, knowing the longer I talked to her, the more likely I would spill all the secrets.

"And you don't want to tell me anymore about your date. I get it. Book club tonight?"

I scowled.

"It'll be good to get out. See some friends and forget about your date."

I nodded, even though I wasn't thrilled with the idea. I liked all the women there, but secrets had a way of becoming public when we were all together.

But Daisy looked excited. She loved having more friends. And I wanted to go for her sake.

Yes, I was being selfish. I felt guilty not opening up to her about Mayor Knight, but I couldn't bring myself to say the words. To admit how badly I screwed up. Maybe one day I could laugh about it, but not yet.

DAISY DRAGGED me down the street toward Book Boyfriends Unlimited with glee on her face. She was so excited to be there. She was good for me, getting me out when I was perfectly content to sit in my room and never leave home.

Finley, the owner of Book Boyfriends Unlimited, unlocked the store and let us in, hugging us both and asking how we were.

"I worked all day, so I'm a little hyper right now," Daisy said.

"You're always a little hyper," I grumbled.

"And you're always grumpy," Daisy shot back with a teasing smile.

"We all have those days," Finley said. "But at least we have cake here."

"It's always a good day for cake," Daisy said.

"Absolutely," Blake said, handing over slices as we joined the rest of the women in the back of the store. "How are you guys?"

"Good," Daisy and I said at the same time.

The others laughed.

"Someone has to have something we can talk about," Elise said, slicing her cake. "How is it possible no one has man trouble?"

I carefully avoided the looks going around the room, not at all interested in being the center of attention.

Thank God Daisy was a good friend.

"I'd have to have a man to have trouble," Daisy said. "I have not had any luck lately. All the men I meet are dads and shopping with their wives."

"No single dads?" Willow asked.

Daisy shook her head. "Nope. I'm starting to wonder if I have to leave the area to find a date."

Karissa chuckled and shook her head. "My app is still getting new downloads every day, so there are people out there. Are you on it? Book Boyfriends Wanted."

Daisy nodded. "I am. Had one guy I was talking to for a

long time. Thought we had a connection, but we met and it was all wrong."

"Ugh, I hate when that happens," Goldie said. "Dating was never easy for me, and it's always worse when you think you have a connection then don't. Sorry that happened to you."

My throat tightened. Daisy was throwing herself under the bus and telling what she knew of my story so I didn't get the focus. Could I have a better friend?

"It was tough," Daisy continued. "But I'll meet someone eventually. Sometimes I don't mind dating, but lately everything has been harder."

"It's the holidays," Finley said. "At least, I'm guessing because of your store. The holidays are always a tough time of year when you work in retail. Even though I'm not going to have anywhere near the same experience as you, I always feel like I'm more drained. Between the days being so short and the work hours being so long, I still collapse into bed at the end of a shift."

Daisy nodded. "That's true. I didn't think about that. It's my first Christmas with the store open."

"How did it go?" Elise asked.

"It was great," Daisy said with a wide grin. "Busy and crazy and so much more work than I expected, but now that it's over I am really happy I opened the store."

"It's like childbirth," Blake said. "After the first one, I forgot how bad it was and was willing to get pregnant again."

Finley scoffed. "Oh, please, you were so thrilled to get pregnant. Especially the trying part."

Blake grinned. "I was definitely up for that."

The others laughed and hooted. I couldn't remember the last time I had something to cheer about. Getting the summer camp going last year was a big project, and this year was going to be even bigger. Dating had definitely taken a back burner, and after my disastrous date, it needed to stay there.

But if I was honest, I missed sex. I missed the connection to someone. I didn't enjoy one-night stands as much as relationships, but I hadn't experienced either in a while.

"I miss sex," Daisy said, as though she was reading my mind.

"Oh, honey, I remember those days," Goldie said. "After my divorce, I didn't care, but before Patrick and I got together, I was so desperate for sex I was leaving work during the day because he would get me so worked up I couldn't stand it."

"No you didn't," Karissa said.

Goldie nodded, chuckling. "Oh, I did. And he knew it, too. He did it on purpose."

"If he was getting you worked up, why did you leave work?" Daisy asked.

"Because she refused to actually date the man," Blake answered for Goldie. "Said he was too young for her. We tried to convince her she was wrong, but Goldie worried everyone would talk. He was young, and she was his boss, and she thought the whole town would be calling for her head."

"My boss was," Goldie said with a scowl.

"The mayor was such an ass," Finley said. "He couldn't see how good things were in this town if he just let well enough alone. Thankfully, Mayor Knight isn't the same. He's wonderful."

"Hot, too," Blake said.

"And he's a good man," Goldie defended. "I've had a lot

of meetings with him and he's always respectable and thoughtful. I just wish he would find someone."

"Is he looking?" Karissa asked.

Goldie shrugged. "I don't know. I know he's divorced, but I don't know the story. He's an amazing man, so I hope he's looking."

"I wonder if he's on my app," Karissa said, pulling out her phone.

"You can tell that?" I blurted, fear tightening my throat.

"She can, but she doesn't interfere anymore," Finley said, reaching for Karissa's phone.

Karissa let Finley take it and scowled at her. "You're no fun. Omar is hot, and I was just curious if he's been matched with anyone." Karissa turned her gaze to Daisy and me. "You two are single. Any interest in the mayor?"

"Not me," Daisy said. "He's too serious for me. Natalie?"

All eyes swung to me, and my ability to lie faded with any hope of keeping my secret. "We've already been matched."

"You what?" Daisy shouted.

Dammit.

11

———

"Was he your date last night?" Daisy asked, digging the hole I wanted out of even deeper.

I wanted to bolt. Just get the hell out of there and not have to tell any of them anything.

But the looks on their faces were warm and open, not judging or snarling. They were curious, but they weren't looking at me like I was not worthy of Mayor Knight.

Not like I looked at myself.

"Yes," I confessed.

"I thought you said he wasn't who you thought he was," Daisy continued.

So much for thinking my best friend in the world was on my side. "He wasn't. He's the freaking mayor of MacKellar Cove. He's my boss's boss. And he's perfect."

"Perfect doesn't exist," Daisy said, throwing my words in my face.

I glared at my best friend. "It does when we're talking about Mayor Knight. He never has anything bad said about him. Everyone loves him. He's exactly what everyone wants.

All of you have been talking about how amazing he is. That's not someone I should date. It would never work."

"Why not?" Finley asked.

I gawked at her. She didn't get it. She was married to a man who owned half the town, and her family was adored and connected. "We're not the same."

Finley shook her head. "Neither are Trent and me. He's town royalty. Everyone knows him and wants something from him. When I found out who he was, I felt the same way you are right now. Except I was pregnant with his kid and he accused me of trying to trap him and get his money."

"You would never do that," I gasped.

Finley nodded. "I know, but Trent didn't know me when we met. We were paired on Book Boyfriends Wanted, had a one-night stand, and I got pregnant. I never thought I'd see him again, but it felt wrong to not find him. It wasn't easy to get to where we are now, but we are proof people who don't think they should go together can work."

"You're different, though. You're friendly and talkative. People like you. I'm none of those things." I pushed my hair out of my face and fought the urge to let my emotions get to me.

"People like you, Natalie," Blake said. "You don't give yourself enough credit. Not all of us can be outgoing and talkative, but that doesn't mean you're not friendly."

"People don't see me that. People would only see me and Mayor Knight and wonder what in the world he could possibly see in me," I said, feeling the panic rising up.

"I think you're wrong. I think people will accept that there are always things about others we don't understand or know. I'm divorced, but Patrick saw through my past and wanted me. Omar was told I wasn't doing my job and should be fired, but he saw past Mayor Levine's hatred and sexism and looked at who I am. Unless he was cruel to you, I see no reason why you should stay away from him," Goldie said, her face open and curious, waiting for my answer.

I shook my head. "He wasn't cruel. I didn't give him a chance to be. I walked out."

"You walked out? Before you even talked to him?" Elise asked. "I get that, but it's harsh."

"No," I said. "I talked to him, but when I saw it was him, I left."

"Ouch," Karissa said.

"I did that to Colin," Elise said. "We were matched, and we had already met and he scared me. I knew he had the power to make me better. To pull me in and make me want things I didn't think I deserved back then. I was not ready to accept that love was in the cards for me. And he made it obvious that he would challenge that. So, I ran."

"What happened?" I asked.

Elise shrugged, a grin lifting her lips. "He didn't give up. He knew we were meant to be before I even accepted he was someone I could trust."

"That's not going to happen for me." I took a bite of my cake, feeling both better and worse.

"Has he reached out since last night?" Elise asked.

I shook my head. "I haven't looked at the app, but I'm sure he hasn't."

"Check now," Goldie said. "Just to see."

I rolled my eyes and grabbed my phone from my handbag. I was sure there would be nothing and I could get back to my cake. Better to get it over with and go back to what I knew.

Mayor Knight was not going to be right for me.

I opened the app and gasped. I had thirteen notifications. It could have been anything, but I opened the messaging section and saw all of them were from him.

BIGCITYCONVERT

I wish you hadn't run out on me. I promised I wouldn't do that to you. I should have asked you to make the same promise.

My cheeks heated at his words. He was right. I was worried he would meet me and leave, but I was the one who did that.

I pressed my hand to my mouth and kept reading.

BIGCITYCONVERT

I'm sorry you were disappointed it was me. I was not disappointed.

I was disappointed you left. I enjoyed talking to you.

Maybe this is better. Talking on here. What do you think?

I guess not.

I looked at the times. The last message came this morning. The others were from the night before. He reached out right after I left, and I ignored him all night, but he kept trying.

BIGCITYCONVERT

I wish you'd give me another chance. I don't know why you thought meeting was such a bad idea, but I'm happy I met you.

I'm the only one. I am happy you showed up, even late. I was looking forward to sitting across a table from you and seeing the smile I always imagined on your face.

Now that I think about it, I feel like I should have known who you were. I was drawn to you in person, too.

Again, I'm the only one. But for the record, you are beautiful and fun and all the things I want in a woman. Awkward doesn't scare me off. It's in your name. I expected it. But I wasn't scared by it.

Dating is never easy, and anyone who isn't interested in you is a fool.

But if you're not interested in dating, or in dating me, then I don't know why I'm pushing. You made it clear how you feel.

I was not disappointed when I saw you. I'm sorry you were.

I won't keep bothering you. I hope you find someone else you are excited about meeting one day. Goodbye.

"Did he message you?" Daisy asked.

I nodded, tearing my gaze from the messages. "Thirteen times."

"What did he say?" Goldie asked.

I could feel the collective intake of breath. I could feel their anxiety and curiosity. I hated that I was going to crush their hopes, the hopes I also felt, stronger than the other emotions.

"He said goodbye," I whispered.

"He what? Just goodbye?" Elise blurted. "What a jerk?"

I shook my head and put my phone away. "He didn't start with that. He started with wanting to talk, but when I didn't answer, he ended with goodbye."

"So there's a chance. If he messaged you, he's interested," Daisy said, forever the optimist.

"No," I said. "It's not worth it. It's for the best that he's going to walk away. We're not right for each other."

"I think you're wrong," Elise said. "But I also know you need to get there on your own. What I will say is I'm sorry for whatever made you think you're not good enough for him. I hope you find a way to heal from that."

I gasped, meeting her gaze and hating that she was able to see through me so easily.

"What are you talking about? What is she talking about?" Daisy asked.

"It was a long time ago," I admitted.

"But it obviously still hurts," Elise countered.

I drew a breath and let it out slowly. "My high school crush was the class president. He was popular and funny and every girl in school wanted to date him. For some reason, he liked me."

"You never told me this," Daisy whispered.

I breathed a laugh. "It's not easy to talk about my first heartbreak. But Tony was it. He was my lab partner in chemistry. Too nice to argue or say anything about not wanting to be my partner. We got to know each other, studied together, and became friends. He asked me to prom. It was like a dream. I never thought a boy like him would want me."

"What happened?" Elise asked.

I shrugged. "It wasn't that bad."

"But something happened." Blake was sure of it.

I nodded. "We went to the dance and this girl who liked Tony got him out on the dance floor. Was all over him. She was pretty and thin and popular like he was. He didn't push her off or tell her he was with me, just kept dancing with her. After half the night, he found me and said he was going to spend the rest of the night with her. That she wanted to dance and they were having fun and I was just sitting on the side."

"What a jerk," Goldie breathed.

"He wasn't wrong," I argued.

"No, but you were sitting out because he didn't make an effort to include you. He pushed you aside, then blamed you for it," Elise said. "What's his last name? I'll go hunt him down."

I chuckled. "He's not worth it."

"But you are," Elise said, her voice full of conviction. "You are worth it, Natalie. Teenage you was worth it. He was a fool for not seeing that. And so is Mayor Knight if he can't tell who you are."

"But—"

"No," Daisy said before I could argue. "Don't you dare speak poorly of my best friend. You have always been quiet and you figure things out inside before you tell others. That doesn't mean there's something wrong with you. It's just who you are. And finding someone who appreciates that is a good thing. Maybe it's the mayor, maybe it's not, but you have to stop hiding and believing some high school jackass was right. You are amazing, Natalie. And you need to trust that."

I looked around at the women I wanted to be friends with but was afraid to let in. None of them had ever been nasty to me or said anything mean about anyone. They were kind and friendly and the kind of people I always wanted as friends.

"Thank you," I whispered.

"You're welcome," Daisy said.

I smiled at her, then lifted my gaze to the others. "Thank you to all of you. For accepting me."

"We will always accept you," Elise said. "None of us are

perfect, but we're pretty perfect together. And we're happy to call you two our friends, too."

"Thank you."

"Now, what are you going to say when you apologize to Mayor Knight?" Elise asked.

I laughed. Then listened to all of their advice.

MONDAY MORNING WAS SLOW. Painfully slow. I was tired from thinking about what I should say to Mayor Knight when I saw him again. If I saw him.

Perspective was tough because it made me wonder if I was wrong about him. What if I hadn't walked out? What would he have said? Was he serious in the messages he sent afterward about not being disappointed?

I owed him an apology, if nothing else. I didn't like it, but that didn't matter. He was right, and I asked him not to walk out as soon as he saw who I was, then I did it to him.

Amelia stuck her head into my office a little before lunch and asked, "Do you want to go grab something to eat? I'm dragging and need to get out of here for a little while."

"Same. You pick."

She smiled and went back to her office.

I grabbed my coat and made my way out of my office. She was waiting at the door for me, keys in her hand.

We were both quiet on the short drive into town. Amelia circled the blocks around Catherine Park before she found a spot near Cove Bakery.

"We need to stop in there before we go back to the office. I can smell the sugar from here," Amelia said, pocketing her keys and heading toward Cracked.

We turned the corner and had Cracked in our sights

when someone stepped in front of us. He was in a suit and had a microphone with a cameraman right behind him.

"We're with channel six news, interviewing residents. Can you give us a comment about the allegations against Mayor Knight?"

Amelia stopped and glared at the man.

To his credit, he blanched but recovered quickly.

"What allegations?" Amelia demanded.

"An article came out this morning stating Mayor Knight is not good for this town. There was a picture of him caught in a compromising position with a woman on her knees at a local bar. And there are questions about his use of town funds."

My cheeks burned, and I turned my head. He had to be talking about the night I fell and grabbed Mayor Knight. The night I was on my knees in front of the mayor at O'Kelley's.

"Mayor Knight is the best thing that's happened to this town in a very long time. I've been a resident here my entire life, and Mayor Knight is professional and understanding and he is a huge supporter of the community. He would never do any of the things you're saying," Amelia said, standing tall and proud.

"You work at the community center, right?" the reporter asked.

"I do. I run it."

"It stands to reason you would support the mayor when the funds that are in question are going to pay for the new summer camp. I'm not sure your word is going to sway voters."

Amelia closed her mouth, looking unsure.

"You don't know what you're talking about," I growled. "Mayor Knight wants the best for this town. He's worked hard to make sure the town is thriving. Mayor Knight has done everything to support initiatives to improve the town, to build tourism back up. If you're calling his character into question, it's because you're grasping at straws to find fault with the man. You're here to stir up trouble where there isn't any. Maybe you should go find a real story instead of trying to bury a man who has no skeletons in his closet."

"Are you sure about that?" the reporter asked me, a smirk lifting his lips. "He's divorced. He has no ties to the community. Why would he be here? Why would he want to run this little town if he wasn't getting something for it?"

"He is getting something for it," I continued. "Personal satisfaction. Pride in his community and staff. Knowledge that he's making a difference. He's making MacKellar Cove better. His personal history has nothing to do with his capabilities as the mayor. He's intelligent and compassionate. He sees this town for what it could be, instead of letting toxic garbage like you drag us down. Why shouldn't he be investing town funds into the new summer camp? If he was only interested in himself, he'd be using that money to give himself a raise instead of trying to help the working families of MacKellar Cove. The parents who either have to quit their jobs for the summer to take care of their children or who need to rely on family and friends to do so. I'm failing to see why this is a bad thing. Except that you want to bury the man. A man who is so much better than you that you don't deserve to even speak his name."

Amelia slid her arm through mine and tugged me toward the restaurant. "If you'll excuse us, we have somewhere else to be."

I wanted to keep fighting with the jerk reporter, but I finally looked around and saw he wasn't the only one there.

A dozen people had gathered and were filming me. Some had phones, but other news stations had arrived.

"How much did they get?" I whispered to Amelia as we walked into Cracked.

"All of it. You were amazing."

If only I felt amazing. Instead, I felt like it was one more piece of evidence I was all wrong for Mayor Knight.

12

OMAR

I stared at my screen and watched Natalie tear the reporter to shreds. I still couldn't believe she did that. But there it was, in a shaky video posted to social media and shared hundreds of times.

When I first saw it late yesterday afternoon, I was sure she was going to agree with the reporter and talk about how bad I was for MacKellar Cove. She obviously thought I was bad for her. I wasn't surprised when Amelia defended me, but Natalie?

I had to have watched it a hundred times. There were four versions, all of them showing the same conversation from different angles. All of them telling me the same thing.

I needed to thank her for defending me.

It felt like groveling after the way things went the last time we spoke. And after the dozen unanswered messages I sent her. I said goodbye, and I meant it. If she didn't want me, I wouldn't push.

But we had to work together. We had a meeting in a week, and MacKellar Cove was too small for us to avoid each other forever.

I owed her my gratitude. I would keep it professional and not think about how much I wanted her.

My morning was productive, and I didn't have any afternoon meetings, so I left the office for lunch. Early January was cold and snowy, but the sun was out and the snow had melted. I needed the fresh air and a chance to clear my head.

I stopped for a sandwich and took it to my SUV so I could drive around a little. I rolled down the window and let my mind wander while I made turns at random and tried to get lost. Not that it was possible in a town as small as MacKellar Cove, but I tried.

After a few minutes, I realized I was getting close to the campground. Amelia wanted to show me the property, but I hadn't made it out there yet. With my job and support of the camp in question, I decided to check the place out and see what it looked like and how much work was really needed to make it functional.

The branches on the overgrown bushes next to the driveway scraped the sides of my vehicle when I pulled in, making me cringe. Those definitely needed to be cleaned up or removed altogether. For a campground, it was nice to have the driveway a little secluded and feel like you were going to a new place. For a summer camp, that was not a great thing.

Once I made it through the brush, the space opened up in front of me.

"Wow," I breathed, surprised at how stunning it was. No wonder Amelia wanted to do so much there. It was perfect for events, and it was going to be great for the kids lucky enough to go there for summer camp.

I continued up what was left of the driveway toward the camper parked next to what used to be the parking lot. A blue SUV was just on the other side of the camper, out of sight until I got closer.

Who was there?

I got out of my SUV and looked around, trying to find someone.

The space was fairly flat, but I still didn't see anyone. I decided to explore, hoping being out there alone wasn't as bad of an idea as I thought it was.

I went to the pool first, standing next to the tarp covered hole in the ground. Water pooled on top of the old cover, doing nothing to actually keep people safe near the pool. Just like Natalie said.

There was a small building next to the pool, but the walls had more holes than solid boards and it was easy to see it was empty.

I continued on, looking at the horizon for signs of movement. Electrical boxes stuck up from the ground at even spaces around the property, leftover from the old camper hookups. Some had been removed and pulled close to the camper at the front. Natalie's work that left her with the injury.

Was she the one out there alone? Again?

With the thought in my mind, I quickened my pace and searched for her. I counted six camper hookups, but I thought Amelia said there were thirty. That meant there were a lot I couldn't see from where I stood, even though the property was relatively flat.

I followed what appeared to be an old road and made my way past the first grouping of campsites. More of the old wiring had been dug up. A second grouping came into view. These were farther from the pool but had a better view of the mountain.

Damn. No wonder it was called Mountain View Campground. It was stunning.

But that wasn't why I was there.

I kept going, finally spotting someone on the far side of the site. Five acres was a huge space, and Natalie had to be close to the edge of it.

"What are you doing?" I called out, catching her attention.

She screamed, then turned to me. "I'm working. Why are you here?"

I waited until I got closer to answer her. Dirt streaked across her forehead. Her boots were brown, but it was definitely not their original color. She was dressed in a flannel shirt that was open and revealed a blue tank underneath. Her jeans were tucked into her boots, hugging her curvy legs the entire way down.

Need slammed into me hard. The need to take care of her, to be there for her. But also need for her. She was stunning.

"Why are you here, Mr. Mayor?"

"I thought we established you should call me Omar."

She didn't reply, just pursed her lips and raised her dark eyebrows, waiting for me to answer.

"I needed to clear my head. I was close and decided to check the place out."

She nodded, then went back to digging the trench she was standing over.

"What are you doing?"

"Saving the town money," she said without looking up. Her shovel dug into the mud, then she pushed it down to lift the mud from its resting place. When she cleared enough away to move the cables forward, she put the mud back into the hole she'd just dug.

"You're doing all this work by yourself? I thought that was how you got hurt."

"I'm fine. Amelia knows where I am, and so does Daisy. If I don't check in with them in an hour, they're going to send someone to find me."

"How long have you been out here?"

She took a breath and stabbed her shovel into the ground. She looked up at me and brushed the hair out of her face with the back of her hand, leaving another streak of mud. "I'm trying to get as much work done as I can by myself. Getting this place up and running is important to me. If I don't do this when the weather cooperates, there's no way it'll be done on time."

"I thought you were going to hire people for this."

She shook her head. "It's not in the budget, Mr. Mayor. We need to save the money the town gave us for bringing in professionals to do things we can't do ourselves."

"How do you know you're doing this safely?"

"There's no power to the property. The utility company came out and told us what needs to be done before they can run new lines and make it safe for the campers. Step one is digging up all of this, but it has to be done by hand so we don't tear more stuff up. That's expensive. But I'm cheap."

"It's not safe for you to be out here alone. You didn't know I was here. Anyone could show up and hurt you."

"I'll be fine," she said, ignoring me and going back to her work.

"Natalie, please."

She spun on me. "What do you want me to do? I can't afford to hire someone. If I only work within the budget you gave me, we'll never have this place open. And Amelia wants to do all these other things, and it's getting bigger and bigger, and if I don't do it, no one will. So I have to, Mr. Mayor. I have to do this."

Her words were punctuated by a rumble of thunder that was so close I felt the ground tremble. "Is it supposed to rain today?"

She shrugged. "I have no idea."

As she said that, the first drops hit the muddy ground hard.

"I guess it is. It'll make the ground softer."

"It's not safe to be out here in a storm."

"It'll be fine," she argued. Another clap of thunder echoed with her words, with a bolt of lightning immediately after and the thunder continuing to roll, alternating with lightning.

"We need to get out of here. We can't be out in the open."

"Shit," she breathed, looking at the sky and closing her eyes to the rain coming down harder by the second. "There's no shelter out here."

"What about the camper?"

She shook her head. "It hasn't been cleaned. It might kill us faster than this storm."

"Come on," I said, reaching for her hand. I was not going to leave her behind.

She slid her hand into mine, and we started to run.

We slipped almost every step, forcing us to go slow. She grabbed onto my shoulder when she almost hit the ground. The camper and our vehicles seemed like they were miles away.

"We can get in my car," she shouted above the roar of the storm.

"Mine's bigger. I already started it up, too. It'll be warm. Get in."

I kept a hold of her hand and opened the passenger door

for her, waiting until she jumped in before I slammed the door and rushed to the other side. I slipped going around the SUV and nearly fell, catching myself on the hood. She pushed my door open from the inside, letting me into the warm vehicle before I slammed my door closed, the sound echoing the thunder that chased us the entire way.

"Are you okay?" I asked her.

The look in her eyes answered before she spoke. "No. I'm not okay. How can I be okay? I'm about to die."

I pointed the vents her way, hoping it would help warm her up. "You're not going to die."

"Yeah, I am. Because I made a bad decision. I'm not surprised. Last time I didn't have my phone or my coat with me, and I didn't have an emergency kit. I thought I was so damn smart. My phone is in my pocket. I had my jacket out there near me. But it doesn't do me any damn good when I'm trapped out here and freezing to death."

"You're not freezing to death. We're not far from town. We can get home."

"We can't drive in that!" she screeched.

"No, we can't. We shouldn't. It's raining too hard to be able to see the road, and we probably won't make it out of the driveway. But you said people know where you are. We can call for help."

Thunder boomed outside, making her jump.

"Natalie, it's going to be okay. "

"No, it won't. I don't know why I thought I could do this. I didn't check the weather, and I would have been stuck out there if you hadn't come and found me. Again. What is wrong with me? No one is going to trust me with their kids. This place is a failure before it even gets started."

She leaned forward and put her head in her hands. Her shoulders shook. She looked so defeated that it gutted me.

I'd seen her unsure, pissed off, and doubting herself, but never completely lost. I wanted to pull her into my arms, but I had gotten that message already. "Parents trust you with their kids because you're amazing with them. You connect with kids and you adore them, and parents see that."

"It doesn't matter because we're going to die out here. They're going to find my dead body in your SUV. With the mayor. There's the scandal they're all looking for. Hopefully, they'll paint you as the hero you are."

"I'm not a hero."

"You're out here saving me. I'm about five seconds away from pulling my hair out and screaming until I can't breathe, and you're just all calm here."

"I'm not all calm, but I know panicking is not going to change anything."

"You sound like my therapist."

"Maybe your therapist is right."

She shook her head. "No, she's not. And it's not like I can help it. I'm scared. And I'm here with a man who doesn't want to be around me. And I'm never going to make this camp happen. And I'm going to die without falling in love and having a family and telling my parents I love them and Daisy will be all alone and—"

It was a bad idea, but the only thing I could think of to stop her panic was to kiss her.

A surprised squeak snuck out, then a low growl. Her arms wrapped around my neck and pulled me closer. Her tongue pushed against my lips.

I opened them for her and slid my hands to her neck. I pulled her closer, wanting to feel more of her.

She grabbed my shirt like last time I kissed her and held on.

I groaned and tightened my grip on her. She inched closer, the center console a frustrating barrier between us.

"Omar," she breathed.

"Yeah?"

"Why did you come out here today?"

I pulled back to look at her. Her face was flushed, her hair tangled from the rain. Her chest heaved with every breath. Her skin was cold to the touch, a reminder that we'd been caught in the freezing rain, even though my body was hot at the moment.

"I didn't plan it. I went for a drive and ended up nearby. I wanted to see the place."

"I am sorry about the picture. The article." She ducked her head, biting her lip and hiding herself from me.

I cupped her chin and turned her face back to mine.

She met my gaze reluctantly.

"That picture was not your fault."

"I'm the one who tripped and assaulted you. I know I need to come forward and explain—"

"No."

She drew back. "Excuse me?"

I shook my head. "That picture was taken out of context, and dragging you into the middle of that will not help anything. It could end up with your reputation damaged and this place not the success I know it will be."

"I can't let you go down for it when it was my fault."

"No, Natalie. It was the man who took the picture's fault. And if someone is coming for me, they'll come for you and anyone else who tries to get in their way."

She shivered at my words. "Do you think so?"

"I wish I knew. I have no idea what's going on. All I do know is I don't want you to end up in the middle of anything. You are going to do amazing things here. And you need to tell Amelia to roll back her big ideas if it's not what you want."

Natalie shook her head, her brown hair tumbling around her shoulders. "I can't. She's been so good to me. I'm horrible with people, but Amelia never makes me feel like I'm a liability. She is amazing, and if she has ideas to improve on this place, I'm going to listen to her."

"If it means you're overwhelmed and can't function, she needs to know."

Natalie swallowed roughly. She turned her head away, tears in her eyes before she hid them from me. "I'm handling it."

"Hey, I'm not trying to say you can't. I want to see you succeed. And not because I'm the mayor. I want to see Natalie Edwards succeed. Even if you don't want me to share in it."

"If I succeed, it's good for the whole town."

"You know that's not what I'm talking about, Natalie. I'm talking about you. I'm talking about this. I'm talking about you not wanting me. I apologize for kissing you again. I have an emergency kit in the back. I'll get it, give you some space."

I twisted in my seat and shoved my body through the too small gap between the seats. I hit the horn with my hip and grabbed the back of the seat, not at all gracefully falling onto the backseat.

What was one more embarrassing moment in front of Natalie Edwards? She couldn't possibly think less of me, so why did I care?

13

NATALIE

Omar leaned into the trunk and grabbed his emergency kit, because of course he was prepared and had an emergency kit.

He sat again, and I quickly looked away before he caught me watching him. He leaned forward and handed me a blanket and a bottle of water.

Silence stretched between us. The warm air from the vents heated the space, but I was still shivering, the cold air outside combined with the rain dropped my body temperature in a hurry.

I shook as I unfolded the blanket he gave me. My flannel shirt was plastered to my wet skin. I glanced back at him, considering taking it off.

He avoided my gaze. He sat behind the driver's seat, out of my line of sight unless I turned to see him.

I tried to pretend he wasn't there, but it was impossible. His scent filled the vehicle, his warmth radiating around me as though it were a part of the heat coming from the vents.

He fought to take his coat off, dropping it to the floor behind my seat. He was drier than me, but not by much.

"You should take off your shirt," he growled.

Was he joking? "Yeah, sure."

"I'm not trying something here. You're freezing. If you don't get rid of some of your wet clothes, the blanket and the heat won't get through fast enough. You'll get sick." He unbuttoned his shirt and dropped it onto the floor with his coat, leaving him in a black tank that caressed his muscles.

My gaze snagged on his chest before I realized I was staring. I yanked my eyes away and pulled off my soaked flannel shirt, tossing it onto the floorboard at my feet. I wrapped the blanket around my shoulders and leaned closer to the vents, willing the warmth to sink deep into my body.

I stared out the window at the storm. We were going to be stuck there for a while. An uneasy silence and temporary unspoken truce between us.

"I was going to find you to thank you. I didn't intend for it to go like this, but I wanted to say I appreciated your words. Your apparent support of me. I... I would never have expected it, but it's greatly appreciated." His quiet confession was as sincere as it was unnecessary.

"I meant every word. You are good for MacKellar Cove. And that picture..."

"It wasn't your fault. The man who took it, and the reporter who published it, they did this for a reason. I'm going to do everything I can to keep you out of it. I hope you speaking up for me doesn't send them looking your way."

"If it does, I'll handle it. I... I don't want that, but it's not fair for you to get punished for trying to help me."

"It's fine."

"Why don't you like me?"

"Excuse me?" he barked.

"I just..."

"You're the one who said we're all wrong and left that night, Natalie. Not me."

"I know." I swallowed. "I don't... Relationships are not easy for me. Being anonymous was easy. You didn't know how awkward I am."

He snorted a laugh. "Your screen name was ThisIsAwkward."

I chuckled. "Okay, fine, maybe you had an idea. But I don't want to end up ruining your chances at re-election because you're dating me."

"And I think dating you will only help my chances. But that's not why I want to date you, Natalie."

I breathed a laugh. "I'm sure there's a long list of reasons you don't want to date me."

He shook his head. "It's the opposite. I have a long list of reasons I do."

"What? Why?"

"Because you're beautiful. You're smart. You care so much about kids, you don't care who you piss off to get what's right for them. You're willing to get filthy dirty and hurt in order to make this a success. You're passionate and kind and creative. Do you want me to continue?"

I shook my head. "I don't see myself that way."

"Maybe you should stop seeing all the things you don't want to see in yourself and see all the things the people who care about you see."

I chewed on my lip. "I've never been very good at that."

"No one is. We are our own worst critics. We always focus on the things we fail at."

"You don't fail at anything," I blurted.

He laughed loud enough that it drowned out the thunder. "I wish."

"Name one time you failed."

His gaze snapped to mine, and the heat coming from him surpassed what was coming from the vents. "Our date."

I gasped. "That wasn't on you."

"It doesn't matter, Natalie. I didn't come here to rehash that. Or to make you feel bad about your choice. I shouldn't have said anything."

He shifted in his seat and faced the window, shutting me out.

I wanted to let it go. Ignore the whole thing. Let him be and not fight for something I didn't think would work anyway.

But I knew I couldn't do that. I couldn't sit there and let him believe I didn't want him. That I was upset when he was the one I'd been talking to and met that night.

Before I could talk myself out of it, I crawled into the backseat with him. He gasped and moved over to give me space, staring at me as I positioned myself next to him and tugged the blanket around my shoulders again.

"I was a jerk. I shouldn't have walked out on you. But more than that, I shouldn't have allowed you to believe I was upset that it was you."

He scoffed and turned away again.

"You're so... You shouldn't be single. You should have women falling all over themselves to date you. I'm sure you do. You're poised and intelligent and so damn good. For this town and in general. You're so much better than me, Omar."

He opened his mouth, but I pushed ahead without giving him a chance to speak.

"I know where I belong. I love what I do. People don't know me. I grew up here, and I'm invisible. I've always been invisible. I... I don't mind that. But you? You're visible. You're up front. You're looked up to and admired and respected."

"And you think you're not?"

I shrugged. "I don't know, but it doesn't really matter. I don't want that." I inhaled a shaky breath and forced myself to meet his gaze. "I built you up in my mind as this man who would make all my dreams come true. Foolish, I know, but I felt like you were... You didn't judge me. You didn't make me feel like I wasn't good enough. But when I saw you, I knew I was wrong about you because I'm not good enough for you."

He laughed mirthlessly. "Wow. I've heard the *it's not you, it's me* thing before, but never in a way that made me immediately want to call bullshit."

"Bullshit?" I gasped.

"Bullshit. Just tell me you don't want to be with me, Natalie. I can handle it. Hell, you already told me without the words. Is it so hard to just say *I don't like you*?"

"It wouldn't be if I didn't like you," I whispered.

"Don't, just don't. Don't say that, Natalie. You made your feelings clear. I wanted to thank you for what you said to the reporter. We can be professional and we can put all of this aside, and when the camp is up and running, we won't have to deal with each other again. But don't make a fool of me. Don't say things you don't mean."

"You think I'm lying to you?"

"I know you are," he bellowed. "I know you are." He sighed and faced away from me again. "We can just sit here until the storm passes. We don't have to talk."

I'd been fighting the way he made me feel since I walked into O'Kelley's, but I couldn't fight any longer. I didn't think I wanted to. "I can think of another way to pass the time." I crawled onto his lap.

His hands went to my thighs immediately, not pushing me away. Shock registered in his gaze, then heat.

I wanted to scramble back to the other side of the SUV

and pretend I hadn't been so bold, but I couldn't. I wanted him. The man was addictive, and I wanted more.

I moved closer slowly, giving him time to push me off.

He sat still, letting my lips land on his. He sucked in a breath, the cool rush of air whipping past my cheek. His fingers curled into my thighs, betraying his feelings.

I wrapped my arms around his neck and slid closer, needing his body heat, his touch, his lips. I licked his lips, and he groaned, thrusting his tongue into my mouth.

His hands slid up my thighs and cupped my ass, dragging my body tight to his. His erection rose between us, sending tingles through my entire body.

He pushed me back, and I realized that wasn't tingles. It was a phone vibrating.

Reality was back.

"Yeah?" Omar said into his phone.

He closed his eyes and sighed.

"I apologize, Jane. I'm not going to make it back to work. I should have called you. I wasn't ready for the storm, and I'm stuck. Yes, I'll be in tomorrow." He sighed, then smiled and nodded. "Thank you, Jane. I don't know what I'd do without you." He chuckled. "I'll see you tomorrow."

He hung up the phone and looked up, his gaze slamming into mine.

"Is everyone okay at work?" I asked him.

He nodded and tossed his phone onto the seat next to us. "I thought you had to check in with Daisy and Amelia?"

My phone rang as he finished his sentence. I dug it out of my pocket and turned it to show him Amelia. "Hi, Amelia."

"Natalie. Are you okay? You didn't call, and it's pouring here."

"Yeah, I got caught in it. I'm... safe. I'm in a vehicle, waiting until I can see out the windows to leave."

"Oh, thank goodness. I was worried. I was about to send my son out to check on you."

"No, all good," I said quickly.

"Okay. You're off the rest of the day, so get warm and stay safe."

"I will. Thanks, Amelia. See you tomorrow."

"Have a good night, Natalie."

I hung up and sent Daisy a text, letting her know I was okay and waiting out the storm.

> I was just about to call you. Glad you're okay.

> All good. Cold and wet but not hurt.

> Good. I'll feel better when that place is done and you're not out there alone.

> Me, too.

"You didn't want them to know I'm here."

I looked at him. "I wasn't sure if you wanted me to."

"Did you want to?"

"I'm not sure about that either."

He nodded, not laughing but not making his case either.

"What do you want me to do?" I asked.

"I want you to do what makes you feel comfortable."

"That's not an answer."

"Natalie, I'm your boss's boss, something you made clear bothers you. I'm not going to tell you to do something. I want you to make choices. It doesn't matter what I think or what I want."

"It matters to me," I whispered.

He sucked in a breath. "Does it? I'm not asking that to be cruel. Just curious. Because before an hour ago, we barely spoke."

"My dating history is spotty, at best. Most of the men I've dated were casual and short-lived. All it takes is one panic attack or one problem because of my anxiety, or one look at my figure, and they're ready to run."

"I'm still here," he said.

I nodded slowly. "You are. But what if I have a panic attack before some appearance you have to make? Or if my anxiety makes us late for something? What if you get exhausted having to take care of me like you did today?"

"None of what you said scares me off. As for taking care of you, I don't think I agree that's what's really happening here."

"You showed up and got me out of the rain. I would have been trapped out there without you."

"I'm pretty sure you were trapped out there anyway. So was I. I didn't do anything to help you."

"You didn't let go."

"What?"

"When we were running to get here, you didn't let go of my hand."

He picked up my hand and wound our fingers together. He brought our joined hands to his lips. "I'm not letting go now either, Natalie. But this is up to you. All of this is up to you."

"You don't get a say?"

He chuckled. "You're cute."

"What?"

"I made my choice when I asked to meet you. When I decided I wanted to meet you. Of course, I wanted to meet

ThisIsAwkward so I'd stop thinking about Natalie Edwards, but karma is funny."

"What are you saying?"

He exhaled a long breath and met my gaze. The depth and emotion in his surprised me. "I'm saying nothing about you has scared me off. I want to see where this can go. I liked talking to you online. And I was drawn to you in person. Putting those two people into one package did not make me want you less."

"Omar," I breathed.

He shook his head. "You get to decide because I've already decided, Natalie. I wanted you to stay when you walked into O'Kelley's. But I wasn't going to chase you down."

I put my hand on his cheek, and he nuzzled against it. I moved closer, pressing my body to his.

He took the hint and slid his hand around my back. "Natalie, you need to tell me what you want. I don't want to do the wrong thing here."

"You're not."

"I want to kiss you again."

"I think we've established that I'm on board with that."

He nodded and moved slowly, waiting for me to stop him.

I had no intention of doing so.

He kissed me slowly, like the cold and the outside world would stay away forever. He licked my lips and gained access, swirling his tongue through my mouth. His fingertips tightened on my back, drawing me closer and closer until I could feel the effect our kisses had on him.

He groaned and thrust up. His hands held me tight and encouraged me to rock against him.

God, this man. He didn't flinch when I mentioned panic

attacks. He didn't say a word about anxiety. He just proved I was a fool to walk out on him.

When I pulled back, I waited until he blinked his eyes open and looked at me. His gaze was fuzzy and loaded with desire.

"Will you go on a date with me?" I asked.

His gaze brightened. A smile curled his lips. I could feel his answer before he spoke. "Yes. I would love to."

"Good."

"I'm really happy I ended up here today," he said.

I chuckled. "So am I."

"Thank you for defending me to the reporters, Natalie. That really meant a lot."

"You already thanked me for that."

He nodded. "Yeah, but I wanted to thank you again. You know... You know about my ex-wife. You know more than anyone else in MacKellar Cove, and knowing you still feel that way makes a difference."

"I meant what I said. You're good for this town. You've put the town ahead of yourself a lot of times."

"I always liked the idea of giving back. There are a lot of people who go into politics for the wrong reasons, but I wanted to help. To make a place better."

"And you are. I know your job isn't easy, and I'm sorry for the times I got upset with you. Especially a few weeks ago when I didn't provide you with the information you wanted."

He laughed. "No, you were right that day. I wanted an excuse to see you. I do want to make sure we're following all the rules with this place, but not because I don't trust you. It's important."

"It is important. I know that. That's why I'm doing what I'm doing here. Saving money for the things we have to pay people for."

"What about the fundraiser?"

I shook my head. "I can't count on that. I hope it goes well, but there's no guarantee. If we earn enough to fix up the pool, I'll be thrilled."

"You don't think you will?"

I shrugged. "The budget you gave us will pay for the electrician and for a fence around the pool, and staff for the first month. I don't want to be counting on the payments from parents to pay counselors immediately. We need a little bit of a buffer."

"That's smart," he said. "But there's still a lot of work besides that."

"Yeah. Amelia talked to her son, and James and his friends are going to help us clean up the basketball and volleyball courts, probably the landscaping, too. We'll be functional but not great."

"What about a building?"

"We don't know," I admitted.

"I think the building is a pretty important part of the whole thing."

"I know," I breathed, feeling angry and agitated. "I know it is. But if I don't have the money to make it a reality, there's nothing I can do about it."

"Do you know how much it would be?"

I shook my head. "No."

He opened his mouth to say something else, then rolled his lips in and gave me a wry look. "I'm being the boss instead of just listening to you."

"You're not wrong, though."

"I didn't start talking about the budget to push you into a corner. I got carried away."

"You're passionate, too. It's good to see."

He laughed softly. "As long as it doesn't mean we're fighting."

"I doubt that's going to stop just because we seem to have reached an agreement."

"An agreement?"

"You can't argue with me if I kiss you."

He tipped his head back and laughed loudly. He nodded and reached for me, pulling me close as he dipped his head. "That goes both ways, you know."

"Oh, I know."

14

I'D NEVER KNOWN A KISS TO MAKE ME SO HOT. IT WASN'T JUST the heat on full blast and warming us up, it was Omar. He had me panting and begging for more in minutes.

And he was happy to deliver.

He lifted the edge of my tank top to get his bare hand on my skin. I arched into him, whimpering at the feel of his warm hand on me. I dropped my blanket and tossed my tank top, leaving me on his lap in a highly unsexy blue cotton bra that did not slow him down at all.

"Blue's a good color on you," he whispered against my breast.

"I didn't intend for anyone else to know I had a blue bra on."

"Tell me to slow down, Natalie."

"I don't want you to."

He tugged my mouth down to his, inhaling me as he plunged his tongue between my lips.

I was frantic, needing him like I needed the heat in his car.

The storm continued outside, raging along with my

emotions. I'd never dared to fool around in a car before. My high school best friend lost her virginity in a car and tried to tell me how awesome it was. Maybe it was the thirteen years since high school, but I could not imagine having sex in a car would be so great.

"What are you thinking about?" Omar whispered.

"Car sex," I admitted.

His cock twitched against me.

"People did it all the time in high school. How was that a good idea?"

He chuckled. "Youth makes us foolish and flexible."

"That's true. I wasn't trying to ruin the moment."

"You didn't. I want to know what you're thinking. I asked."

"Because I was distracted."

"I've been distracted since we met, Natalie."

I grinned, finding his simple confession tingle-inducing. And this time, there was no phone ringing. "It's a good thing that photographer can't get a picture of this. The two of us in another compromising position."

"Worth it," he whispered.

I smoothed my hands down his arms, enjoying the twitch of his muscles and the way his cock responded in kind. I caught his hand, threading our fingers together and bringing them to my lips.

He thrust against me, a moan escaping my lips. My eyes fluttered close and the months of resisting him fell away.

"Natalie?"

"Please," I whispered.

"Hold on to me," he said, putting my hands on his shoulders.

I gripped his shoulders and trembled when he cupped my hips and brought me into contact with him.

His jaw tightened. His fingers dug into my hips. Determination set in his eyes, and he took me on a ride.

I wasn't sure I'd be able to come through our clothes, but Omar was not giving up. He shifted his position to find what worked for me. He licked my bare skin when I got close to him. And when my bra strap fell off my shoulder, he yanked one cup down and brought my bare breast to his mouth as an offering.

And sent me soaring.

"Omar," I gasped, the first waves crashing over me with my nipple pinched between his lips.

He bit harder, sending a bolt through me and everything in me shook.

"Oh, fuck!" I shouted, losing myself to the pleasure I'd been chasing for months. I didn't allow myself to think of him when I was alone, but I was. I always was.

"Fuck, Natalie," he growled, twitching beneath me.

"Did you?"

He shook his head. "Almost, but no."

"Do you—?"

"One day, but not today. That car sex you were just talking about wouldn't be any easier if you were on your knees. But damn, that's an image I'll want to hold on to forever."

I laughed softly, feeling self-conscious and greedy.

"Hey," he whispered, lifting my jaw to meet his gaze. "What's in that head?"

"I took advantage of you."

"Not even a little. Relationships shouldn't be about keeping score. I'm not going to start this one like that."

I nodded.

"But we probably should head out soon before someone actually does come out here."

I looked around and saw the rain had almost completely stopped. The thunder and lightning had completely passed.

And my boob was on full display if anyone came up to the window.

"I didn't even notice."

He smirked. "Good."

Omar helped me get my clothes back into place, then asked for my keys.

"Why?"

"I'll go start your car so it'll warm up before you have to get in it."

"You don't have to do that."

He smiled. "I'm being selfish. It means I can spend a few more minutes with you if we're waiting for your car to warm up."

"Well, in that case..." I handed him my keys.

He kissed me, then opened the door and climbed out in his tank without his coat. He closed the door against the cold air already seeping in, then raced to my SUV.

It took him a minute to unlock the doors and climb in. It burped to life, then Omar was getting back out and running to me again.

He climbed into the backseat with me and pulled me close. "I need you to warm me up. It's cold out there."

I laughed and climbed onto his lap again, wrapping myself around him and kissing him until the windows fogged up and we were both panting again.

"Was this a dream?" he asked.

I shook my head. "Not a dream."

"So you really did ask me on a date?"

"I did."

"I'm going to hold you to it."

"I'm counting on it."

We kissed a few more minutes, then admitted we needed to get out of all of our wet clothes.

He walked me to my SUV and made sure it wasn't stuck before he went back to his own vehicle. He followed me down the muddy driveway and out to the street until he flashed his lights and made a turn where I'd gone straight.

A few minutes later, I pulled into my driveway. I grabbed my wet clothes and Omar's blanket and hurried to the door.

"Oh my God! You're alive!" Daisy yelled, rushing to me.

I was hoping to have time to dissect the day without having to talk to anyone about it. We crossed a line. A line I wanted to cross, but it changed everything. And I needed time to process that. Time I didn't have before Daisy was going to want details that I wasn't sure about sharing.

But it was Daisy. If I could tell anyone, it was her.

"I'm okay. I got caught in the rain."

"How are you not frozen?"

"We sat in the car."

"We? Who's we?"

"Omar came—"

Daisy punched her fist into the air. "Yes! Hell, yes. Tell me everything. What happened? Why was he there? Did you share body heat?"

"You are such a child," I teased her.

She nodded solemnly. "Yes, yes, I am. That's why I own a toy store. Trying to recapture the youth I never got."

I smiled, knowing it wasn't just what she said. She meant it. And I hated it for her, but she would never let anyone show her pity. "And every kid in town is going to have a better childhood because of you."

"I sure hope so. Now quit stalling and tell me about your day."

I let my breath out in a rush and told her about Omar

showing up at the campground and finding me digging up connections. She swooned when I told her he grabbed my hand and refused to let go as we ran back to the parking lot. And when I shared our kissing and conversation, she sighed happily.

"I'm so happy for you," she said when I was finished with my story.

"Thank you. I know there's a lot between now and wherever, but we agreed we liked talking on Book Boyfriends Wanted. We got to know each other, and that connection is still there."

"I tried to tell you that."

I nodded. "I know, but I wasn't ready to hear it. Especially when I was so sure he hated me for walking out."

"But he doesn't?"

I shook my head and smiled. "No, he doesn't."

"Well, good. I'm really happy for you. He is a lucky man."

I snorted. "Uh huh."

Daisy shook her head. "You, my friend, are amazing. I wish you could see that, but I'm really happy Omar does. Because you deserve someone who sees all the things that make you special."

"Thank you. You know I feel the same about you."

Daisy cocked her hip. "You better. Because I'm awesome, too."

I laughed, the sound fading. "I'm nervous."

"Of course you are. Dating isn't easy. But it seems from all those other people who've found their perfect one that it's worth it when you get to that point."

"Do you think you'll ever find that one?" I asked her.

She exhaled through her nose. "I sure hope so."

"Me, too."

"Go shower. You have to be freezing, and I know you're dirty. I'll fix dinner and we can watch something."

"Sounds good. Thanks."

"You're welcome."

Daisy went to the kitchen, and I turned to go to my room. Our house was perfect for us, with a bathroom in each bedroom. I got the room with the bigger bedroom and smaller bathroom, which worked well for me. Daisy liked the big bathroom, but didn't care about having a large bed.

I went past my bed to the bathroom and stripped out of my soaked and muddy clothes for the second time in two weeks. At least this time, I wasn't doing it with an injured ankle. Which was likely only because Omar was there to help me.

I saw a different side of him when we were trapped together. He was the man I talked to online. Emotional and kind and supportive. I needed that in a way I didn't see before.

I stepped into the hot shower. I closed my eyes and let the water run over my body. I washed myself quickly, letting the bubbles from my body wash carry away the dirt and sweat from my day. God, how embarrassing. We spent all day crammed in his SUV and kissing when I was so gross.

But he didn't mind.

I couldn't help but wonder what he was doing. If he was in the shower, thinking about me. His large hand wrapped around the thick erection that had been pressed against me all day. Stroking and tugging and whispering my name as he came.

The thought of him touching himself made my pulse race and my body tingle. The slam of something on the other side of the wall, in the living room, pulled me out of the moment before I got too worked up.

I washed myself again, making sure I was clean, then got out of the shower. I dressed in warm, cozy pajamas and met Daisy in the living room. She had food hot and on a plate for me, the remote in her hand and a movie ready to go.

"Do you feel better?"

"Tons," I said honestly. Orgasms made everything better.

OMAR and I messaged the next few days, but before we could make plans for the weekend, Amelia confirmed arrangements for James to meet me at the campground to remove the tree from the basketball court. When I showed up Saturday afternoon, James wasn't alone.

"Jude!" I called, surprised to see one of my campers standing there. "How are you?"

"Hi, Ms. Natalie! Dad said I could come help."

"Of course," I said, hugging the boy. He was almost as tall as me and still growing. Jude was a sweet kid who was always looking out for the other kids during summer camp. He made sure everyone knew how to play the crazy games I made up and he was a big fan of anything different.

"Hi, Mr. Bailey," I said, shaking his father's hand. Derek Bailey was as nice as they came. I'd been taking my SUV to his auto shop forever, but I didn't know Derek until Jude came to summer camp.

"Please call me Derek," he said. "I feel like I know you after how much Chelsea talks about you. She likes you as much as Jude does."

Derek and Chelsea did not have the easiest start to their relationship, but once they got to know each other, everything changed. Chelsea was my hair stylist, someone Daisy made me go to kicking and screaming.

Thankfully, I listened. Chelsea was amazing, and she gave me a confidence I had never had before. Not that it made me totally confident, but it was an improvement.

"The feeling is mutual," I told Derek. "And James, thank you for doing this."

James grinned. "I'm happy to help. Mom is so excited about this place. She hasn't stopped talking about it. We came here when my brother and I were young, but it's been forever since I was back here. I hope you don't mind that I brought help."

I shook my head. "Of course not. I appreciate it more than you know."

"How's the ankle?" Derek asked.

My cheeks heated. "You heard about that?"

The men nodded.

"I'm good now. I should have been more careful."

"Mom feels bad that you got hurt. She blames herself for letting you come out here."

"It wasn't her fault. Just a bad step. But there's a lot that has to be done, and not a lot of money."

"Well, what else can we do?" Derek asked. "We can be here as long as you need us."

I shook my head. "I couldn't ask you to do more than you are. We just need to get this tree out of the way so we can see if the court is in decent shape."

"It looks like there's a lot more to do," James said. "Let's get the tree and go from there. Are you saving the wood?"

"Um, yes?"

The men chuckled.

"If you're going to use some of those fire pits, you might as well keep the wood so you can use it for that. If you are, we will cut it up into pieces that are small enough for someone to carry. If not, we can just leave it in logs," James explained.

"Oh, well, yeah, I was thinking about that. I want to take down the fire pits out there and make one bigger one using the bricks. Hopefully something to cook on. Your mom also has a lot of big ideas about how to use the space, and I think using the fire pits in one way or another is something she wants to do." I didn't want to create more work, but if it meant I could save money down the road, it was smart.

"We will cut the logs small," Derek said. "You saw, I'll chop?"

James nodded.

"What am I going to do?" Jude asked.

"You are going to help Ms. Natalie stack these wherever she wants them. Make sure there's a neat pile somewhere so everything is all together," Derek said.

Jude nodded, sliding his hands into gloves his father handed over.

I grabbed my gloves, and the two men pulled tools from their vehicles. James handed me a pair of earplugs, and Derek offered me a pair of safety glasses. Both men donned their safety equipment, and Jude followed suit. I'd learned my lesson and did the same.

James cranked up the chainsaw he brought, the loud zipping noise cutting through the otherwise quiet space. He set it against the trunk of the tree, a line forming immediately.

James sawed the tree into three pieces, being careful not to get too close to the basketball court. After those pieces were cut, he turned off the chainsaw and set it on the ground.

"Let's get these off the court and I'll cut them up smaller. I don't want to risk damaging the court."

Derek moved to help, grabbing one end of the biggest section. Jude stood by, watching them, and grabbed one end of the smallest piece.

"I'll help, Jude," I said, walking to him and knowing it was going to be a challenge for us to lift the large log.

We tried, getting absolutely nowhere.

James and Derek came back and carried off the second piece.

"What if we roll it?" I suggested, noting there weren't a lot of branches sticking out from the piece we were trying to move.

"Let's try it," Jude said.

We got on one side and pushed. The log didn't move right away, but after a few seconds, it did. Jude and I grinned at each other and pushed harder, getting the log to roll right off the court and next to the other pieces.

"Have you seen the court?" Derek asked from behind us.

I stood and shook my head, anxious about what I would find.

"It looks good," James said, walking around the surface. "Could stand to be sealed and definitely needs to be cleaned up around the edges, but it's a lot better than I expected."

"I agree," Derek said. "I have a service contract with a local crew that does paving and sealing. I can reach out and see if they can do this, if you're interested."

"It's on my very long list. I need someone to do the driveway and parking lot."

"I'll give them a call and have them get in touch with you. I know you're on a budget, so I'll ask if they can do it for cost."

"You don't have to do that," I argued.

"Yeah, he does," James said. "Because you are on a budget. There's nothing wrong with that."

I drew a breath and nodded. I needed to get that through my head. I grew up not asking for handouts. There were times when it might have helped, but my parents always said there were families worse off than us. And they weren't wrong. I never went without meals like so many kids at MacKellar Cove Elementary did. I always had my parents around, and they made sure I knew how much they loved me.

It was a point of pride for me. But it wasn't about my pride anymore. It was about the kids I was helping to serve. If I refused help from others, I was going to have to accept that I couldn't do as much for the kids as I wanted.

And I wasn't willing to do that.

"Thank you," I said to Derek. "That would be really helpful."

"You're welcome," Derek said.

James nodded, as though he understood how hard that had been for me, then he put his safety glasses and earplugs back on and went back to work cutting the tree into pieces.

15

OMAR

I was looking forward to my date with Natalie but was not happy we needed to wait another week. When she was done with the work at the campground, she was exhausted and her ankle was sore.

If she lived alone, I might have picked up dinner and gone to see her, but she had a roommate, and that would have been awkward.

So, I had to wait.

Sunday night, I needed to get out of my house. I went for a drive on Saturday, but it didn't take away the unsteadiness I was feeling. I needed to be around people.

Once more, I found myself walking into O'Kelley's and seeking out Hudson.

"Evening, Omar. What can I get you?" Hudson asked when I took a seat at the bar.

"Are you always working?"

Hudson chuckles. "It just seems like it."

I smiled. "Can I get a burger and a beer?"

"On the way."

Hudson poured my beer, then left to put my dinner

order in. I sipped my beer and looked around the bar. Groups were scattered around the room. Some played pool, others lined up at the darts boards, and many more pulled tables together and expanded their group.

I sat alone.

A few people waved or said hello, but no one approached or invited me to join them.

It hadn't bothered me before, but the closer I got to my re-election, the more I saw how much I'd separated myself from the town. I loved MacKellar Cove, but I wasn't really a part of it.

Maybe that would change with Natalie.

She was showing me pieces of the town I had never paid attention to before. The families, the kids, the need. Even the others close to my age, I felt more of a connection to the men on Thursday night after admitting to them that I had a thing for her.

The irony was I thought she'd ruin my chances at re-election, but she seemed to be the best thing for it. And that was before she defended me and shut down the reporter who wanted dirt.

"Here you go," Hudson said, sliding a plate in front of me. "Need anything else?"

I shook my head and focused on my food.

"You doing okay?" Hudson asked.

"Yeah. All good."

Hudson hesitated for a minute, watching me as I tried to keep it together.

"Actually, no. I'm wondering if I'm really what's best for this town. Maybe someone like you should be mayor."

Hudson laughed loudly. "No. Not happening."

"You're someone everyone knows. Everyone likes. You're considerate and good with people. Why not?"

"I don't want to be mayor. I like what I do. There's no pressure. And you're good at what you do, Omar. Why are you doubting it? Because of that article?"

I shrugged. "I enjoy it, but the only person talking to me is you, and you're sort of required to do so."

Hudson grinned. "Do you want to talk to people because you want them to elect you or because you want to be friends with them?"

I tilted my head and considered his question.

Someone called his name, and Hudson glanced away from me. He held up one finger, then looked at me. "When you decide on your answer, you'll know what you really should do. Everyone here likes me because I provide them with beer and food and a place to hang out. Everything changes when everything changes."

I chuckled, nodding when he walked away.

He wasn't wrong. If he was the mayor instead of the local bar owner, people would see him differently. But what about me? I was never a part of the local community. I moved here and put my head down and worked. I liked my coworkers, but I never spent a lot of time getting to know them.

But why did I want to know people?

Getting elected mattered to me, but it wasn't why I wanted to talk to people. Without anyone running against me, I would be elected.

But I wanted more. I wanted to live in MacKellar Cove instead of just existing there.

I finished my burger and beer and thanked Hudson for the advice and dinner, leaving him a big tip for his help.

I walked out of O'Kelley's and ran right into someone walking past.

"Oof," she grunted.

Instinct had me grabbing onto her, catching her before

she hit the ground. I hugged her to me, her softness matching my strength the same moment her strawberries and marker scent filled my head.

Her hands were on my biceps, gripping life I was her lifeline.

"Are you okay?" I asked.

"Omar," she breathed, my name coming out in a whisper.

"Natalie." My voice dropped, desire I hoped I hid sneaking in. My fingers tightened on her back, pulling her closer.

"Be careful or you'll be the next one in a compromising picture with him," Daisy teased from a few feet away. "Are you okay?"

Her words had Natalie extracting herself from my arms. She removed her fingers from my biceps and took a step back.

My hands fell from her body, the heat of her wiped away in an instant.

"I'm fine. Just slipped when Omar came out of O'Kelley's."

"I apologize. I wasn't paying attention to where I was going. I should have been more careful."

"It's fine." She took a step to go around me, putting more space between us.

I didn't want her to go, but it was clear Daisy didn't know anything about us. I told Natalie it was up to her if she told anyone about us, and I had no right to be upset that she hadn't.

But I was.

"Are you okay?" I asked again.

She nodded. "Yes. Thank you for catching me."

"It was..." I glanced at Daisy, who was watching us with open curiosity. "Could I have a word with you?"

"Daisy! Natalie!" someone called from the other side of Book Boyfriends Unlimited.

All of us turned to look as Trinity and Willow approached.

I groaned inwardly.

"Mr. Mayor," Willow said when they got closer. "Are you coming to book club?"

I took a step back and shook my head. "Uh, no. I was heading home. Just not watching where I was going and ran right into Natalie. You all have a good night."

"You, too," they all said.

I walked away, hating that I was still a secret from her friends. Would she ever want them to know about us? Or was that her way of saying there was no us?

ANOTHER DAY, another article about how bad I was for MacKellar Cove. This time, I didn't fight it and get pissed. I read the article and accepted what it said.

Things like *biased* and *favoritism*. Again, the article claimed I wasn't doing what was best for the entire town and only focused on certain departments and action items.

There was even an interview with a former employee. Supposedly. The person remained anonymous and said I'd fired them after they questioned my integrity.

I couldn't think of anyone it could be. But it didn't matter because public perception was what mattered, and the article was making it clear the author thought someone better than me was out there.

So much for thinking the election was the least of my concerns.

Maybe the worst part of it was I hadn't heard from Natalie. After getting trapped at the campground together, we talked a little online, but I hadn't heard anything from her since we ran into each other outside O'Kelley's on Sunday night.

And it pissed me off more than it should have.

We had a meeting scheduled with Amelia, but I couldn't ask Natalie what was going on with her boss standing there.

I paced my office waiting for them to arrive, my mind bouncing between Natalie and the election and whoever was trying to sink my election chances. If the former mayor hadn't been run out of town, I'd think it was him, but I didn't think even he was dumb enough to try something like this. Not with the information Patrick had on the man.

A knock on my door stopped me in the middle of my pacing. "Yeah?"

Jane opened the door and flashed me a tentative smile before she let Amelia and Natalie into my office.

I thought I was hiding my frustration well until Natalie stopped dead when she caught sight of me.

"Omar, are you okay?" Amelia asked, walking right up to me and putting her hand on my arm.

I worked to smooth my scowl and the tightness in my shoulders. I certainly failed if the two of them could see how wound tight I was.

I hung my head and nodded. "You saw the latest article?" I glanced at Natalie.

"We saw it this morning," Amelia said. "I would have thought these reporters would have tried to get something more truthful than garbage no one who knows you would believe."

"It said they have a former employee. That's a pretty good source."

Amelia scoffed. "If it's true."

"I can't comment on that. I have to believe they wouldn't print something that would open the paper to legal action."

"Well, they stepped in it," Amelia continued. "You have been so good for this town, and people will see that. Besides, you're running unopposed."

I snorted. "I think that's the point. Someone is planning to run against me and wants to wait for the right moment to announce it."

Amelia gasped. "Really?"

I shrugged. "It's the only thing that makes sense. They sat on that picture for a while. Possibly the same with this new source."

"The picture was real?" Amelia asked.

I nodded but didn't look at Natalie. "It's real. But it was taken out of context and was not anywhere close to what it looked like."

Amelia shook her head. "It doesn't matter to me. What you do in your personal time is your business. Even if the picture wasn't taken out of context, it's no one's business but your own. As for you firing someone, disgruntled former employees are never seen as reliable sources because they have a grudge. The paper should have known that."

"Thank you, Amelia. Your support means a lot."

I glanced at Natalie, but she stayed silent.

"Enough about all of that. Do you have an update on the budget?"

Amelia nodded and took a seat across from my desk. "Natalie has all the numbers."

My gaze swung to Natalie. She stepped closer, clutching a file folder in trembling hands. She sat next to Amelia and opened the folder. "Um, so, this is the budget. It's all the things we want to do, broken down into the three phases we are hoping to have."

"It's almost entirely blank," I said.

She glanced at Amelia, and Amelia simply raised her eyebrows for Natalie to respond.

"Yeah, um, the weather hasn't been cooperating lately, so we haven't been able to get the work done. And phases two and three we know we won't be able to do for a year or two, so I haven't priced those out."

"But phase one needs to be done by summer. Things need to be moving or it'll never happen."

"Yes, but the weather—"

"Can't be the excuse for everything. Contractors are working on their spring schedules now. If you don't get people lined up, there's no way any of this will actually happen. I was hoping to see more progress. What has the money already spent gone to?"

Natalie fumbled with the folder again, flipping pages. She grabbed a paper clipped section and lifted it from the folder. "So this is— Crap!" She dumped the entire folder on the floor. Papers went flying everywhere, scattering to the carpet and sliding underneath my desk.

Natalie dropped to her knees, snatching sheets from the floor.

"Let me help you," Amelia said, leaning down and gathering the papers closest to her.

I heard Natalie inhale sharply and wanted to help her. To tell her it was all going to be okay. I retrieved the papers that slid under my desk and pretended I couldn't hear Natalie and Amelia whispering on the other side of my desk.

"Are you okay?" Amelia whispered.

"No. I thought you were going to talk about some of this."

"You are doing fine," Amelia said.

"Yeah, I'm crawling under his desk and making a fool of myself."

"Just take a breath, Natalie. You know what you have here. It's all okay."

Amelia sat up, smiling at me before turning her gaze back to Natalie. I saw the worry and the pride on Amelia's face. She was letting Natalie fail. Letting her fumble and be awkward. Because it was how Natalie would be better.

And Amelia was trusting me to not attack her.

Natalie hugged the folder and all the papers to her chest and avoided my gaze. She tried to sort through things without dropping all of it again, but there was no way she would be able to do that.

"Why don't you use the desk to organize your paper-work?" I suggested.

She looked up at me like I was offering her so much more than a temporary flat surface. "Thank you."

I nodded, handing over the sheets I'd gathered for her.

"Should we start over?" I asked.

Natalie swallowed audibly. "Thank you, but I know you're busy and don't have time for me to be all..."

"Awkward?" I asked.

Natalie looked up at me with a gasp.

I smirked, a secret shared between us.

She exhaled a laugh, and her body language changed. "Yeah. Awkward."

"I think I'm already aware of that one. Why don't you just tell me what's going on?"

She drew a breath and nodded. "James, Amelia's son, and Derek Bailey helped me to remove the tree from the basketball court over the weekend. They spent all day at the property with me, and we dug out the rest of the connections. We're ready for the electrical crew to come out and remove everything the rest of the way."

"That's huge progress from a week ago."

"It is," Natalie said. "I also got the camper cleaned out this week. We rented a dumpster and paid a company to get rid of everything in it."

"Natalie was trapped at the campground in the storm last week," Amelia told me. "We were in contact, but she was still stuck out there."

"Getting the camper cleaned was a good idea."

Natalie's lips twitched with suppressed humor. "Derek Bailey put me in touch with Total Paving. They're going to do the parking lot, driveway, and seal the basketball court in April or May."

"So you do have some things set up?" I asked.

Natalie nodded. "Because our budget is limited, I didn't want to commit to anything I didn't know we could pay for. That's why I'm not further along than I am. Until the fundraiser, I haven't been able to confirm everything with these contractors."

"Okay, I understand that. It makes sense to me that you wouldn't want to take up space on their schedules and then back out and risk them missing out on other jobs. Have you been in touch with some of these companies?"

"Yes. I have a pool company that agreed to clean up the pool if we can pay them. I am still unsure about a building, but that's a big ask. The camper was the biggest piece since we have to have a weather-safe location."

"You're making progress. And the fundraiser is less than a moth away?"

"It is. We have been getting calls from local companies

wanting to donate items for a raffle, and we have information going out so everyone in town will know about it," Natalie said.

"Good. Last we spoke, you seemed unsure."

"I'm—" She gasped. "I was, but I realized last week that if I let my pride get in the way, I am only hurting myself."

My brows jumped high. Was she talking about us? Or something else?

Did it matter?

"Well, I'm happy to hear that."

I held her gaze for a long moment. Long enough that I forgot Amelia was sitting in the room with us.

"Okay, Omar, we'll get on everything and be back for our next meeting in two weeks. The fundraiser will be almost here by then, and we'll have all the details together." Amelia stood and shook my hand. "And please know people are behind you. Anyone who does come out of nowhere and starts their campaign with lies and half-truths and an attempt to shame you isn't someone I want running this town."

"Thank you, Amelia."

She nodded, then walked out, leaving Natalie and I alone for a minute.

"I'm sorry about the article," Natalie said.

"Thanks." I wanted to pull her into my arms and hold on.

"Do you still want to get together this weekend?"

I looked up at her. "Do you? You haven't told anyone about us, so I assumed—"

"Daisy knows," she blurted. "She didn't know how to act when we saw you. And the others at book club know."

"Really?" I couldn't contain my grin.

She nodded. "Is that... is that okay?"

"Yes, it is."

"Good."

"So, does that mean you still want to get together this weekend?" I asked.

"Very much."

"Good. It's a date."

She grinned. "Yes, it is."

16

———

"SHOULD I BE OFFENDED THAT YOU'RE LATE AGAIN?" I ASKED Natalie as she took a seat opposite me.

We were on a date. Our first official date. Where we both agreed to it and knew we were meeting each other.

She pressed her lips together in a smile. "I had a long day. It wasn't that I didn't want to be here."

"Well, that's good. For once." I smirked at her.

She shook her head. "Yeah, yeah. I told you I was awkward and anxious. You should have expected it."

"And I wasn't upset. Not even a little. Not last time and not this time. You look amazing, by the way."

She did. Stunning. We agreed to a casual dinner, nothing overly fancy, and she was beautiful. Jeans that clung to her legs and tucked into short boots, a light pink sweater that brought out the pink in her skin and glowed against her dark hair.

"Thank you. So do you." The way her cheeks darkened told me she wasn't sure if it was okay to say that.

"Thank you." I ditched my suit and went for jeans of my own and a lavender long-sleeved button-up shirt, untucked with no tie. It felt like a stretch after so long watching every little thing I did, but after two articles came out about me, trying to discredit me and gaining zero traction, I was done catering to my critics and ready to step into my own power.

"You look like you made a decision about something," Natalie said, sipping her water and watching me over the edge of the glass.

I nodded, smiling at her insightfulness. "I was just thinking I'm happy to be here with you."

She looked around, catching a few people watching us, and ducked her head, letting her hair fall in front of her face.

"Are you not feeling the same?"

Her gaze snapped to mine as her head shook quickly. "No. I am very happy to be here. But I... being the center of attention is not my usual."

"People will forget about us soon enough," I assured her.

She smiled and glanced around. "I hope so."

The server approached and took Natalie's drink order and asked if we were ready to order.

"I haven't even looked at the menu," Natalie confessed, opening her menu.

"I'll give you a minute," the server said, smiling before checking on another table.

"I've never been here," Natalie said without looking up from her menu. "Do you come here a lot?"

I shook my head. "Jane mentioned it. Said she and her husband like to come here when they have a date night."

"Everything looks good."

"Get it all."

She scoffed. "No. That's a waste. I'd never eat it all."

"Well, what are you thinking? Maybe we can share."

She looked up at me, a hopefulness in her gaze that hit me square in the chest.

This woman had the ability to undo me. I couldn't remember that ever happening before. The complete and total surrender to her and the way she made me feel. It was terrifying and exciting all at once.

"Okay," she whispered.

We talked about the food options for a few minutes, and when the server returned, we ordered two dinners, two appetizers, and one extra side because Natalie couldn't decide what she wanted.

"That's too much," she said when the server collected our menus and left.

I shook my head. "Worst case, you can take some home for dinner another night."

She smiled and met my gaze. "Thank you for wanting to do this."

My eyebrows shot up. "A date?"

She nodded, looking away from me. "I haven't been... easy to deal with. Between walking out the first time, assaulting you before that, getting you caught in a storm, and then not knowing how to tell people about us... I don't know why you wanted to go out, but—"

"Because I like you, Natalie. A lot."

She rolled her lips in and smiled.

I reached across the table and took her hand. She fidgeted, but turned her hand over so our palms slid together.

Her eyes closed, and her shoulders dropped just enough to tell me it helped. "I'm sorry I wasn't very nice to you the last time we went out. When we met at O'Kelley's."

"You were surprised," I said. "And we weren't on the best of terms."

"But we are now?" One brow rose in question.

I laughed. "We're getting there." I sipped my water. "If I'm being honest, I was fighting my attraction to you. I was pretty sure you hated me, so I was trying to keep my distance."

"I never hated you," she whispered. "I was intimidated by you. Still am."

"Why?"

She raised an eyebrow.

I chuckled. "Okay, fine, but I'm just a man."

She laughed. "There is nothing *just* about you."

"What does that mean?"

She shook her head, then realized I was serious and sobered. "You're the mayor of our town, which means you have power. People want to be close to you. But it's not just because you're the mayor. You have this way of making people feel like they're safe around you. Like they can be honest and you won't judge them."

"Except you," I said, knowing she didn't feel that way when we met.

She breathed a self-conscious laugh. "No. When you found me at the campground... I would have panicked if you weren't there. I froze when that storm came in. I had no idea what to do, and you took charge and got us to your car. That's sort of what I'm talking about."

"It's a good thing I take over instead of offering people to think for themselves?"

She chuckled. "No. Well, yes, when the situation warrants it."

"And if the situation doesn't warrant it, then I'm an over-bearing jerk?"

She shook her head. "No. You just know what makes sense. You think farther ahead than others and know where things need to go. I live in the moment more, which works out well with my job. That's how kids are, and it allows me to be on their level more easily, I think."

"You really love kids." It wasn't a question, but she answered anyway.

A dreamy look lifted her lips and had her eyes unfocused and staring past me. "I do. I always have. I guess it's a symptom of my childhood or something."

"Did you grow up with a bunch of younger siblings?" I asked.

She shook her head and laughed. "Not even close. I'm the youngest, but my dad was married before me so my older sisters didn't grow up with me. They're eight and thirteen years older than me."

"Wow."

"Yeah. I was always jealous that they had each other. I begged my parents to have another kid, but it wasn't in their plans or in the cards or whatever. Whatever the reason, I'm the only one. But I was always drawn to the younger kids. Any of my friends who had younger siblings I would spend as much time with their siblings as my friends. I always felt more comfortable with them."

"There's nothing wrong with that. A lot of people go into education because they want to be there for younger generations."

She nodded. "Yeah, that was part of it. I just wanted to have someone to play with."

I laughed. "Well, that works, too. Now it's what you do all day."

"Not all day. There's this guy who won't give me money and has me working on all kinds of different things." She laughed.

I fought the unease inside me. Was that why she wanted to date me?

No, it couldn't be. I was the one who pursued her. But was I a fool?

"I was just joking," she said softly, drawing my attention.

I pressed my lips into a smile I didn't feel. The server came over with our appetizers and distracted us for a moment, but the moment wasn't over.

The server left, promising to return to check on us soon, and Natalie looked at me.

"I am not here to ask you for more money. Or anything like that. I really was joking."

"Okay," I said, but it was hard to believe her. I picked up a potato skin and took a bite, resolving not to let her bad joke ruin the night.

She followed suit, choosing her own appetizer and turning the conversation away from work to things less full of landmines.

"I ruined this, didn't I?" she asked after our dinner was served.

I sighed, knowing I had to be honest with her. "I'm trying not to let it. My ex was a master manipulator. She would tell me one thing but do something else, then accuse me of not paying attention to what she said. She had multiple affairs. She made me doubt everything I knew about myself."

"I'm not like that," Natalie breathed.

"I know. I want to know. I believe you. But..."

"Everyone wants something from you. And it makes you wonder if anyone is ever honest with you."

I nodded, surprised she was able to capture my thoughts so succinctly.

"It was a bad joke, but I promise it was a joke. I love

playing with the kids. I love being able to come up with new games and try different things. To be creative and expressive in a way I never could be when I was teaching. I thought teaching was going to be the right thing for me. I loved the idea of it, but when I was a student teacher, I started to see it wasn't what I expected."

"In what way?"

She shrugged and pursed her lips as though afraid to tell me what she thought. "Teachers are amazing, and it's a valuable career. I wouldn't be where I am without amazing teachers who were willing to see all of me."

"You don't have to extoll the benefits of teachers to me, Natalie."

She pressed her lips up. "I know. Maybe I'm doing it for me. I spent a lot of time in school. I have a degree that would change things for a lot of people. But I don't use it. It feels like I wasted my education, like I took something that was given to me and threw it away. It's not always easy to be objective."

"I think we all go into college with the best of intentions. We think we know what we're getting into, but not everyone is going to come out with the same thoughts we walked in with. I know I didn't."

"What is your degree in?"

"Political science."

She gave me a look that said I was full of crap.

I laughed. "Okay, yes, I'm using my degree, but I'm not normal."

She smirked.

"Ha ha. I'm just saying it's hard to make a choice when you're seventeen that will rule the rest of your life. A lot of people can't do it."

She nodded thoughtfully. "I guess. I wish I'd been able

to. I think teaching would be amazing if I could do things my way."

"Instead of following the state guidelines?"

Her head bobbed side to side. "Somewhat. I get that there are things kids need to learn every year so they're prepared for the following year, but not everyone learns the same. Some kids do better with action included in their lessons. Some kids need music. Some kids need to read or listen or write things down. There's not space for all of that in schools."

I shook my head. "No, there's not. You're right."

"That's why I love working at the community center, and now the rec center. I love being able to make recreation the biggest part of the day. Whether that's physical activity or fine motor skills when they're crafting with Trinity or any of the things they do. Amelia said when Trinity came in, it opened the eyes of a lot of the kids to other things. Some of them refused to do her crafts, but over time more and more have joined her. Now, it's something the kids ask for and are so excited on the days she's there that we can barely contain them."

"That's good. It's good for them to have a variety of activities."

She nodded, smiling softly. "It is. It's very good."

We finished our dinner and talked about the fundraiser. I relaxed and accepted that she was being honest about her intentions. She wanted the best for the kids, and she was working hard to get it.

I found myself wishing I had more money to give her to support her project. That was the danger of dating something within my hierarchy. An attachment could mean impropriety.

"What happens if you don't get enough money to do everything you want to do for the summer camp?" I asked after I paid the check. We were finishing our drinks and not in a hurry to leave.

"Honestly, I don't think we will get enough money. It's a huge project, and it's expensive. But if we don't get enough money, then Amelia plans to put forth a proposal for the budget for the next fiscal year. She said there might be a way to get more. She's full of ideas." Natalie chuckled, her eyes wide like Amelia's ideas were crazy.

"What other ideas does she have?"

"The one she keeps trying to talk me into is to hold a community building party. Like some charities do where they have volunteers come in and build a house or something. She wants to do the same thing but have people help out with constructing the building."

"Is that possible?"

Natalie snorted. "I doubt it. We would need someone who knows what they're doing to run it, and even the material costs are going to be pretty huge."

"What if there were people who knew how to make that happen? And if we could get materials at cost?"

Natalie shook her head as I spoke. "I don't want you getting involved. It's not why I told you about it."

"I asked."

"I know, but still. I can't ask you to do more than you've already done."

"I'm not the person who knows how to do that. I meant Knox Randall or Sofia Frank. Sebastian Parks might be another one. They might have their contractor's license."

"Yeah, but a building is going to require an engineer and an architect and a lot of people."

I shook my head. "I'm not so sure. There are prefab buildings that come with instructions to assemble them."

"We're going to be putting kids in this," she said, not sounding convinced.

"I know. I really think it might be worth looking into. It might be more affordable, too."

"I will look into it. But back to your original question, we would probably have to delay opening the camp for a year. It might be the better option anyway."

"But it's not what you want."

She shook her head. "No. It's not. But we don't always get what we want when we want it. It'll happen. The camp will open. And if I have to wait a year so we can do it right, that's okay."

I studied her. She smiled and set her glass on the table. She stood and pulled on her coat, then slung her handbag over her shoulder.

She looked like she meant what she said. It wasn't a manipulation. It was simply the truth.

"I hope you don't have to wait a year."

"Me, too."

I followed her outside into the cold night and realized I hadn't thought about what would come after dinner. I wasn't ready for the night to end, but I wasn't going to be presumptuous.

"So, um, I parked over here," she said, gesturing toward the parking lot.

I nodded and followed her. She fiddled with her keys as we got closer to her car, then unlocked it with a beep.

"I had a good time," she said.

I brushed the hair out of her face so I could look into her eyes. "I don't want to say goodnight yet."

She tilted her chin up and smiled. "Neither do I. But I have a roommate."

"I do not."

"That's... nice for you."

I laughed with her. "Would you like to come back to my place?"

She ducked her chin and nodded.

I lifted her chin, waiting until her gaze hit mine before I spoke. "The choice is yours, Natalie. I don't want you to feel pressured."

She bit the inside of her lip and smiled. "Would it help to know I told Daisy I was hoping to not be home tonight?"

My dick twitched at the thought. I nodded, then cleared my suddenly thick throat. "Yes, that helps."

"Should I follow you?"

I nodded, leaning closer to her. She smiled, her back pressed against the side of her SUV and me to her front.

I leaned down slowly, holding her gaze until the last minute when mine dropped to her lips.

Her lips parted with her quick inhale, then they were on mine. Hungry, desperate kisses passed between us, give and take and give again.

My erection thickened against her stomach, and her whimpers told me she was almost as ready as I was.

I found her hand and clasped it in mine, holding tight to it. Her fingers were cold, her lips warm, and her body willing.

I pulled back reluctantly, knowing it would be worth the wait to get back to my place.

"Follow me, Natalie. I'm just over there."

She nodded, her chest heaving with her attempt to catch her breath.

I kissed her fingers, then released her hand and waited for her to get in her SUV. When she closed the door and turned on the vehicle, I jogged to mine and cranked it up, not needing the heat before I was pulling out of the lot and ready to get home.

Now.

17

———————

I PULLED INTO MY GARAGE AND LEFT THE DOOR OPEN FOR Natalie to walk in after me. She locked her car with a soft beep, then was back in my arms.

"I don't want you to feel like I'm here because of your position. Because you're my boss's boss. I'm not here with the hope of getting money or support or anything like that from you," she whispered, her face against my chest.

I nodded. "I know."

"Do you? Because I saw the way people looked at you in the restaurant. The way people always look at you. The man who took our picture when I fell, and the other article about you. We don't fit together, and I don't want you to doubt me when you realize that."

I pulled her tight in my arms and held her close, feeling her curves fit to my body. "We fit together, Natalie. In every way that matters. You have your career and your life, and I don't expect you to give all of that up to stand at my side and be some figurehead of propriety or something. I don't want that in my life. I'm not looking for a woman who's a statue and isn't allowed to be independent. I'm looking for a woman who challenges me and wants to be with me and makes me excited to rush home from work every day."

"You didn't have that with your ex?"

I exhaled and shook my head. "Let's go inside." I released her and led the way toward the house. I hit the button to close the garage door, then held the door for Natalie to go into my house.

I hadn't had many people in my space. A few women before I was the interim mayor, but no one since. Dating felt risky, and I didn't have much time for it the first year. I was starting to get my feet under me when the first article about me came out, casting doubts on my hope of dating while running for mayor.

"Do you want a drink?" I asked her, heading to the kitchen.

"Your home is beautiful. Very cozy," she said instead of answering me.

"Thank you. It's my escape. That and my car."

She laughed. "I know all about your car."

"What does that mean?"

She smirked. "You have this appearance of wealth and power. You have that car and you wear suits every day and you're fit and gorgeous and people talk."

"About me?"

"All the time. Good things. People admire you. Look up to you. Want things from you. I think that car made you seem more real to some people."

"What about to you?"

She smirked. "Honestly?"

I nodded. "I always want you to be honest with me."

"Honestly, I don't get cars. I'm indifferent to them. So for me, it makes me think you're a little bit of a tool."

A laugh burst from me. "Don't hold back."

"You said to be honest!"

I laughed again. "I did. And I get it. My car was always the only place I felt like I didn't have to put on a show. Before I moved up here, I had a job my ex wanted me to have. I worked in town politics, but I wasn't doing anything I really believed in. My drive to and from work was the only time when I felt like I could breathe. When I could relax."

"She had no idea what she was throwing away when she cheated on you."

My chest swelled with gratitude. My throat tightened. "Thank you."

"You don't believe me?"

"I've never been told that before," I confessed.

"Why not? She's the one who cheated. Why would you be to blame?"

"Men cheat all the time. When they do, it's dismissed as the woman's fault. She wasn't doing all the things he needed. It's bullshit. The only one to blame when someone cheats is the one who cheats."

"I agree, but I would also guess your marriage wasn't great before then."

I shook my head. "No. It wasn't. But I never stepped out on her. I was faithful."

"Which says who you are."

"That's not what others have said. She was cheating on me, but I was blamed for it. Told I was the problem. I had people ask if I was gay or just a shitty lover who never pleased her. Every single person said it was my fault she felt the need to go somewhere else. Not one person said she was the problem."

"She was the problem," Natalie whispered. She moved closer to me. "She should have seen the amazing man in front of her and realized what a gift she had in you. She was blind, and she didn't deserve you. She doesn't deserve your anger now, or your time or focus or regret."

"I don't regret divorcing her."

"But you regret marrying her."

I nodded slowly, agreeing reluctantly. "I do."

"You can't do that. It helped you become the man you are. The man who took over as mayor of this town and made it a place where everyone has a place."

"Someone's trying to take that from me."

"We're not going to let them."

"We?"

She raised an eyebrow and took a step back. "Unless you don't want me to help you."

I grabbed her before she could get farther away. My arm slid around her waist and tugged her to me.

Her hands went to my chest, smoothing over my shirt and wrapping around my neck.

"I don't want you to feel obligated to do anything that makes you uncomfortable."

She laughed. "Everything makes me uncomfortable."

I leaned down and kissed her neck. "Does that make you uncomfortable?"

She hummed and tilted her head to give me better access. "No."

I licked her throat. "How about that?"

A groan slid from her throat.

I nibbled her ear, slicking my tongue around the shell. "Does that make you uncomfortable?"

Her grip on me tightened. "I think I'd be more comfortable in your bed, Omar."

I scooped her up and turned toward the bedroom.

"Stop! You're going to hurt yourself."

I shook my head. "Nope. You said I'm fit and gorgeous.

I've been wanting to drag you to my bed since those words left your beautiful lips."

"I hope it's close."

I growled and stomped through the house, kicking the door closed behind us a second later. "Very close."

I eased her body down, holding her tight until her feet touched the floor. Her hands relaxed on my neck and slid around to my chest. She opened the top button of my shirt.

"Natalie," I groaned.

She kissed the skin she exposed, then opened another button. And another, and another, kissing my bare skin with each button she opened.

When she opened the last button, she looked up at me from her knees.

"That night I fell into you, I was so embarrassed. I looked up at you and wanted to melt into the floor."

"I wanted to yank you to your feet and never let anyone ever touch you again."

Her eyes widened. "Why?"

"You were beautiful. Still are. I hated that you were hurt. If that guy hadn't taken our picture, I'm not sure what I would have done."

"What do you mean?"

"You have no idea the way you make me feel. The day I came to the community center to meet with you—"

"I made it awkward. I'm sorry for that."

I chuckled, shaking my head. "No, beautiful. You didn't make anything awkward. I did. I wanted to kiss you that day. I wanted to sit there all day and listen to you talk about kids and how passionate you were about the rec center."

"You ran out like I scared you off."

"Ha, no. I ran out because I couldn't control myself

around you. I had to get away or risk you suing me for sexual harassment."

"I wouldn't have done that."

"You would have had grounds for it."

"And now?"

I sucked in a breath. "I hope this is consensual."

She kissed my stomach and licked around my belly button.

I groaned and resisted the urge to thread my fingers into her long hair and hold her there. I needed to know she was on board with what was happening.

"It's definitely consensual, Omar. I want to be here. And I want to feel you inside me. I haven't been able to stop thinking about it since we were trapped at the campground."

"Neither have I."

She slowly raised to her feet, kissing my chest on her way up. Who would have thought quiet, awkward Natalie Edwards was secretly a seductress?

I lifted her chin, bringing her lips up so I could claim them with mine. She parted them, licking my lips as my brain fought to keep up with her.

I groaned and thrust my tongue into her mouth, pulling her close. The feel of her top against my bare chest reminded me she was still fully clothed. I needed to do something about that.

I bunched her shirt in my hand, pulling the fabric high enough to touch her bare skin. I spread my fingers wide on her lush body. I lifted my hands, drawing her shirt up until it snagged on her plump breasts. I moved my hands around to the front, pausing to rub circles below her breasts, and pulled back.

"Are you sure?" I whispered against her lips.

"You've seen me topless before," she replied.

"Yes, but we were in my SUV, not my bedroom."

She stepped back from me, her shirt falling back into place without my hands to hold it up. She reached the edge of her shirt and pulled it up and off in one motion.

I nearly lost all thoughts as she stood there in a pink lace bra with her gorgeous globes spilling over the top.

Then her hands went to her jeans, and I did lose all thought.

I hurried to catch up to her, dropping my shirt to the floor and unbuttoning my jeans to give my throbbing cock a bit of relief.

Her jeans hit the floor, and she stood in front of my bed in matching pink lace.

"Holy shit," I breathed. "You're gorgeous."

Her cheeks darkened, the pleasure and shyness on her face a reminder of all the conversations we had before I knew who she was. The confessions about not being very good at dating and not wanting to date and men not choosing her once they knew who she was.

I was a lucky son-of-a-bitch. It was painful for her to go through that, but it gave me the chance to have her.

"Omar?"

All I could do was stare at her. My gaze slid down her body and back up, my cock thumping with every beat of my heart. I wanted her. More than I thought possible. More than I expected.

I was looking forward to our date, but I had no hope in mind that we might end up in my bedroom at the end of the night. It hadn't crossed my mind. Now that it was here, I was stunned.

"Do you want me to...?" She reached for her clothes, avoiding my gaze.

"Dammit," I hissed, closing the distance between us and grabbing her hand. "Natalie, no. I was trying to figure out how I got so lucky tonight."

"I'm not anyone special."

"Yes, you are. You are incredibly special." I brought our joined hands to my lips. "You keep saying we don't fit. That we're not supposed to go together. And you're right, but not in the way you think. I'm not worthy of you, Natalie."

She scoffed.

"You can disagree, but I've been divorced. I thought I met the woman I was going to spend my life with. Coming to MacKellar Cove was running away. I thought if I hid here, I'd figure out my next move one day. But I fell in love with this town. I wanted to stay, but that was when I became interim mayor. I'd always kept my distance from others because I thought I'd be leaving. Then I was the boss of half the town and kept my distance because of the way people saw me. You are beloved. People adore you. When you stood up for me, people listened. I have a chance of winning this election because of you. Because no matter who is behind those stories, with your word, no one is going to doubt me."

"I'm not important."

I tucked her hair behind her ear. "But you are, Natalie. You're so important. You're more important than me because you're changing things for the next generation of residents. You're making this town better for families and kids. You are the one with the power and the authority here."

She chuckled and shook her head. "I don't have any power."

"You do over me."

Her eyes widened.

"I'm stalling right now because I know when I get my

hands on you, I won't be able to slow down. I'm going to lose my mind and the night will be over too fast."

"Then we make sure the night lasts," she said.

Before I could say anything else, she stepped into my arms and raised up on her toes. She kissed me soundly, pulling me down to her.

I responded instantly, needing to let out the passion she unleashed in me. Our movements were frantic, tugging at the last pieces of clothing we both wore. Her hands shoved at my jeans. I unhooked her bra. She wrapped her leg around my hip. I slid my hands into the back of her panties and cupped her perfect ass.

We moved together to the bed, falling onto the mattress with my jeans around my ankles and her bare breasts pressed to my chest. She slid up to rest her head on a pillow, and I groaned at the sight of her, dark hair a halo on my pillow.

I crawled off the bed and got rid of my jeans and boxer briefs, then hooked my fingers in the sides of her panties.

She lifted her hips to let me slide them off her, and I got my first look at all of her.

"My God, you're beautiful," I whispered.

She reached for me, nodding. "Same."

My hand went to hers, and she tugged me onto the bed. I stretched out next to her, kissing her and teasing her stomach with one hand. My hand drifted to her breast, drawing faint circles around her nipples before tweaking them gently.

She moaned into my mouth, her hips rising.

I slid my hand down her body, barely touching her until I reached the apex of her thighs. She parted them for me, letting me feel through her curls to her soaked, slick skin.

She moaned again, tightening her fingers on the bedding.

I pressed one finger into her, groaning at the way her body sucked it in. I added a second on my next stroke and brushed my thumb over her clit.

"Omar," she breathed, breaking our kiss. "Please."

"Are you already going to come for me?"

"Don't tease me. Please."

I kissed her hard, letting her feel my erection against her hip, and wasted no time drawing pleasure out of her body. She writhed against my hand, her hips rocking with each stroke of my fingers into her.

Within seconds, she was moaning and whimpering and pulled away from me to cry out as an orgasm hit her. She clutched at my shoulder, her nails digging into my skin.

"More," I whispered as she built toward another orgasm.

The second one hit her harder. She rocked with me, then wrapped her hand around my erection and stroked it as she came.

"Inside," she demanded, trying to pull me into position with her hand on my dick.

"Condom," I reminded her, rolling the other way to grab one.

"Let me," she said, rolling with me and reaching for the packet when I took it out of the nightstand.

I handed the condom to her and stood next to the bed.

She looked up at me with a dangerous gleam in her eyes. Before I could ask what she was thinking, she wrapped her lips around my cock and sucked hard.

"Fuck, Natalie," I hissed, unable to stop myself from pumping into her mouth. "I'm sorry."

She swirled her tongue around the tip of my cock, then

released me and opened the condom as though she was never sucking my dick.

I counted to ten and thought about budgets while her hand smoothed the condom down my length. She pumped twice, and only stopped when I jerked in her palm.

She laid back down, spreading her thighs and watching me crawl over her.

I positioned myself between her legs, once more wondering how in the hell I got so lucky.

"I want you, Omar," she whispered.

I locked eyes with her and pushed inside, both of us moaning at the feel of me sinking all the way into her.

"Wow, you feel good," she breathed.

"So good," I agreed. I withdrew until I was almost out, then eased back in, wanting to feel her entire body tighten around me again.

"Don't hold back. Please."

"Natalie?"

She looked up at me, her gaze glassy but determined. "Let me feel you, Omar. Don't hide from me."

Those words were so simple, so innocent, but not coming from her. She knew what she was asking me. She knew what it meant to me to be able to share my entire self with someone. And she was asking me to trust her. To let it be her.

I took one hand in mine and lifted our joined hands above her head. Her breast rose with her arm, perking up on one side. I grabbed her leg with my other hand, spreading her wider and holding her knee up and away from my body.

I sank in deeper, something I didn't think was possible, but I did. My balls hit her body, and something inside me unleashed.

I stared into her eyes as I pounded into her body.

She looked back at me, taking it and encouraging it and moaning through it with each thrust. She lifted her hips to meet mine and squeezed her hand to tell me she was right there with me.

And when her body clenched my dick, when she shouted her orgasm, when she screamed and came and nearly broke my fingers, and when I followed her right over the edge, I knew the guys were right.

That damn app had a way of knowing something the rest of us would never be able to figure out. And I was damn happy I found it.

And Natalie.

18

NATALIE

Omar unleashed was otherworldly. It was magic and inspiration and eroticism all at once.

I'd never been fucked the way he fucked me. That was the only word I could think of for it. He didn't hold back. He didn't try to make things balanced or equal or resist his own pleasure for mine.

He just let loose. And it was so damn good.

"Are you okay?" he whispered, holding himself above me.

I enjoyed sex. I always had. Not every experience had been great, but overall, sex was fun for me.

That was so much more than sex. It was emotional and pleasurable and joyful. I felt a connection to him deeper than any other man I'd ever been with. And not just because he was deeper than any other man ever, but because he was Omar.

"Natalie?" he said, his voice lifting in tone and fear.

"I'm amazing," I whispered. "I didn't know it was possible to feel this good."

"Are you sure?"

I looked up at him and cupped his chin with my free hand. "Your ex-wife was a fucking idiot."

A laugh popped out of him, making all of him shake. Yes, even his cock, which set off another mini-orgasm inside me.

"Damn," I breathed, trembling at the way he rubbed my body without even trying.

"I don't mean this as an insult, but you were pretty easy to please." He rolled off of me and sat on the side of the bed. The snap of rubber said he removed the condom, and the tissue he pulled from the box confirmed it. He went to the bathroom I hadn't noticed before and disposed of the condom, then washed his hands.

"I've never come that easily before," I confessed when he laid next to me. "It usually takes me a little while."

"I never would have guessed that."

"I think you're good for my vagina."

He snorted a laugh. "Words I've never heard before."

I smirked at him. "Mind if I use your bathroom?"

"Please be my guest." He rolled off the bed with me. "Water?"

"Yes, please."

He let himself out of the room before I made it into the bathroom.

I debated closing the door or leaving it open. Open felt very domestic and close, but closed felt like I wanted a barrier between us. I opted for half-closed and hurried to use the bathroom and wash my hands.

Only after I opened the bathroom door did he come back into the bedroom.

"I wasn't sure how you felt about me being in here," he said, handing over a water bottle.

"I wasn't sure either," I admitted.

He sat on the edge of the bed. I sat next to him. Was this the awkward dismissal time? When I wasn't sure what to do and he was waiting for me to leave?

"I don't want you to go," he said, as though reading my mind.

"How did you know I was trying to figure out what to do?"

He shook his head. "I didn't, but I didn't say a lot of things to you that I wished I'd said. I am trying to do better now and tell you how I feel."

"I think you've said a lot to me."

"Maybe online, but not in person."

"Ah, well, that's probably true."

He chuckled.

"Will you tell me about your ex?" I asked.

He turned to look at me. "Why?"

"I want to know more about you, but I also want to understand why you're okay it's over."

He sighed, then sat on the bed with his back against the headboard.

I wasn't sure what I should do, but he raised his arm for me to sit next to him, so I crawled up the bed and rested my head on his chest.

"We bonded over a proposal that came into town hall one day. We both wanted to support it, but not a lot of other people did. We started working together to figure out how to make it happen, spending a lot of late nights together. One thing led to another, and we ended up together by the time we got the proposal approved."

"You had common interests."

He nodded. "We did. And for a while, it worked. But if we disagreed on anything, she would get angry. If I worked later than her, she would get angry. I thought getting married would silence some of that. That maybe she would see I was committed to her instead of thinking about other women, like she always accused me of."

"That's ironic," I said. I regretted it until he chuckled.

"Right?"

"How long were you married?"

"Three years."

"How long have you been divorced?"

"Seven years."

"Wow, really? How old are you?"

"Thirty-five. How old did you think I was?"

I did not want to answer that question. "Um..."

"How old, Natalie?" he demanded. The sharp, commanding tone of his voice sent a shiver through me.

"Over forty."

"Seriously?"

"I didn't know!"

He shook his head and groaned. "Am I allowed to ask how old you are?"

"I'm thirty-one."

"Is that one reason you didn't want to get involved with me?"

"Maybe."

"Can I ask you a question?"

"Sure." I wasn't sure what he was going to ask, or if I was going to want to answer, but I felt like I had to agree.

"What was your first thought when you saw me at O'Kelley's?"

I closed my eyes and thought back to that night. I was ashamed of the way I ran out on him. After I asked him not to do the same to me. "I thought you looked attractive from behind."

"Okay," he said with a chuckle.

"And when I sat down and saw it was you, I felt foolish. All that time I'd been telling you things, and you were my boss. My boss's boss. You were this larger than life man I'd already manhandled and I'd confessed all this stuff to you, and the only thing I could think was I needed to go before I made it worse."

He squeezed me tight against his side. "You wouldn't have made it worse. I was surprised it was you, but I wasn't disappointed."

"I'm sorry I ran out on you that night. I made you promise not to do that to me, then I did it to you, and I'm sorry."

"Thank you." He kissed the top of my head.

"I'm really happy you were willing to give me another chance."

"I'm happy you wanted one."

We sat there for a few minutes, then he stirred.

"Come on." He got off the bed and reached his hand out to me.

"Where are we going?"

"Get dressed. We're going for a drive."

"A drive?"

He nodded. "I know you don't like cars, but I want to take you for a drive. You said you like nights as much as I do. We can drive north and look at the stars over the water. Are you up for it?"

I looked up at the excitement on his face. The joy. He wanted to share something with me that meant a lot to him. Something he prized, if the way he stared at his car when we walked into the house meant anything.

"Sounds good," I said, putting my hand in his and letting him help me off the bed.

"Good." He smiled, then grabbed his clothes and got dressed.

HOLY SHIT, I was a convert. Sinking into those seats, and feeling the rumble of the engine was enough to have me wondering if I'd been missing something my whole life. Then Omar opened it up on the back roads, and damn, I understood the appeal.

"Wow," I breathed when Omar slowed down and pulled into a parking lot. "I might have to insist you take me out in this car again someday, Mr. Mayor."

He laughed, a cautious, wary laugh. "Back to Mr. Mayor?"

"I'm just teasing you. But this car is amazing."

"I agree." He put the car in park and let out a breath. "I'm glad you enjoyed this."

I nodded, turning toward him in my seat. "I did. I never thought I would, but I get why you love this."

He grabbed my hand and brought it to his lips. "Thank you for letting me take you for a drive."

"Is this how you used to get girls in high school?" I teased him.

He laughed. "Not exactly. I was pretty nerdy and didn't get a lot of dates in high school. I wasn't really interested in girls for a long time, and when I finally was, I was the nerdy, dorky kid no one wanted to date."

"Aw. I can't see that, though. You're too..." I waved my hand at him. "Too sexy."

He smirked. "You think I'm sexy?"

I scoffed. "I mean, you do have some appeal."

He laughed. "Thank you."

I leaned across the console, smiling when he met me in the middle for a kiss. It didn't take long for the kiss to become heated and the windows to fog up.

"I think we should go back to your house," I whispered against his lips.

"You read my mind," he said.

The drive back to his place was much faster than the drive out there.

WAKING up in a strange bed with a hand on my stomach was not a regular occurrence for me. When I stretched, and his hand moved, I had a moment of panic before I remembered where I was and why someone else was there.

Then I smiled.

My body ached in places it hadn't ached for a very long time. And my heart clenched at the memories of our night.

Omar Knight was quickly becoming so much more than I thought he would ever be. I wanted to protect myself from him, keep my distance and remember we would never work, but every moment we spent together had me hoping I was wrong.

When we got back from our drive, we left a trail of clothes from the garage to his bed. We were frantic and passionate. He held my hand and my gaze as he plunged into me and the whole time he made both of us come.

After, he tucked me under his chin and held me close as our breathing slowed and our skin cooled. The next time he slid into me, it was slow but no less passionate. I'd never had a lover who could make me come every way he touched me. Who could send me to the edge with a look.

Who I had a strong suspicion I was falling in love with.

"You're thinking very loudly over there," he whispered, alerting me that he was awake while my thoughts raced through my head.

"Sorry," I said.

He tugged me closer, moving to meet me in the middle of his bed. His hand circled my waist. He kissed my shoulder. His erection nestled against my butt. "You don't have to apologize for anything. Are you regretting last night?"

"No," I said quickly, turning to face him. "Not even a little."

His eyes closed like he'd been worried about my answer. When they opened, the dark brown drew me in.

"You were worried."

He nodded. "You're not the only one who struggles to date, Natalie. All night I've been wondering if I'd wake up alone or hear you trying to sneak out or if you'd avoid eye contact in the morning and make up a reason you had to leave immediately."

I shook my head and moved closer to kiss him. I poured all the thoughts I was having into my kiss. About how much I enjoyed our night and how worried I was that I was falling for him. I kissed him with every shred of passion I was feeling.

And he responded in kind.

I crawled on top of him, feeling bold and sexy. His erection flattened under my body, the hard ridge of his cock hitting my overly sensitive clit. I moaned, my hips shifting to increase the friction.

"Use me, Natalie," he growled, his gaze trained between our bodies.

He pushed me up with his hands, holding on and supporting me while I rocked on his cock.

"Oh, God," I moaned.

"Yes, Natalie."

I kept going, letting the feel of his erection on my clit drive me forward. Closer and closer, faster and faster, I rode his erection, taking what my body needed from him.

"Omar," I whispered, tipping from sane to not. My movements were frantic, demanding, taking everything from him.

"Fuck, Natalie. You're beautiful. Keep coming for me."

"Inside. I want to feel you inside."

He grabbed a condom from the nightstand. I lifted myself off him, making a move to roll over. "Stay," he commanded, that delicious shiver racing down my spine.

I watched as he rolled the condom on, then positioned myself over him. He held himself still while I sank onto him, my first orgasm making it easier for him to slide into me.

He thrust up as I sank deep, and we both moaned. "Fuck me," he groaned.

"Yes," I replied.

He grabbed my hands again, supporting me as I started to move. His gaze went back to where we were joined, watching himself slide in and out of my body.

"I wish I could see what you're seeing."

"I wish you could, too. I love seeing my dick disappear into you. Watching you stretch to let me in. Accepting me. Then watching my dick appear again, your body holding on like you don't want to let me go."

"I don't."

He looked up at me and smiled. "I'm not going anywhere, Natalie."

"Good."

He sat up, bringing me closer and kissing me hard.

The closeness made it harder for me to move, but I didn't care. I had him. Right there, I had him. And he had me. Heart and body, I was his.

He fell back onto the mattress and thrust up into me. I gasped at the feel of him, and he did it again and again.

I met him with every stroke, matching his pace and losing my mind as our bodies slapped together and my heart traveled into his body. He owned it now. He owned me.

"Natalie," he groaned.

My gaze snapped to him, and I saw the same feelings reflected back at me. Love. Desire. Lust.

I couldn't look away from him. I couldn't hide my feelings. I couldn't do anything but stare into his beautiful brown eyes and lose every piece of me to the man I never thought would look at me, let alone look at me like that.

"Come, Natalie. Let me feel it."

My body listened, as though it had forgotten what we were chasing. All of a sudden, I shook and exploded. My orgasm tore a scream from my throat. It ripped all thought from my mind. It left me flopping on top of him, my bones turned to goo and my body a puddle.

"Fuck, Natalie," Omar groaned. "Yes. God, yes. Natalie!"

He swelled inside me and released. His cock twitched, and he surged upward, kissing me sloppily. His hands held me to him, his body soaked and vibrating just as much as mine was.

His kisses slowed and drifted to my cheeks, my eyes, my neck. "I have no words for that."

"Same."

He leaned back far enough to look me in the eyes. I saw his thoughts on his face. The words he was holding back just like I was.

One date. That was all we'd had. One date couldn't possibly make people fall in love. It wasn't realistic. It wasn't natural.

But none of that mattered.

"Thank you," Omar said after a minute. "For not sneaking out on me. For being here this morning. For giving me another chance. For... For being honest with me."

I wrapped my arms around him, needing to hide the tears welling in my eyes. I nodded against his shoulder. "Thank you," I whispered.

There was no way he missed the emotion in my voice, but he didn't call me on it. He just held me until our hearts slowed to a normal pace and his dick slid from my body.

"Let me take care of this, then I'll start coffee and breakfast while you use the bathroom. Is that okay?"

"Perfect," I said.

And it was. I never thought perfect existed, but there he was. Perfect for me.

19

OMAR

THE WEEK AFTER MY DATE WITH NATALIE, I BRACED MYSELF for a third article to come out. After two weeks in a row, I figured one had to be coming.

I searched the paper, twice every day, and saw nothing new about how bad I was for the town. By Wednesday, there was nothing.

Relief was a strange feeling because I didn't trust it. Someone was out there trying to destroy me. Having Natalie on my side helped, but that didn't mean the threat was done.

Or that I knew who it was coming from.

Jane smiled at me when I made it to the office on Wednesday morning. She'd been doing that more and more lately. I wasn't sure why, but I knew everyone in town was aware of my new relationship with Natalie. We hadn't tried to hide it after our date, and I had no intention of doing so.

"How is Natalie?" Jane asked, proving my thoughts.

"She's good. Why?"

"You never told me if you enjoyed the restaurant I recommended."

"I apologize. I should have. It was excellent. Great food and wonderful service. I appreciate the recommendation. Natalie did, too."

"Good. I think she's good for you."

I smiled. "I think so, too."

Jane went back to her work, and I continued into my office.

We were less than a month to the first fundraiser for the campground, and I was seeing more and more about it around town. I was determined to do whatever I needed to do to make sure it was a success. Including reaching out to Goldie Spear to check with her on the progress.

Five minutes before my meeting with Goldie was scheduled, Jane buzzed me through the intercom.

"Mr. Mayor, your next appointment is here."

"Thank you, Jane. She can come right in."

A knock on the door proceeded Goldie as I stood to greet her.

She approached quickly, her hand extended to shake mine. "Good to see you, Omar."

"You, too, Goldie. I hope things are going well. Patrick seems to be doing well."

"We are both good. Thank you. And the tourism department is running as designed. We have a lot of events planned for the summer, and we're really excited about the fundraiser."

"I know it's not within your normal job, but I appreciate you helping out."

"We're all happy to. My son worked at the summer camp last year. He adores Natalie. He's really excited about the idea of moving to the campground. Not that he remembers the campground, but he can imagine the fun things Natalie will come up with."

"She seems pretty amazing at what she does."

"She is. And if you're looking for me to tell you something else, you're asking the wrong person."

"What do you mean? Why would I be asking for you to tell me something else?"

"Can I be honest, Omar?"

"Please."

Goldie took a second, gathering her thoughts. Her blonde hair hung long and loose, tumbling when she moved her head to focus on me once more. "Natalie is a friend. I really like her. I was happy to help her out because I believe in what she's doing. I think you feel the same, but I also know things between you two didn't start out that great. I was surprised when Jane called and asked to meet, especially when she said you wanted to know about the fundraiser. Natalie has it well in hand. She's very organized and methodical. I trust her completely with this. And I'm not sure if you're asking me about it because you don't trust her or if there's another reason, but I'm not going to tell you she's not doing what she's supposed to do."

I leaned back in my chair and absorbed what Goldie said. I laughed softly. "You're right. I apologize. I know how nervous she's been about the fundraiser. She didn't want to do it, and she doesn't tell me much unless I ask directly because of the conflict of interest."

"Conflict of interest? Because you're dating?" Goldie asked, leaning forward and resting her forearm on my desk.

"No, not that. If I'd had a bigger budget for the summer camp, she wouldn't have needed to do a fundraiser. She made a joke about it, and I got defensive."

"Ah, I see. So you're trying to get information out of me because you don't want her to fall flat on her face but you can't ask her."

I chuckled. "Pretty much, yeah."

"Well, I think that's sweet, but it's unnecessary. For one, Natalie is amazing. For another, you should just ask her. She's probably avoiding talking about it for the same reason, but that doesn't mean you shouldn't."

"You're right. And I'm being ridiculous."

"No, you're not. You have a lot going on. Speaking of, how are you?"

"I'm fine. What do you mean?"

Her brows shot high. "The article from today? And the last two."

"Today? I didn't see one from today." I unlocked my computer and pulled up the paper.

"It's not online. Print only."

"What? I didn't know that was possible."

"It's in the free paper they have out in boxes. I brought it. I figured you were going to ask me about that."

I shook my head as I reached for the paper she offered.

Goldie was silent as I read through the latest edition of Omar Knight sucks.

It was more of the same with new quotes from the supposed former employee and more fake evidence that I was playing favorites and supporting my girlfriend's initiatives only.

"You know this isn't true, right?"

Goldie nodded. "Of course. Everyone in my office does, too. I've been drug through the mud before, but mostly it was within this building and not in public. Mayor Levine made sure everyone he spoke to believed I was incapable of doing my job. But he never went so far as to get an article published saying so."

"No, he was just going to cut you off at the knees and replace you with a man who would do as he said," I replied.

Mayor Levine was a piece of work. And a piece of shit. He couldn't see the value Goldie brought to the tourism department, or the value of most women who worked for him. He was a tyrant, and not a day went by that I wasn't happy he was gone.

"Exactly. So who did you piss off?"

I chuckled. "I wish I knew."

"You have no idea?" She seemed surprised by that.

I shook my head. "Not a clue. The woman in the picture—"

"Natalie."

"How did you—?"

"We all know. Maybe not the people who are writing these articles, but Natalie is a friend. She admitted it. But she wouldn't do this. She didn't do this. You know that, right?"

I hadn't considered Natalie until Goldie said that, but I shook my head even as the thought entered. "She wouldn't. I know that. She wasn't always a fan of mine, but she would never do something like this."

"You didn't think she was a fan? Did you see the way she went off on the reporter a few weeks ago? Before you started dating?"

"Yeah, I saw it. And she made it clear she didn't like me."

"That's all in the past, though. Natalie is young and a little scared, and she doesn't think she's good enough for you."

"She told me the same, but I don't understand that."

"People are not always logical. Like whoever is behind these articles. Who is the former employee? Do you know that?"

I shook my head. "No. I fired one person since I've worked in this building. He was using the town computers for personal use and getting to websites that were supposed to be inaccessible."

"Oh. Well, that's interesting. And could be your person."

"It's been years, and he left the area."

"It doesn't matter. These reporters will dig up all kinds of things. Someone also could be following you. See where you go, who you spend time with, checking to see if you're hiding anything."

She was right. And it was likely how they knew Natalie and I were dating. Calling her out and saying I was only supporting her project was pulling her into the middle of all of this. "Natalie doesn't deserve to be dragged through the mud on this."

"I agree. Which is why I think you might need to sit down with a reporter and get your side of things out there."

"I'm not sure that's a good idea."

"I do. Not the one who's been publishing these articles, but someone who's going to actually listen to you."

"I don't think I know anyone."

"A friend of a friend is a new reporter. Worked for the paper years ago, then quit when she had her daughter. She just got divorced and is back working there."

"And you think she'd actually listen to me?"

"Absolutely. She's a good friend of Melody Holland. You know Ramsey, right?"

"Yeah." The idea was getting more appealing.

"Melody said Casey is pissed about the articles. Considering finding a new job because she doesn't like being tied to a place that would try to ruin someone who's doing good things for the town. She also has a daughter who will be going to the summer camp."

"So there's a conflict of interest."

Goldie shook her head. "Not if you're talking about your job instead of the summer camp."

"True."

"How does the rest of your week look? Do you have time to meet with her tomorrow?"

"I'll make time," I said. Clearing my name was too important not to.

"Do you mind if I call Melody right now? I don't have Casey's number, but Melody watches Casey's daughter after school. She sees her every day and can get in touch with her."

"Please do."

I listened to Goldie's side of the short conversation. From what I could tell, Melody was on board and was excited to let Casey know I'd asked for her at Goldie's suggestion.

"Melody is going to have Casey call Jane and get an appointment with you," Goldie said as she put her phone away.

"Then we better tell Jane to make it a priority," I said, getting up from my desk. I opened my office door for Goldie, who stopped at Jane's office with me. "A woman named Casey..."

"White," Goldie provided.

"Thank you. Casey White is a reporter and is going to call to get on my schedule. I want you to set an appointment with her as soon as possible. She's a friend of a friend."

"So she'll put out a good article about you for once?" Jane asked.

Goldie laughed. "That's the plan."

"Exactly."

Jane's phone rang, and we all stared at it. Jane answered and winked at us before clicking over to the calendar. After a minute, she hung up.

"Tomorrow at nine," Jane announced. "She's going to have a photographer with her and said she wants to highlight all the good you've done for MacKellar Cove since you took over as interim mayor."

"Good. Thank you, Jane. And you, Goldie. I appreciate you coming by, and being honest with me."

"Any time, Omar. Have a good rest of your day."

"I think it's good you're doing this," Jane said. "It's good for people to see who you are."

"Thank you, Jane. I hope it's good."

"It will be. Goldie wouldn't have recommended it. She's your biggest fan. Well, maybe second biggest. I think Natalie might have top spot these days."

My lips lifted into a smile at the thought of Natalie. I was definitely her biggest fan.

And there was no one I wanted to talk to about the article more than Natalie.

WITH NATALIE'S late nights at the community center, we didn't see each other during the week very often. I let her know about the article, and she wished me luck. She also asked to hear all about it on Saturday, when we had another date planned.

I was more nervous than I expected to be when I got to work Thursday morning. I knew this one article could have a bigger impact on my future than anything else I did for the next few months. I hated that it was true, but it was how politics worked. If a candidate looked horrible once, it was the only thing anyone remembered.

Thirty minutes before Casey White was supposed to arrive, Jane buzzed my office. I'd closed the door to focus and avoid distractions. I wasn't excited about one, but I answered in case it was Ms. White there early.

"Yes?"

"You have a visitor, Mr. Mayor. She promises to be quick."

"Okay," I said, my heart jumping. A smile lifted my lips even before the door opened and revealed Natalie. "What are you doing here?"

She walked right to me and stepped into my arms without hesitation. "When I have something big like this, I get nervous. A hug from someone I care about helps. I took a risk that it would be good for you, too."

I held her tight and inhaled the strawberry and marker scent of her. My heart rate slowed and my body relaxed. "How do you do that?"

"Years of therapy and lots of meds," she said with a chuckle.

"Really?"

She shrugged, looking embarrassed about her admission.

"No judgement. I just didn't know."

"Anxiety is a bitch. Sometimes it's worse than others. I don't do well when I have to talk to strangers. Adults. I'm fine with kids, but I had a panic attack and threw up before my first open house night when I was a new teacher. Same before parent-teacher conferences. First day of school, I was fine. Kids only? I'm set. But parents? Nope."

"I'm sorry."

"Don't be sorry. It's just a part of my story. And I'm not here to complain about me. I'm here to help you relax."

I quirked an eyebrow at her. "Oh, really?"

She pushed me away. "Not that relaxed."

"Aw, man."

She chuckled and smoothed the lapels of my suit. "Are you ready?"

"No," I admitted. "Goldie was here yesterday and suggested it. Said she thought it would be good to get my side out there."

"She's right. I wouldn't have thought of it, but it's a good idea."

"I was checking up on you," I confessed.

"You were what?" she blurted.

"I wanted to know how things are going with the fundraiser and afraid to ask you. Goldie set me straight. I want to know about the fundraiser. And about your day. And everything about you."

Natalie's face softened. She nodded and stepped into my arms again. "Okay."

I held her tight, letting her presence relax me and remind me I was good at what I did and I believed in not only myself, but my staff and the town.

"You're going to be amazing," Natalie whispered. "You are so good for this town, and people know that."

"Thank you for coming."

"You're welcome."

She pulled back and lifted on her toes to kiss me. We kept it chaste and simple, but I wanted more. I always wanted more from her.

"I'm gong to go before the reporter comes, but good luck. Kick ass. And remember how awesome you are."

"Thank you, Natalie."

"You're welcome." She smiled, holding my hand as she walked toward the door. When she was too far away to hold on, she squeezed my hand, then let go.

I watched her leave, knowing the article was going to be a success.

Casey White arrived a few minutes after Natalie left. Casey and the photographer set up quickly, then we jumped in, exchanging pleasantries.

"Tell me what the most important thing about this job is, Mr. Mayor," Casey said.

"I believe my job is to make every situation best for as many people as possible. To use the town's funds to support the residents and find ways to bring more money into the town to help support it."

"The articles lately have been pretty hard on your position to help out with the new summer camp. Can you comment on that?"

"The new summer camp will be on land that was donated to the town by a very generous family who wanted it to be used for the town. The original idea was to use the property for summer camp. It was the owners' suggestion, and I agreed that it was excellent."

"But it is taking money to fix it up," Casey prompted.

"Of course. We had a very small amount of money in surplus that I directed toward that project because we're getting toward the end of our fiscal year and the money didn't have any other uses. Putting that money into the new summer camp and having the ability to open it up to more students will be a huge benefit to the parents of MacKellar Cove."

"It will be, yes. It'll also bring in some jobs, won't it?"

"Yes. Amelia Rucker, the director of the community center, has some amazing ideas about what can be done with the property. We intend to use it for more than just summer camp. It's going to be an asset to the town, and it's easily going to pay for itself. But first it has to be functional."

"What other projects do you have going on right now?" Casey asked, a gleam of approval in her eyes.

"We are working to get the gazebo in Catherine Park repaired. The River Walk needs some small repairs after the storm a year ago. And our tourism budget expanded this year to help bring more people into town. Goldie Spear is amazing at coming up with events that draw guests to town."

"But doesn't that put a strain on local resources?"

"There is a balance, yes. Always. MacKellar Cove Inn is almost completely booked through summer, from what I hear, and the hotels just out of town are getting close. The other towns in the area are seeing the boost from our town as well, with more of their hotels filling up and more money going into their towns."

"Is that a good thing? Money going to these other towns?" Casey asked.

"Absolutely. As we elevate the overall awareness of the area, people come to all the towns and see the variety. Each of the towns along the Saint Lawrence River has something a little different to offer. We don't compete with each other. We work together and support each other. Goldie has reached out to the other towns and a few of her events this year include visitors traveling the whole length of the Saint Lawrence River from Lake Ontario up to Canada. Everything we do is beneficial for MacKellar Cove and all the other towns."

Casey's grin widened. "That sounds like a lot of fun. Family friendly but not exclusive to families. You've created an amazing team, Mr. Mayor."

"I'm very fortunate. The people who dedicate their time to this town are truly special people. They work hard to make MacKellar Cove not just an amazing place to live, but a great place to visit. And it shows. It's because of that we've not had to raise taxes since I became interim mayor, and I don't see any reason to do so going into next year, either. It's all a team effort, and I am able to do all the things I do because of the team around me."

Casey nodded. "Thank you for your time today, Mr. Mayor. I think I have everything I need. It was a true pleasure to meet you. And I will say I will be voting for you."

"Thank you, Ms. White. That means a lot."

"You mean a lot, Mr. Mayor. Thank you."

"Thank you."

They cleaned up their things and headed out. Jane gave me a thumbs up after they left. I couldn't stop smiling.

If the article was as good as the interview, I was feeling good about my chances at election.

20

———

THREE WEEKS AFTER MY INTERVIEW WITH CASEY WHITE, I had my last meeting with Natalie and Amelia before the fundraiser. Everything was set, everyone was ready, and I had to admit they'd pulled together an amazing event.

"I think we're going to hit our goal, Omar," Amelia said before we ended the meeting.

"I think you might, too. It was a great idea to have the baskets for people to bid on. It's very generous of Hudson to provide food and drinks at cost, too. I know that's a lot of money he's losing, especially on a weekend," I said.

"He was happy to help. He's paying his staff their regular salaries, but everyone who comes gets a drink ticket and a food ticket," Amelia explained.

"He's really looking forward to it. He was talking about it last week. Everyone is ready."

"I just hope we get the money we need. The building kit we want is not cheap, but I think it'll be ideal for us," Natalie said. She studied her notes carefully. "We have some presale tickets, but not enough to cover everything."

"People will come," Amelia assured her.

"Yes, they will. It's going to be a huge success. Everyone wants the summer camp to work." I was completely on board.

"That interview you did a few weeks ago helped. We had a lot of calls from people who wanted to help out after that article," Amelia said.

"I'm happy to hear that. And I'm happy the article was a success," I said. A bad article about me hadn't come out since. That didn't mean I was safe, or that whoever was behind the other articles was done, but it meant things were moving in the right direction.

"What time are you able to be at the fundraiser?" Amelia asked.

I looked at Natalie to answer. I suggested we go together. I wanted to support her, and that meant being there for as much of it as she wanted me to be.

"He's going to come with me at four," Natalie said.

"Perfect," Amelia answered. "Thank you for your help. We definitely could not have done all of this without your support."

"I'm looking forward to the fundraiser," I said, meaning it. It was going to be a fun night, and I had no doubt they would meet their goal.

"We'll see you then," Amelia stood, making her way out of the office and giving Natalie and I a minute alone.

Natalie glanced at her boss, then turned back to me. "I'm nervous about Saturday."

"It'll be good. The scholarships are all set up, and we will announce that on Saturday with the understanding that the summer camp needs to be funded first and anything above your goal will go toward scholarships."

She drew a breath and let it out slowly, nodding and chewing on her lip.

"What else is going on?" There was something.

"How do I act around you?"

"What do you mean?"

"Well, it's a work function, and we've been very professional when either of us is at work. But it's also a social function."

I reached across my desk for her hand, smiling when she didn't hesitate to meet me in the middle. "I think we will do whatever feels right at the time."

"Are you okay with everyone knowing we're together?"

"Yes. Without question. I am not looking to hide from us."

"Okay," she whispered.

"What about you?"

Her gaze snapped to mine, her hazel eyes widening as if the question was ridiculous. "Me? You think I would be ashamed to tell people I am dating you?"

I shrugged. "You asked first."

"No," she said with a laugh. "I think people will be more shocked than anything."

"I wish you could see yourself the way I see you."

"Me, too."

I rubbed my thumb along her wrist. She sighed, then pulled back and stood.

"You're going to make me want to stay here all day."

"Home would be better." I followed her to the door.

"Maybe we can do that on Sunday, after the fundraiser."

"Pack a bag and stay at my house. I'll pick you up Saturday so you don't have to worry about your car."

"In the blue car?" she asked, her eyes wide with excitement.

I chuckled. "In the blue car."

She squealed softly. "I'll see you then."

"Bye."

"Bye."

I watched her walk away, knowing I would do anything for her. She came out of nowhere, but I wasn't sure I could go back to a life without her in it.

I hoped I didn't have to.

O'KELLEY'S WAS PACKED. I could barely move through the bar and wondered if someone was going to call the fire marshal for how many people were in there.

Natalie was immediately swallowed up by Amelia when we arrived, and I'd barely seen her since. She was smiling and talking to people, but I could see the anxiety in her eyes when I did catch a glimpse of her.

"Have you seen Natalie?" a perky blonde woman asked me. It took me a minute to realize it was Daisy.

I shook my head.

"I'm Daisy, by the way. We haven't officially met."

I grinned fully, nodding and extending my hand. "It's so nice to finally meet you. I know I've stolen Natalie away a lot over the last month. I've heard such great things about you."

"Well, I hope my bestie is singing my praises. She better be."

"She's not the only one who adores you. It sounds like you'd give me a run for my money if you decided to run for mayor."

She shook her head, blonde hair tumbling everywhere. "Oh, no, Mr. Mayor, I don't want your job. Not enough play."

I laughed. "There definitely is not. Why don't I help you look for Natalie? I know she's running around and talking to a lot of people. She could probably use a break."

"Uh oh. That's not good because it's time for her to give her speech."

"Does she know she has to give a speech?" I asked.

Daisy shrugged and turned into the crowd.

I followed her, doing my best to look over the heads of the people around us and find Natalie.

Daisy was blindly searching through the crowd, not tall enough to see anything but the person in front of her. She turned at random and made it nowhere.

I finally spotted Natalie to our right and tapped Daisy's shoulder. She turned to look up at me, and I pointed to the right.

Daisy nodded and forced her way through the crowd. A minute later, we were in front of Natalie.

"I brought you a drink," Daisy said, handing over the glass she was carrying. "It's just water."

"Thank you," Natalie said, taking it and sucking half the water down in seconds. "Is it hot in here or it is just me?"

"It's always you, babe. But yeah, it's hot. There are a ton of people. How close are you guys to hitting your goal?" Daisy shouted to be heard above the noise.

Natalie shrugged. "Amelia has been keeping track of everything, mostly. Last I saw her, we were about halfway there."

"That's great news! Hudson has a microphone for you," Daisy said.

"For what?" Natalie screeched.

"Um, you're supposed to give a short speech, hun. Thank everyone for coming and tell them what you're using the money for."

Natalie shook her head as Daisy spoke. "No. I can't do it. No. No. I'll make a fool of myself. I've already been talking to people all night, and I told one couple they should have a party in their shower, and I told another man he should work on making some kids so they can come to my camp. I can't talk to people."

"Yes, you can, Natalie. This is your night. You have been doing amazing. This is going to be nothing for you," Daisy encouraged.

"No. Daisy, I can't. I can't. I need a break. I can't do it. I can't get up in front of everyone and talk. I can't breathe. I can't—" Natalie wheezed, sucking in air and pushing it out quickly. Her eyes were wide with fear. She clutched her throat, clawing at it. Panic was all over her.

"Let's go," I said, grabbing Natalie's arm. "Delay," I told Daisy.

Natalie let me pull her toward the exit and push her outside. She continued to struggle to get air, even though we were outside.

I steered her a few feet away from the door, away from the crowd spilling out of the bar. I pushed her head down, encouraging her to put her hands on her knees. I rubbed her back and hunched down beside her.

"In, two, three, four. Breathe with me, Natalie. Out, two, three, four. Inhale, two, three, four. Good. Better. Exhale, two, three, four."

She took over, breathing without the prompt from me. Her body shook less and her breathing was more controlled and less panicked.

"Take your time."

"I can't do it, Omar. I can't talk to all those people," she said, the panic inching into her voice again.

"Keep breathing for me, Natalie." I waited for her to inhale a deep breath and let it out again before I continued. "You don't have to give a speech."

She jerked upright. "Yes, I do. You heard Daisy. All those

people. They're there. And they're donating all this money. They're supporting my summer camp. They're doing all this, and I have to say something."

"What's the worst thing that happens if you don't?"

She inhaled sharply. "I can't. I can't stay out here and not say something."

"What if I say something instead?"

"What do you mean? Why would you do that? Would you do that?"

I shrugged. "If you want me to, absolutely. I know what the money is going to be used for. I know what you're doing at the summer camp. I know how important it is. I might as well use my position as the mayor for something."

"I can't ask you to do that."

"Sweetheart, I don't mind talking to a group of people. It doesn't bother me. I'm used to addressing a crowd. If you want to do it, I will not tell you not to. I know you can go in there and you can say what you want to say and you can make it amazing. I know you are articulate and intelligent, and you can do anything. I know it. All I'm saying is if you're dead set against it, if you're going to have a panic attack again, I will help you. But I believe in you."

Natalie shook her head. "I don't know if I can do it."

"I do," I said simply. "I know you can do it."

She looked up at me, her hazel eyes trusting and anxious. "How do you know?"

I tucked her hair behind her ear and cupped her jaw. "Because I've seen you in action. I've watched you challenge me, handle contractors, and take on a building full of kids. That last one would scare almost any of the people in that bar, but you do it with ease and grace. Every single person inside is here because they believe in you. They want to see you succeed. They're not here to boo you or tell you that you're not good enough. We all know you are the perfect woman to run this camp and to make the old campground amazing."

"There's no such thing as perfect," Natalie said wryly.

I smiled. The panic in her eyes was almost gone. "Maybe not, but you are definitely the best person to be taking this on. And we all know it. You care, Natalie. You adore what you do. You want this project to be a success. And you will do anything to make sure that it is. Even if it means facing your fears and standing up in front of all those people and telling them you're grateful for their support."

"Will you go with me?"

"Absolutely, sweetheart."

"Will you stand next to me and take over if I freak out?"

"Yes, but I don't think I'll need to. You got this."

She smiled, her eyes lighting up with confidence. "Thank you."

"This is all you, Natalie. Go out there and be you, and it'll all be great."

She surged upward, surprising me with a firm kiss. Her arms went around my neck and pulled me down.

My hands went to her hips and held her close, letting her lead the kiss and take it where she wanted it to go. When she parted her lips and licked mine, I groaned and slicked my tongue alongside hers. She kissed me back, inhaling and bringing her chest into contact with mine.

When she eased back, I released her without hesitation. She rested her head on my chest and shivered.

"Let's get you back inside. It's cold, and you have a crowd to address," I said, kissing the top of her head and turning her back toward O'Kelley's.

Natalie nodded, looking far more sure of herself than when we walked out. She nodded to the man at the door, then took my hand and led the way inside, going right to the bar.

Hudson was talking to a very worried looking Daisy and nodded toward Natalie. They both made their way over. Hudson reached us first.

"How's it going?" he asked.

"Good. Daisy said you have a microphone for me," Natalie said.

Hudson nodded, glancing at me before reaching under the bar. "You're welcome to climb up on top and address everyone. If you want. The ceiling is high enough."

Natalie nodded. She turned to Daisy and smiled, then turned to me. "Thank you."

"All you, Natalie. I'm right here if you need me."

She nodded, then took my hand and climbed on the stool in front of her. She sat on the edge of the bar, then positioned herself to stand.

Once she was up, Hudson handed her the microphone.

Natalie tapped on the end, the sound echoing through the bar and quieting the crowd.

"Hello, everyone!" Natalie said loudly, her voice making the speaker screech.

"Argh!" the crowd replied.

"Sorry about that," Natalie said softly. "For those of you I haven't spoken to or met yet, I'm Natalie Edwards."

A few cheers went up from the crowd, making Natalie blush.

"Thank you, everyone. Um, I just wanted to say thank you to all of you. For supporting the summer camp. For being here tonight. For proving what an amazing community we have."

Everyone clapped, cheering for Natalie and her words.

She was amazing, just like I knew she would be.

"I'd like to offer a special thank you to Harry and Sue, who donated the property we will be using for the new summer camp."

The crowd cheered loudly, even though Harry and Sue weren't there. It was a nice touch from Natalie, and no doubt something they would hear about.

"Summer camp was always my favorite time of the year. I loved being able to play while I was learning. I loved having a chance to share my passion for that with your kids. This camp, and the things we're planning, will help us to be able to expand that to more kids this year."

Again, everyone cheered for Natalie.

The more she spoke, and the more the crowd responded to her, the more confident she looked. My heart swelled with pride. She was doing it.

"There are renderings of what we hope the camp to look like around the bar, and I hope you've had a chance to check them out. Our goal tonight is to raise enough to make the pool and volleyball court functional, to add a building we can use for lunch and when the weather doesn't cooperate, and provide scholarships to camp. When the building is not being used for camp, we will be able to use it for town events and it can be rented out for private functions. We want this to truly be a space that is for the town."

Once more, everyone cheered.

"Next month, if we meet our goal, we are going to have a week of volunteer time. We will be erecting the building we're going to buy. There are signup sheets everywhere, and if you can commit to a few hours, a day, a week, we will definitely be able to use your help. We intend to do the same thing in May. That week we will be working on the landscaping and cleaning up and making the campground more functional and maybe a little prettier."

"Did we meet the goal?" someone shouted.

"Did we meet the goal?" Natalie looked out at the crowd, searching. "Amelia is keeping track of the numbers. Amelia?"

"Here!" Amelia called out. She waved to get Natalie's attention.

"Amelia! Did we reach our goal?"

"We have more than doubled our goal!" Amelia shouted.

The people close whooped loudly.

Natalie's eyes widened. "No. We doubled our goal?"

The crowd went crazy.

"We did!" Amelia shouted over the roar.

Natalie's eyes welled up. She wiped at her lashes, then looked down at me.

"You did this," I shouted.

She put her hand over her heart. "Thank you," she said into the microphone. "Thank you to all of you. For your support. For your generosity. For your trust and belief and commitment. I can't tell you how much this means to me."

Once more, the crowd erupted, cheering and celebrating.

"Nat-a-lie! Nat-a-lie! Nat-a-lie!"

Natalie kissed her fingertips and blew a kiss to the crowd. Her face was red with joy, her eyes overflowing with happy tears.

She handed the microphone back to Hudson, then took my hand to climb down from the bar and fall right into my arms. She buried her face in my neck and let her tears fall.

"I'm so proud of you. So happy for you. You are amazing, Natalie. Amazing."

"Thank you. I couldn't have done any of this without you."

"Still a lot to do, but you will make it happen."

She pulled back. Her eyes were bright and tear-filled. Her cheeks were red and plump from her smile. "I will make it happen. Thank you."

I leaned close and whispered, "Tonight, we celebrate."

She looked up at me, her eyes sparkling. She nodded. "Can we leave now?"

I chuckled. "Soon, my love. Soon."

21

NATALIE

LOVE? HE SAID *MY LOVE*. DID THAT MEAN WHAT I THOUGHT IT meant? Or was I reading into it?

I didn't have time to dissect it before I heard my name in the crowd.

"Natalie! Natalie!"

"Mom?" I turned in Omar's arms and found my mom leading my dad through the wall-to-wall crowd of people.

Mom waved. "Natalie!"

"Mom!"

Omar released me, letting me hug my parents.

"What are you guys doing here?" I asked them.

"Amelia told me about it," Mom said. "She was surprised you didn't. Why didn't you tell us? We wanted to be here to support you."

"I didn't want to make you feel like you had to come. You didn't have to come."

"We wanted to, Natalie. You were great up there. Always knew you had it in you," Dad said.

"Thanks, Dad."

"Bet you showed that jerk you had a date with last

month how wrong he was about you, too. No one's too good for my girl," Dad continued.

My cheeks burned at his words, especially when I felt Omar behind me and knew he not only heard what Dad said, but completely understood he was the jerk in question.

"Um, yeah. Anyway, Mom, Dad, this is Omar," I said.

"Nice to meet you, Mr. Mayor," Mom said. "We're happy to hear you're running this fall. Excited to support you."

"As long as you're good to our girl." Dad crossed his arms and looked Omar up and down. "Are you?"

Omar shook Mom's hand, then let Dad appraise him. "I am doing my best, Mr. Edwards."

"Is your best good enough?" Dad asked.

"Dad!" I hissed.

Dad raised his brows at me. "I don't care how old you are, I'm still your father, and I'm going to make sure any man who kisses you the way he did is holding up his side of things. There's more to life than what happens between the sheets."

"Oh my God. Dad!"

Omar chuckled, his body shaking with humor. "I agree, sir. I'm divorced, but my first marriage was not a good one. I'm not going to make the same mistakes I made then. But I do intend to keep seeing Natalie for as long as she wants to date me."

Dad leveled me with a look, one I knew meant he was waiting for me to answer.

"Dad, we're fine."

Dad nodded, then jerked his chin at Omar. "I'm watching you, Mr. Mayor. And if I find out you hurt my baby girl, we're going to have a very different conversation than this one."

"Da-ad!"

Omar just nodded. "I'd expect nothing less, Mr. Edwards."

"Dean, leave the mayor alone," Mom said. "This is a party. Get me a drink."

Dad kissed Mom's cheek, then left to get her a drink, leaving a withering stare behind for Omar.

"Don't mind him," Mom said. "He's harmless."

"A father is going to do anything to protect his daughter, Mrs. Edwards. I respect that."

Mom smiled at Omar. "I like you. Better than the man who sent you running to our house. How long have you two been dating?"

"About a month," Omar said, holding Mom's gaze and letting her know the truth.

My entire body flushed hot.

Omar slid an arm around my waist. "The beginning was rocky, with a misunderstanding between us. One I have worked hard to correct. I care a lot about Natalie, Mrs. Edwards. I would do anything to make sure she knows how I feel about her."

"And how do you feel about her?" Mom asked.

Omar looked at me. His brown eyes twinkled in the dark bar, the depth of them drawing me in. "I love her, Mrs. Edwards," he said, his gaze locked on mine. "But this is the first time I've said those words to her."

Mom gasped. "Natalie! You have to say something back."

"I would if you would allow me to," I said.

Mom inhaled sharply, watching us like we were the only entertainment around.

"You love me?" I asked Omar.

He nodded. "I didn't intend to tell you like this, but yes, I love you. I have for a while and wasn't sure how to say it. I think I fell in love with you the night we went for a drive.

Maybe when we were trapped at the campground. Or maybe the day you landed on your knees in front of me and nearly castrated me. It doesn't really matter to me when, just that I love you, Natalie."

"I love you, too," I whispered.

"Yeah?" His lips lifted on the edges.

I nodded, pulling him close.

He erased the distance between us and sealed our declaration with a kiss that promised so much more once we were alone. He pulled back long before I was ready for him to, but we had an audience. A large one.

That included my parents.

"Oh, I'm so happy for you, Natalie," Mom gushed. She cupped my jaw, then hugged me tight. "I'm glad you worked things out."

"Me, too," I admitted. I knew one day I would have to tell them the whole story, but not now.

"What happened?" Dad asked, joining us with a drink for Mom and one for himself.

"They're in love, Dean. He just told her for the first time that he loves her." Mom took a sip of her drink, then looked at me with wide eyes. "You were the woman in the newspaper article."

She couldn't have had that revelation without my father next to her? I nodded, but before I could say anything, Omar jumped in.

"Mr. and Mrs. Edwards, that picture was taken out of context. I was walking down the hallway, coming from the bathroom. Natalie walked out of the women's restroom, and a man was racing past. He bumped into her and knocked her down. I tried to catch her, but she fell. That's when the picture was taken."

Dad looked at me with a glare that bordered on murder. "Is that true?"

I nodded. "Yes, that's exactly what happened. It was the night of that engagement party I told you guys about."

"For the hair stylist?" Mom asked.

"Yes, Haley and Knox from Al's Hardware."

Dad nodded, knowing who we were talking about.

"I tried to grab onto something and ended up grabbing onto Omar. But he was just trying to help me. He didn't do anything wrong," I explained, pleading for them to understand.

"That's very kind of you to try to help her," Mom said. "Right, Dean?"

Dad grumbled something that was supposed to be an agreement.

"We should go mingle. And I'm sure you need to talk to people, too. We're so proud of you, Natalie. And Omar, we're so happy to meet you. Hopefully, we'll be seeing a lot more of you. You should come for dinner this week. Tuesday night?" Mom wasn't asking, she was just making it sound like she was.

"We'll do our best, Mom," I answered for us.

"Good. We'll see you then," Mom said before turning Dad to go back into the crowd.

"So, I met your family. Does that mean we're more serious now?"

I shook my head. "No. It means I love you."

He grinned and pulled me in for a kiss. "I love you, Natalie."

"Natalie!" someone else called in the crowd.

"Go shine, Natalie," Omar said, kissing me softly before releasing me to the crowd.

And for the first time, I wasn't afraid to face them.

Because I knew I could do it, and I knew he would be right there with me.

I was quiet on the drive to Omar's after the fundraiser. I was drained and exhausted and needed quiet. He held my hand and allowed it.

I couldn't remember anyone ever allowing me to be quiet. Not my parents, not Daisy, not anyone I'd dated or been friends with. They wanted me to talk.

Omar wanted me to be myself. If I wasn't already in love with him, that would have sealed it.

"Thank you," I said when he pulled into the garage and closed the door behind us.

"For what?"

"For not asking me to talk on the drive here."

"I assumed you were trying to decompress. It was a lot of people and a very busy night and everyone wanted to talk to you."

I nodded. "Most people wouldn't understand that it meant I needed quiet."

He leaned across the center console and kissed my cheek. "I guess I'm not most people. Are you ready to go inside?"

I nodded, releasing his hand and letting myself out of the SUV. Because we were just going to O'Kelley's, he drove the SUV, but he promised we'd take the Bluebird out soon.

Yes, I called his car the Bluebird. He vetoed Blueberry.

Omar held the door open for me, then followed me inside. I was almost ready to crash but a part of me was energized from how successful the event was.

"Water?" Omar asked, going to the kitchen.

"Yes, please."

He poured two glasses and met me on the couch. I'd kicked off my shoes, needing to stretch my toes. I wasn't used to wearing shoes that weren't sneakers, and my feet were killing me.

Omar sat on the couch next to me and handed over my water, then set his on the side table and pulled my feet onto his lap.

I tried to pull them back. "My feet are smelly."

He lifted one to his nose and inhaled deep. "No, they're not. But I'm guessing by the way you keep moving them around, they do hurt. Let me rub them for you. You find something to watch." He handed me the remote and went to work on my aching feet.

I found a movie and moaned my way through the best foot massage of my life. By the time the movie ended, I was a puddle on the couch and barely conscious.

"Let's go to bed. Do you want to change alone?"

I shook my head. "I don't have to."

"Okay." He followed me into his bedroom, where I'd left my bag earlier.

I grabbed my bag and pulled out the outfit I packed for the night. I was feeling spontaneous and sexy, and even though I was exhausted, those earlier feelings were coming back as I changed from my jeans and pretty top into my loose-fitting tank and barely-there shorts. There was nothing overly seductive about my outfit, but both were edged with lace and nearly see-through.

When I caught the look on Omar's face, I could tell the outfit did not miss the mark.

"You're going to kill me." His tone was gravelly and overflowing with desire. The erection he was sporting only added to the impact.

"That was never my intention."

"What was your intention?"

"Celebrating the night, whether it was a success or not."

"It was a hell of a success. And that's a hell of an outfit."

"Do you like it?" I spun so he could see the extra low droop in the back and the way my cheeks were almost exposed.

"Fuck me, Natalie." He crossed the room in three quick steps, not pausing before he captured my lips. His hands went to the low back, scorching my bare skin with his need.

I kissed him back with the same urgency. He'd stripped out of his pants and button-down shirt and was in his boxer briefs only. His skin was warm and smooth and inviting for my fingers.

He cupped my ass with both hands, finding the lace and flesh and groaning when he got his hands on me. He guided us to the bed, pausing to get one more look at me before he nudged me to climb onto his bed.

I crawled to the top and laid down, drawing him on top of me. He positioned himself between my thighs and kissed me again, his hands exploring my body as mine did his.

He thrust against me, revving me up before either of us was out of clothes. He lifted my shirt between us, getting his hands on my exposed stomach before breaking our kiss and dragging his lips down my throat, across my collarbones and over my top to suck hard on my nipples.

He left wet spots behind from his mouth and kissed my stomach, nudging my shirt up until he could access my breasts without a barrier. He nibbled and teased my nipples while I panted and writhed, wanting more and wanting him to never stop.

"I love you," he whispered against my breastbone.

"I love you."

He shoved at my shirt, and I leaned up to remove it. He devoured my fully exposed top half, his lips everywhere at once and driving me wild. When he dipped a finger beneath my panties, I went even more crazy.

"Omar," I moaned.

"You are so beautiful," he replied. "I love watching you."

I pried my eyes open and found him. He was kneeling between my legs, one hand invisible as he played under my shorts. The other hand cupped my breast, teasing my nipple and playing with me.

"I need you."

"I'm not going anywhere." He pressed his fingers into me, and my hips rose in response. "I want to watch you. Then I want to taste you. Then I want to feel you."

I whimpered at his words, desperate for all of it. His thumb rubbed over my clit, then pressed down as his fingers curled deep inside me. I went flying without notice, my body popping like a balloon as I came instantly.

The next moment, my shorts and panties were gone, and his face was buried between my legs. He sucked at my clit and pumped his fingers deep into me, taking me from one peak to an even higher one. He refused to let me fall, holding me on that edge until I tried to nudge him out of the way to finish the job myself.

He growled at my hand and grabbed it with his free one, wrapping his fingers through mine and ruthlessly pounding into me with his other hand.

I flushed hot, then came with a shout, my hips bucking against his face as he fought to hold on and take everything I had inside me.

"Fuck, I love you," he said as he licked back up my body, leaving wet trails all over my stomach. His fingers stayed inside, teasing me and keeping me reaching for more.

"Please, Omar," I begged him.

He grabbed a condom from the nightstand and handed it to me. He kneeled next to me, keeping up the delicious torture between my thighs while I rolled the condom down his length.

As soon as it was on, he crawled between my legs again and replaced his fingers with his cock.

"Oh, God, that feels good," I moaned.

"Yes, you do, my love. So good," he said.

"I love you."

"I love you, Natalie. So much. I need to feel you. Are you ready?"

I nodded, bracing myself.

He withdrew, then slammed hard into me.

My body tightened, the feel of him sending me back up the cliff.

He did it again, his rhythm increasing in speed with every stroke. He pounded into me, losing himself in the moment, but never losing me.

"I love you, Natalie. Love you." He repeated the words, like a chant, his hips matching his words as he took me somewhere I'd never been before.

Up and up, higher and higher, more and more, we climbed together. My throat tightened. My body reached. My orgasm raced for me, needing to let go before I passed out.

"Omar," I breathed. "Omar," I whimpered. "Omar!" I screamed, coming so hard I worried I peed a little.

"Fuck, yes. Natalie!" he shouted, surging and releasing with me.

He pumped into me a few more times, twitching and shaking as his muscles tightened and his body emptied into mine.

He collapsed onto me, and I wrapped myself around him to hold him in place. He trembled in my arms, matching the way my body shook.

We laid there forever, our bodies cooling and steadying, our hearts blending. And I knew, without a doubt, he was the one I was meant to have in my life forever.

I just hoped I got to keep him.

22

OMAR

Natalie amazed me every single day. After the fundraiser, she seemed to own how much people liked her and wanted her thoughts and opinions, and by the time the volunteer week rolled around, she was managing everything like a boss.

Summer camp registration was full in less than twenty-four hours, and she was able to award twenty-five scholarships to kids who wanted to get in but couldn't afford it. The tears in her eyes when she called each of the families personally to tell them said it all.

She was changing lives.

"I don't know how you're so amazing, but I'm grateful you chose me," I told her the first morning of the volunteer week. It was the third week of March, and summer camp was three months away.

She smiled at me over her shoulder and shook her head. "I'm not amazing. I'm just me."

"And you are amazing," I said, walking up behind her and wrapping my arms around her waist. I kissed the back of her neck and enjoyed the shiver that went through her. "Let me know when you're ready to go."

She nodded and went back into my room. She spent about half her nights with me and half at her house with Daisy. I'd stayed with them a few times, but I didn't want Natalie or Daisy to feel like I was invading their space. Or for them to feel like they couldn't have time together without me around. Friendships were important, something I learned over the last month, too.

I'd become a regular at guys' night at O'Kelley's and was getting to know the local men. They were smart, funny, and good men, and I was honored they made me feel so welcome.

All of them, all the women from book club, and so many more people were signed up to help Natalie construct the building for summer camp. The whole thing was coming together.

"I'm ready," Natalie said, pulling a sweatshirt over her head as she headed for the door. She was in faded jeans and a paint-stained tee and had her muddy boots at the door.

And she was stunning.

"You're not supposed to look so hot in those clothes."

"Would you rather I changed?" she asked with a smirk.

"No. I just can't wait to strip you out of them later."

She laughed and tipped her head back for a kiss.

I kissed her soundly, lingering long enough to have my body debating hiding out in bed all day instead of working at the campground.

Natalie, far smarter than me, pulled back with a chuckle. "You're going to make us late."

I shook my head and followed her out the door. "I would never."

She laughed, knowing it was a lie.

She decided to ride with me to avoid having one more vehicle there. I had to convince her I didn't mind if she drove my SUV, or my car for that matter, if she needed to. She finally agreed.

"Have you thought of a name for the summer camp?" I asked as I drove toward the campground.

"I... No. Does it need a name? I thought it would be MacKellar Cove Recreation Center."

"It can be. I thought you might want a name for it. It's going to be so much more than a rec center."

"Hmm. That's true. But do you think I should come up with a name?"

"I do. Natalie's Retreat?"

She wrinkled her nose. "I don't want my name on it. It's for the town."

"What about something with Mountain View?"

"That could be a good idea. I like honoring Harry and Sue and what they built here."

"I bet they would love that."

She nodded. She looked out the window, thinking as I drove the rest of the way to the campground.

Amelia was already there, as were a few other vehicles, when we arrived. Natalie greeted everyone, thanking them for attending.

I followed behind her, letting her shine. Knox, Sofia, Sebastian, and Teddy, who worked for Knox, were all there for the first day of the build. Each of them had extensive knowledge and experience. They divided up the rest of the days of the week, and each was managing the project for one day solo.

Natalie coordinated with the four of them and assigned each of them a color for the day so she could tell volunteers which team they would be working with. It was going to be a big day, but with their skills and Natalie's organization, it was going to be good.

The first volunteers arrived shortly before eight, and Natalie quickly assigned everyone a leader to work with. She joined Sofia's group and started working.

I was assigned to Sebastian's group with a dozen others. Sebastian gave clear, easy-to-follow instructions to the volunteers who were helping.

"When we get this panel done, we're going to raise it up and brace it so it doesn't move. Before we can secure it, we will need to make sure it's plumb and level so everything matches up when all the panels are in place. Then we'll move to the next panel. Each team has four panels to start with." Sebastian met the gazes of everyone in the group.

Natalie had a concrete foundation poured right after the fundraiser, and with inspections done, the building was ready to go up. A sill was installed on top of the concrete for the walls to be attached to, and as a barrier between the concrete foundation and the walls.

Sebastian paired me with a man I didn't know to assemble our part of the wall.

"I'm Omar," I said, offering the man my hand.

"Whoa, the mayor. I know who you are. I'm Andre Davidson."

"Nice to meet you, Andre. How did you get involved in this?"

"I live in Sofia's building. In Knox's fiancée's old apartment, actually."

"Haley," I said.

Andre nodded. "Yep. She decided to move in with him, and I finally managed to sneak out of my parents' house."

"Sneak out?" Andre had to be close to my age.

He chuckled. "My dad had a stroke a few years ago. I was

floundering a little and trying to figure out what I was doing with my life. I moved back home to help my mom out since it was a lot at first with my dad."

"Wow. I'm sorry. How's your dad now?"

"Great, actually. You'd never know anything happened. But my parents didn't want me to leave again, so they kept coming up with things I needed to do to help them out."

"Ah, hence the sneaking out."

Andre laughed. "Yep. I think it went over better that I stayed local. I hated it here when I was younger, but coming back I realized it's not a bad place to live."

"I agree. I can't imagine being anywhere else."

Natalie laughed, and I looked over at her. I loved seeing her relaxed and enjoying herself. Not that her anxiety was gone, or she would ever be cured. I knew it didn't work like that. She still struggled, but she had a new confidence since the fundraiser. It was amazing to watch.

"You two are pretty serious, aren't you?" Andre asked, bringing me back to our task.

I nodded. "We are. I'm lucky."

"You are. Not that I'm looking to steal her from you or anything. I've never looked at a woman the way you look at her. She's lucky, too."

"It's that damn app," I told him.

"What app?"

"Book Boyfriends Wanted," I confessed. "I met her on there. There's some weird luck with that app. A bunch of local guys get together every Thursday night, and all of them met their women on that app."

"All of them?" Andre asked.

I nodded. "All of them. Sebastian, James, Knox. Many more."

"Tell me the name of that app again."

I laughed. "Book Boyfriends Wanted. But be careful. You might get more than you bargained for."

"I'm counting on it," Andre said. He tapped his screen, then tucked his phone away. "Thanks."

I nodded. We returned to our task, doing our part to construct the wall panel before attaching all the sections together and raising the panel.

Sebastian verified the position of the panel, then secured it in place. As a group, we moved to the second panel, finishing it as lunch arrived.

Tailgates were dropped, folding tables appeared from nowhere, and music poured from the speakers of one truck. Everyone grouped together to pass around bottles of water, bags of chips, and sandwiches from a local shop.

Laughter echoed all around, conversation flowing. Natalie walked toward me, thanking every group as she made her way through the crowd.

"Hi," she said, leaning down to kiss me.

I captured her, pulling her onto my lap with a squeal and a laugh. I nuzzled against her neck and tugged on her ear with my teeth.

"Omar," she hissed. "People are watching."

"No one cares," I said. I'd chosen a seat a little away from the crowd in case she needed a break from the busyness of all the people.

She wiggled on my lap, then sat next to me on the tailgate of my SUV.

"How do you think everything is going?" I asked her.

"Really good," she said with a happy smile. "I'm amazed we've gotten so many of the outside walls done already."

"There's still a lot to do, but you have a great team here."

"Well, thank you," Andre said, appearing in front of us.

"Didn't mean to interrupt, but I wanted to say how excited I am about this place."

Natalie smiled at him. "Thank you. Do you have kids who will attend?"

Andre laughed loudly. "No. No kids for me yet. I know how good this will be for the town, though. I'm Andre."

"Are you the Andre who moved into Haley's apartment?"

"Guilty as charged."

"Nice to meet you. Haley speaks very highly of you," Natalie said.

"Well, I think very highly of Haley. And Knox. I'm very happy for them."

"Are you single? I have a friend I should set you up with."

"I am single," Andre said. "And very interested in single friends of yours."

Natalie laughed. "I'll talk to her tonight. Thanks for being here, Andre. We need all the help we can get. What do you do?"

"I have a small landscaping company. Mostly residential, but I'm trying to get into some commercial stuff. I just got the contract for MacKellar Cove Inn for the summer," Andre said.

"I didn't know that," I said.

Andre nodded, looking shy and humble for the first time since we spoke. He never once mentioned his job or that he probably wanted the contract for town hall.

"Would you be willing to help me out with the land-scaping for this place when we're done with the building?" Natalie asked.

"Absolutely. I knew this week was all about the building, so I didn't bring my trailer, but I was going to ask if you needed any help with landscaping. It's a quiet time of year right now. I plow driveways and parking lots in the winter, but snow is pretty much gone and we're not ready for a lot of outdoor work yet."

"It'll be here before you know it," Natalie said. "Can I get your number?"

"Definitely." Andre took her phone and added his information. "Andre Davidson, and my company is Davidson Outdoors, so you know who that random guy in your phone is. And so he knows." Andre jerked his head toward me with a wink.

"Ha ha. I will remember you."

Andre laughed. "I'm not sure that's good or bad. You're a powerful man to know my name. Should I be worried?"

"Have you done something that requires it?"

Andre chuckled. "Good point, Mr. Mayor."

"I'm going to call you, Andre. I have a crew coming out to pave the driveway and parking lot in two weeks, but I'm going to need the landscaping cleaned up before we open."

"I can bring my trailer later next week if there would be a good day. Trim back everything at the road to start with and take care of the volleyball court. Make sure everything is out of the way for the paving company. Then I can come out before you open and spruce it up a bit."

"I don't know if I have a budget for sprucing up, but we can talk about a few ideas," Natalie said.

"If you let me put up a sign here, or a flyer where the parents sign kids in and out, I'll do it all for free," Andre said.

"Free?"

"The number of people who will be in and out of here every week will more than pay for my expenses. I'll even maintain the property for you, again for free, for the first three years."

"Three years?" Natalie gasped.

Andre nodded. "Like I said, I believe in what you're doing. I know it's going to be good for the community. Families need this. My expenses are small, and my work is quality. I'm hoping to hire a few new people, but I have a good relationship with Landon at Blossom & Grow. If he knows it's for you, he'll likely give me everything for free or very low cost. If you're open to whatever we come up with."

"I love that place," Natalie breathed. "And yes, of course I'd trust you both. That's very generous of you."

Andre smiled. "It would be my pleasure, Natalie. Truly. Thank you for what you're doing here. This guy's mostly pulling his weight, but I'm kind of carrying him." Andre mock-whispered the last part.

I scowled at him.

Natalie chuckled. "Well, I keep him around for other reasons, too."

Andre's eyes got big, and Natalie clapped a hand over her mouth.

I chuckled.

"I didn't mean it like that. Oh my God. That's not... I'm going to stop talking now," Natalie said.

"Probably for the best," I told her. "And I think most of your volunteers are ready to get started again, if you're ready."

"Yes, I'm ready. And I need to go nail my mouth shut, so I'll say thank you, Andre. It was wonderful to meet you, and I look forward to working with you more."

"You as well, Natalie."

Natalie walked back to the center and spoke to Sofia before their group got back to work.

"I like her," Andre said.

"I love her," I told him.

"I sort of figured. This place is something special. So is your woman."

"Yeah, she sure is."

THE REST of the day brought a skeleton of a building, including the framing for the roof. The building was massive, with three panels at each end and six panels down each side of the building. When the volunteers left, the crane rolled in.

Knox, Sofia, Sebastian, and Teddy were working with Teddy's old crew to get the metal roof on the building. Natalie didn't want any overheard crane work done with the volunteers around, and everyone offered to get it done at the end of day one.

When that was in place, and the building looked even bigger, everyone called it quits for the night.

Day two was punctuated by the constant sound of hammers as plywood was wrapped around the entire building, then vinyl wrap was secured over it. Windows went in that afternoon, followed by the first rows of siding.

The siding was finished on day three, doors were installed, and plumbing and electrical went in through the entire place. Another inspection gave us the go-ahead for insulation.

If my position had one advantage, it was that I could have an inspector on standby when we needed one. He came back first thing on day four to check the insulation so we could move on to drywall.

"It looks like a real place," Natalie said as drywall was screwed into place by teams of four. She hired a crew to work on the ceiling since it required scaffolding, but everything that could be reached by ladders was handled by the volunteers.

"It is a real place. It's going to be amazing."

"It is. I can't believe what we've done this week. And Andre is going to come out next week to clear the landscaping at the front so I can get the camper moved."

"Where are you going to move the camper?"

"I'm going to stick it over by the tree line while we're paving, then figure out the best place for it."

"Are you sure? Those trees look like they could fall at any time."

Natalie shook her head. "It should be fine. It's the best place for it while they're paving, and I want to move it anyway. Since we're going to make the site available for other town functions and private events, I think it would be better if the camper was not the first thing people see when they drive in."

I laughed. "It's not the prettiest thing ever, but it's functional."

"Yeah, it is. Eventually I want to replace it with something a little nicer, something with more bathrooms and a better office. Possibly a permanent structure, but that's low priority."

"You have a lot going on."

She groaned. "I know. I feel like I'll never finish it all before summer."

"You will. I know you will. First the building, then the parking lot."

"Yeah, the asphalt company is coming in a few weeks to pave the driveway and parking lot and seal the basketball court, then we need to stay off all of it for at least three days."

"Still plenty of time before you need to open," I said.

She nodded. "Yeah. We'll get lines painted for parking, and we'll get the camper moved back into place by the end of April. The pool company is going to come out in early May. Andre will finish the landscaping whenever he can get out here."

"That was really great of him to offer to help like that."

"Yeah, I hadn't planned on a lot for landscaping, but it'll definitely add something to the place."

"It will. And so will your second group of volunteers."

"I forgot about that! See, so much going on."

"Good stuff, though. One thing at a time. For now, stand back and look at what you're creating. What you've put together. What this town has done."

She smiled and looked out at the landscape. Tears filled her gaze. She nodded. "Wow."

"This is all thanks to you, Natalie. And so much more is coming."

23

NATALIE

THE CHATTER AROUND ME BOTHERED ME LESS THAN THE FIRST time I walked into Serenity Salon. Not that I wanted to admit to Daisy that she was right about setting a regular appointment with Chelsea to have my hair cut and styled. I would never hear the end of it.

"How's the summer camp coming?" Chelsea asked as she washed my hair.

"So good," I admitted. "I'm so impressed with all the work we've been able to do so far."

"This town is special, isn't it?"

I nodded. "It really is. I still can't believe people not only donated so much but also gave up their time to help bring the building to life."

"Haley and I are coming again for the second week. Only for a day, but it looked like you have a full week of volunteers again."

"I do. It's blowing my mind. But I'll need them. We're going to be putting up a fence around the pool and making things look nice. Planting around the office and decorating the building. I haven't been able to get in there much, and I want it to be a fun place for kids but also a nice place for adults."

"You'll figure out that balance. I'm working on it myself with Derek and I moving in together. Of course, with Dozer, I don't have nice things anyway," Chelsea said with a laugh. She wrapped a towel around my hair and pointed to her chair.

I sat up and moved across the salon to the chair next to Daisy, where a very pregnant Haley was at work on Daisy's new cut.

"Tell Haley she's glowing," Daisy said when I sat down.

I looked at Haley in the mirror and smiled. "You are. You look very happy."

Haley scowled. "I feel like I'm a million pounds and giving birth to an elephant."

"You are not going to be pregnant for twenty-two months," Chelsea said in a tone that told me Haley had been complaining a lot.

"I don't know. It seems like it," Haley said.

"Please talk some sense into her," Chelsea said to Daisy, meeting her gaze in the mirror.

Daisy chuckled. "I'm not sure what I can say. I've never been pregnant, so I don't know what she feels like."

"Same," I said when Chelsea looked at me.

"Even if you were, no one had an elephant baby," Haley said.

"You are so dramatic," Chelsea said, laughing at Haley.

Haley scowled. "Just wait until Derek decides he wants more kids and you are pregnant forever."

Chelsea's eyes got wide, and she stopped what she was doing. "We haven't talked about more kids."

Haley, realizing she hit Chelsea's panic button, came over. She took Chelsea's hands and breathed with her. "I was joking. You guys will talk about kids together. You have to decide if you want them."

"Did you and Knox talk about it?" Daisy asked.

Haley nodded. "We did. We weren't planning to get pregnant so soon, but we both wanted kids."

"I've always wanted kids," I said. "Ever since I was little. My sisters are a lot older than me, and I thought it would be fun to have a sibling to play with."

"Me, too," Daisy said. "I have twin brothers, and I spent my entire childhood watching them play hockey. I didn't do any activities because they took up so much time. I always wished I'd had a sister so I had someone to play with."

"That's so sad," Haley said, dabbing at her eyes. "I didn't have siblings at all. Oh my God, I have to do this again. I can't have a kid who doesn't have any siblings. It's not fair to them. I was so lonely growing up, and—"

"Breathe, Haley," Chelsea said loudly. "Your kid will be fine. Everyone is different. Haley and Chelsea just said they had siblings and were lonely. I didn't, but I had a cousin who was like my sister. You were an only child and were independent because of your parents. You and Knox are not going to be like your parents. And your kid will grow up with a town full of people who want to know him or her."

Haley nodded with Chelsea.

I smiled at them in the mirror, then caught Daisy's gaze. She smiled back. We always talked about having kids at the same time and raising them like cousins.

"You're right. You're right," Haley said. "God, these hormones. I don't love it."

Haley moved back behind Daisy and returned to her task.

Chelsea started on my hair, combing through it and pinning up one large section so she could begin.

"You don't know if it's a boy or a girl yet?" Daisy asked once things were back on track.

Haley shook her head, a smile on her face. "Knox wanted to be surprised. We talked about it a lot, but he said he doesn't care. The most important thing is knowing our baby is okay, or knowing what to do if there is a problem. So far, everything is going really well."

"I don't know if I could do that," I admitted. "I think I would want to know."

"Are you and Omar talking about kids?" Chelsea asked.

I shook my head, narrowly missing a catastrophe when Chelsea was about to cut my hair.

"Don't move," Chelsea said, eyes wide. "Okay, no kids yet. But things are still going well?"

"Yeah," I said, keeping my head still. "He's nothing like I first thought he would be."

Chelsea laughed. "Oh, I so feel that. I hated Derek before we met. Thought he was such a jerk. I'm glad I was wrong."

"We are all glad you were wrong. But he was kind of a jerk before you two got together," Haley said. "Those notes he left on your door?"

Chelsea laughed. "Whenever he gets on my nerves, I remind him about those. He stops complaining real quick. It's pretty much a lifetime apology."

"Oh, you're mean," Haley said.

Chelsea shook her head. "Nah. He knows I'm just messing with him. We're good."

"Have you set a date yet?" I asked her. Derek proposed not long ago at a party in Chelsea's backyard.

"We're thinking about early summer," Chelsea said.

"Whoa, that's fast," I blurted.

Chelsea laughed. "Yeah, it is. But it's easier for us to do

something when Jude isn't in school. He'll be at your camp, but we're thinking about a long weekend away for a short honeymoon and then a family trip sometime later. My parents want Jude to stay with them when we're gone, but I need someone to watch Dozer. There's no way my parents could handle him."

"I'll do it," Daisy said, waving at Chelsea. "I love that dog."

"I couldn't ask you to do that," Chelsea said.

"Oh, please? I really would love to. He's such a sweetheart, and I love dogs. Another thing we never had growing up. Because of the hockey tournaments, we were on the road all the time, and my parents said we couldn't have a dog," Daisy explained.

"Have you ever had a dog?" Chelsea asked, her face betraying her worry.

"Nope, but I love them. I can stay at your house, if that's okay, so he's comfortable. Natalie will help me, right?" Daisy met my gaze in the mirror.

I shrugged. "Sure. We had a dog when I was in high school. I like dogs."

"He needs to be walked a lot. Twice a day at least," Chelsea said.

"Chelsea, I promise you, I will do everything you ask me to do. I will take really good care of him." Daisy smiled, pleading her case without more words.

Chelsea sighed and shrugged. "Okay. Thank you. But if you change your mind, let me know. Dr. Harris offers boarding if we have to do that."

"Nope, I will take care of Dozer. I'll come over before then so he can get to know me." Daisy focused on the mirror in front of her again so Haley could finish her cut.

Chelsea smiled, but there was stress around her eyes.

She focused on my hair, staying silent while the shop around us stayed busy.

When Haley turned on the dryer to style Daisy's hair, I nodded to get Chelsea's attention. "She'll be great. She adores Dozer and will take really good care of him."

Chelsea nodded. "I know. I'm anxious about leaving him. I was trying to talk Derek into going somewhere we could all go so we didn't have to leave Dozer behind. He's been through a lot, and it hasn't even been a year since I've had him. I don't want him to think I've abandoned him."

"He'll be so happy when you guys come home. Maybe we can meet up with Jude and your parents so they can see each other," I suggested.

Chelsea's eyes brightened. "That's a good thought. I'm so ridiculous, worrying about my dog."

"No, you're not," I assured her. "Dogs are a part of the family. You love him. There's nothing wrong with that. Plus, you know your parents will take excellent care of Jude, so Dozer is the concern."

Chelsea nodded. "It'll be fine, though. Thank you."

I smiled, happy I could ease her worries.

Chelsea grabbed her hairdryer to finish my hair when I felt my phone buzzing in my pocket. I ignored it, letting her start, but it rang again right away.

I held up a finger for Chelsea to stop and dug out my phone.

The hairdryer stopped.

"The pavers. Hang on. They're painting lines at the camp today. They must want to confirm something."

Chelsea nodded and stepped away so I could answer.

"Hello, this is Natalie."

"Hey, Natalie, this is Chuck with Total Paving. Uh, sorry to bother you, but we just got here, and there's a problem."

"What's going on, Chuck? I thought you guys were good to paint today."

"We are, and we can. But the camper thing you have?"

"Yeah?"

"Uh, a tree fell on it."

"What?" I screeched.

Every machine in the salon turned off, the dryers, the shampoo, everything. Silence echoed in my ear.

"Yeah, I kind of figured you didn't know yet."

"Uh, no, I didn't know a tree fell on my office. Dammit."

The collective gasp around me reminded me I wasn't alone.

"Sorry, Natalie. Do you still want us to paint lines? We can hold off if you want to come out here and look at it before we get started."

"Yeah," I said, tugging at the cape Chelsea had around my neck. "I'll be right there."

Chelsea stepped forward and unsnapped the cape as I hung up the phone. "Are you okay?"

I shook my head, a mirthless laugh escaping. "No. I... Crap. Omar said the trees looked like they were going to fall and told me not to put the camper where I did. I thought it was fine."

"You couldn't have known," Haley said.

"He knew," I spat.

"What can we do?" Chelsea asked.

"Nothing." I drew a deep breath and let it out slowly. "I need to go look at this and see if it can be saved. I'm sorry I'm rushing out. Let me pay you before I go."

"Don't worry about it," Chelsea said.

"I'll take care of it," Daisy replied. "I'll meet you out there in a few minutes."

"You don't have to do that," I told her, grateful my hair was done besides drying and styling.

"I'll meet you out there soon," Daisy said firmly. "Go. See what it looks like."

I nodded and thanked them, then left.

My heart raced the entire drive over there. It was only a few minutes, but I imagined the worst the entire time, trying to figure out a backup plan.

The easiest thing would be to put a table in the building for parents to sign kids in and out.

But without the camper, we didn't have bathrooms.

Dammit.

I turned onto the newly paved driveway from the road and wanted to cry. It was stunning and exactly what I wanted, but then I saw the camper.

And I did start to cry.

I parked near the trucks and closed my eyes, hoping it was all a dream and when I opened them again, everything would be fine.

No such luck.

I wiped my tears and climbed out of my SUV. There were voices all around me, the painting crew getting ready to start their day. Chuck said they only needed one day, and I was sure they had other jobs to get to, and I was holding them up.

Chuck and two other men were out by the trailer. I made my way across the grass to where they were, my throat tightening with each step as I got closer and saw the damage more clearly.

"Wow," I breathed when I reached them.

Chuck turned and nodded. "Sorry, Natalie."

One of the other men came from the backside of the camper and walked right over to us. "Worst-case scenario," he said, nodding to me. "The framework is snapped. It can be fixed, but it'll be cheaper to buy something new than it will be to fix this thing."

"Crap," I said with a sigh.

"Johnny, this is Natalie. She's the owner," Chuck said in a stern tone.

"Shit, sorry," Johnny said. "I didn't mean—"

"It's okay," I told him. "I would have found out eventually. Nothing you can do about it."

"Sucks, though. Boss, you want us to get those chainsaws?" Johnny asked.

Chuck nodded. "Yeah."

Johnny and the other guy walked back toward their trucks and Chuck turned to me.

"We're going to get the tree cut up and off the camper. I know it doesn't help much, but I figured we could at least help with that. No charge, of course."

"Chuck."

He shook his head. "My grandson got one of the spots here. My daughter was so happy. He didn't get in last year, and they had to go down to A-Bay for summer camp. Having it here is huge for her and my son-in-law. If I had a camper to give you, I would. If I had anything I could give you, I would do it. Getting that tree out of the way isn't much, but it's what I can do right now."

"Thank you, Chuck," I said, my eyes filling with tears and my words coming out as a whisper.

He nodded and squeezed my shoulder as he walked past, giving me a few minutes alone by the camper.

I stared at it through my tears and wondered what I was going to do. The only money I had left was for the pool repair. It wasn't enough to buy a new trailer, not for a decent price. Anything I would buy would probably look about the same as the smashed one I was standing in front of.

Voices approached, and I knew I had to move so Chuck's guys could cut the tree down. My mind raced with options, but I couldn't come up with one. I couldn't run a camp without a bathroom. Without the camper, I didn't have one.

"Natalie," Omar said from right behind me.

"What are you doing here?"

"Daisy called me. Are you okay? I'm so sorry."

I scoffed. "You can say I told you so."

"What? Why would I do that?" Omar asked.

"Because you told me not to put the camper here. You were right. I should have listened to you. If I had, then I'd still be able to open up camp this summer."

"You're opening camp. Why would you not open it?"

"That's my one and only bathroom, Omar," I shouted, throwing my arms wide at the broken camper. "I can't have a summer camp without giving the kids and staff a place to use the bathroom."

He closed his eyes and let out a sigh. "I didn't think about that. Nothing by the pool?"

"Nope. The pool has changing rooms, but no bathroom facilities."

"Dammit," he breathed.

"Exactly. Which means this is over. All this work. All these kids. All for nothing."

"Natalie," he said as I walked away.

"Chuck's guys are going to cut the tree away. We need to give them space. And I need to figure out how I'm going to tell all the families that were planning to send their kids here that it's not going to happen and they need to find another summer camp. Two months after every registration in the area opened. Dammit!"

"Natalie," he said again.

"Omar, I can't right now. I just... I need to figure this out."

He stopped following me.

I stopped to tell Chuck to go ahead, then went to my SUV. Daisy pulled in just as I was about to get in and leave.

"How bad is it?" Daisy asked.

"Worst-case scenario. Camp is done. Before it even starts, it's done. I need to get out of here. They're painting lines, so you need to go, too. Although I don't know what the hell good lines are going to do when there is no camp, but whatever. I'll see you later."

Daisy nodded, not arguing with me as I climbed in my SUV, slammed the door, and drove off.

With only my tears for company.

24

OMAR

ALL I COULD DO WAS WATCH HER WALK AWAY. I DROPPED everything to go to her, and she didn't want me there. She was angry at me for something I had no control over.

"She's broken," Daisy said, approaching without me noticing. "What are we going to do?"

"She doesn't want my help. She blamed me for this. Said I told her not to put the camper here and is mad at me for not listening to me."

Daisy stepped in front of me, blocking my view of Natalie's SUV disappearing onto the road. "She will get over it. Her world just got rocked, and not in the way you've been doing lately."

I snorted a laugh that made Daisy smile.

"See? It's not all bad."

"It is if she can't open the camp."

"She can't open the camp?" the man who appeared to be in charge asked. "Why not? What are the kids going to do?"

I pointed at the demolished camper. "That was the only bathroom out here. Without it, she can't open."

"You can't let that happen. You're the mayor, right?" the man asked.

I inhaled sharply. He was right. I wasn't useless. I wasn't helpless. I might not have a camper in my back pocket, but I could get out there and do something. "Don't say anything to anyone about the camp not opening. We're going to figure something out."

"We are?" Daisy asked.

I turned to her. "We have to. We can't let something like this stop her. Stop all of this. She's worked too hard."

Daisy grinned. "That's what I'm talking about. What can I do?"

"We need to find a new camper."

"Seriously? Where do you think we're going to find a new camper? Why don't we just buy another one of those prefab buildings? That'll be cheaper," Daisy said.

"She wants a permanent structure, but that's going to require a lot more. There's already a septic system here from the old campground, but it needs to be upgraded before putting in a permanent building."

"This just gets better and better," Daisy said.

"We will figure it out. We have to. There has to be someone who isn't using an old camper."

"Okay. Okay, we can do this. How old?"

I chuckled at the disgusted look on her face.

"You weren't here before that one was cleaned. It was hideous."

"I heard. And I don't care what condition the thing is in as long as the bathroom is functional. It would be better if we could find something with more than one bathroom, but we'll do what we can. At worst, we'll have to bring in portable bathrooms."

Daisy wrinkled her nose at that one. "That's worse."

"But it works. We aren't going to let these families down, and we're not going to let Natalie down. Are you with me?"

"For Natalie? Absolutely."

"Thank you for calling me, too. Even though she wasn't happy to see me, I'm glad I knew about this."

"I'm sorry she was so mad. Give her a few days."

I nodded, hating that I had to stay away from her. I wanted to go to her and tell her it would all be okay, but if she didn't want me around, I'd give her the space she needed.

Back in my SUV, I knew I needed to go back to work, but I had to make another stop first.

O'Kelley's was quiet at noon on a Tuesday, but Hudson was there. His wife, Anna, was at the bar, smiling at him as she enjoyed her lunch. Hudson straightened when he saw me marching over to them.

"Mr. Mayor. Omar. Don't typically see you here during the day."

"Sorry to barge in on you two. Hi, Anna."

"Hi, Omar. What's wrong?"

"The camper Natalie was going to use for the office and bathroom at the summer camp is crushed. A tree fell on it. She said there's no chance at making it work. It's bad."

"Oh, shit," Hudson breathed. "No bathroom, no camp."

I nodded. "Exactly. I know a lot of people come through here every day. If you hear of anyone mention a camper or trailer or something with a bathroom they're looking to get rid of, will you let me know? We have time, but we have to figure out something. Preferably not portable toilets."

"That is an option," Hudson said.

"Yeah, but I'm hoping it's not the only option we have. Give me a call if you hear of anything."

"We will. Sorry, Omar. I know Natalie has to be pretty upset."

I nodded and left it at that. I couldn't bring myself to admit she wasn't speaking to me.

I went back to the office and called Amelia.

"Have you heard about the camper?" she said when she picked up.

"I did. That's why I'm calling you. Don't let her tell the families camp won't happen."

"What why?"

"We'll figure out something."

"Why can't you tell her that?"

"She's upset with me. And I get it. I'm giving her space because she asked me to, but I'm going to figure something out."

"I hope so because she walked in here and went right to her office, grabbed some stuff, and left again. I've never seen her look so defeated."

"I'm going to get a portable toilet out there today for the people working on the parking lot. Do you happen to know who it is? I wasn't thinking, but without the camper, they don't have a bathroom right now."

"It's probably Total Paving. Chuck is the foreman. Do you want me to give him a call?"

"Yeah, if you could, I'd appreciate that, Amelia. I'm going to have a toilet there ASAP. Tell him to have it set wherever they want it."

"Okay. Thanks, Omar. We'll figure something out for our girl."

"Yes, we will."

I HAD NOTHING. Not a damn thing. A full week of searching every dusty corner of the internet and reaching out to everyone I knew in the area, and I hadn't come up with any good options for a camper for Natalie.

I was starting to worry.

Her pool guys were starting in a week, and the portable toilet I paid for out of my own pocket was still there, but it was a horrible option for the entire summer.

A hot summer and a bunch of kids. It spelled disaster. And disgusting.

The phone on my desk buzzed. "Yes, Jane."

"Derek Bailey is here to see you, Mr. Mayor."

"Send him in. Thanks, Jane." I stood, walking around my desk to greet Derek. He was a good businessman and a better friend, but he wasn't on my calendar.

Derek knocked once, then opened the door and came in. He approached me with his hand out for a shake. "How are you, Omar?"

"Good. Thanks. What can I do for you, Derek?"

Derek grinned. "It's actually what I can do for you."

"What are you talking about?"

"How flexible are you on that camper you've been looking for?"

I gasped. "You found something? Really?"

Derek nodded. "Last week of the month, so we have a lot of inspections coming in. A family had a trailer that didn't pass inspection."

"Yes. I mean, sorry for them."

Derek chuckled. "I know. They told me they haven't used it for four years, and have kept up the inspection, but that's as much as they've driven it. It's okay, but it needs work to get it road-worthy."

"But if we're not putting it on the road..."

"We would have to make some modifications to it, though. So it can't be on the road."

"Which means?"

"Removing the wheels."

"Put it on blocks?"

Derek chuckled. "Basically, but we would have to have some kind of foundation for it. Something that says it's no longer a vehicle."

"Can we do that?"

Derek nodded. "We can. And even better, the family is willing to part with it for next to nothing."

"How next to nothing?" I asked.

Derek told me a number.

"Done."

Derek grinned. "I had a feeling you would say that. The only other catch is we have to get it onto the camp property by the end of the month, since May first it's no longer legal to have on the road."

"So, Saturday is our deadline."

"Yep. Can you make that happen?"

"Know anyone with a truck?"

Derek nodded. "I think I have a friend."

I chuckled, feeling like all this was going to work. As long as Natalie would take my call and let me help her out.

DEREK AGREED to keep the trailer at his shop until I had a chance to let Natalie know about it. When he got back, he took a bunch of pictures and sent them over.

It was rough. It was an old trailer, but it had a decent sized bathroom and could be functional. Both sides slid out, but the mechanism to slide didn't work, so they had to be shoved with brute force. But once they were out, they were secure.

It had to work.

I sent Daisy a text, asking her if Natalie was going to be home that night and if she thought I could stop by. Daisy said Natalie was working until five, but would be home after that.

I told her I'd be there at five-fifteen.

I traded cars after work, then drove the Bluebird to Natalie's. With any luck, she would be willing to go for a drive with me and I could show her the trailer.

Daisy said to park on the far side of the driveway so Natalie wouldn't see my car from the door, so I did, then walked up their driveway. I rang the bell and wiped my sweaty hands on my pants.

"Coming!" she shouted from the other side of the door. Then she was there. "Omar."

I wasn't sure if the look on her face was a good one or not, but I wasn't there for me. "Will you let me take you somewhere?"

She shook her head. "No."

All my hope faded. I took a step back.

"Not until I apologize for the way I treated you last week. I was upset, and I took it out on you, and I never should have said what I said to you. I know you weren't there to rub it in that you were right. I was a jerk. And I hope you'll be able to forgive me eventually."

I surged toward her, capturing her jaw in both hands and inhaling her. I stopped just before my lips touched hers. "There is nothing to forgive. You had every right to be upset. But I love you. I'm here for you. The good and the bad, Natalie."

She nodded, her throat working as she swallowed hard.

"I... I love you, too. I'm not used to that. To having someone who wants me to succeed as much as I want you to succeed."

"You have Daisy. And your parents."

"Yeah, but they're family. They have no choice."

"I have no choice either, Natalie. That's what love is."

She nodded, her eyes filling with tears. She tilted her jaw and eliminated the distance between us. Her lips were warm and soft and inviting.

I groaned, feeling right for the first time in a week. Her hands slid around my waist and pulled me closer. I wasted no time doing the same, cupping her butt in one hand and threading my other hand into her hair.

"I guess she likes the camper, huh?" Daisy interrupted.

"Not funny, Daisy. You know the camper is crushed," Natalie said, pulling back from me. "But it wasn't Omar's fault."

Daisy looked at me with wide eyes.

Natalie caught her look. "What's going on?"

"Let's go for a drive."

"What is she talking about?"

"Why don't we go for a drive?"

Natalie turned to Daisy and pulled out of my arms. "What are you talking about? What camper?"

Daisy gave me a panicked look.

I shook my head, but she sighed.

"He bought you a new camper. I thought he was showing you pictures of it. I didn't know he was going to take you to it. I'm so sorry," Daisy gushed.

"You bought me a camper?" Natalie shouted.

"I... Yes. If you want it. Technically, it's not purchased yet, but if you think it'll work, then I'm going to buy it."

"The town doesn't have any money for a new camper," she said.

I snorted. "It's not new."

She grinned. "How bad is it?"

"Yeah," Daisy said, "how bad is it?"

"Do you want to go look at it with us?" I asked Daisy.

Daisy shook her head. "No. I'm good here. You two go. Text me later. See you tomorrow!"

Daisy grabbed Natalie's handbag and pushed us out the door. She slammed it behind us, locking it for good measure.

"You know I have keys," Natalie called through the door.

"You know you'd rather be out there with him than in here with me. Go enjoy. You have a week to make up for, and I don't want to be around to hear it," Daisy said.

Natalie looked up at me and burst out laughing. "I guess you should show me this camper."

I nodded and stepped into her personal space. She smiled right before I kissed her, meeting every stroke of my tongue with one of her own.

We were panting by the time we pulled apart and headed for Bluebird.

"How in the world did you find a new camper?" she asked.

I told her about Derek showing up and the family who doesn't use it anymore. I explained everything Derek told me on the way to Stone Auto Repair. When we pulled into the lot, I crept around to the back, where Derek said it would be.

Natalie gasped when she saw it.

It was so much uglier than I thought.

I turned off Bluebird and got out.

Natalie climbed out and came around to stand next to me. She burst out laughing. "It's hideous. But I love it."

I let out a breath and chuckled. "It is pretty ugly. The inside might be worse, though."

"Do you have the keys?"

I handed her the key Derek gave me earlier. He kept one in case they needed it, but wanted Natalie to look at the whole thing.

Natalie unlocked the door and opened it, holding her breath for a minute. "Well, it smells better than the last one."

I exhaled. So far, it was okay.

Natalie walked inside. There was no power, so she pulled her phone out and turned on the flashlight. I turned mine on so we could get a look at the place.

We walked into the main living area. A gray couch was to the right and had definitely seen better days. To our left was the world's smallest kitchen, with an even smaller banquette taking up most of the walkway. The vinyl on the banquette seats was ripped. The appliances were yellow. Through the kitchen was a bathroom that was surprisingly spacious for a trailer.

"And you're sure they don't want this?" Natalie asked.

I nodded. "That's what Derek said."

She nodded, then put her face in her hands and sobbed.

Shit.

I was at her side in two steps and gathered her into my arms. She wrapped her arms around me and buried her face in my chest. My heart broke as she cried.

So much for hoping this would be what she needed. It wasn't right for her.

"I'm sorry this isn't good enough, Natalie. We'll find something else."

She pulled back and looked up at me. Her face was

streaked with tears, but she was smiling. "Not good enough? This is amazing."

"What... Then why are you crying?"

"Because you did this for me. I was a complete jerk to you, and you've been working your ass off to find something like this for me. I don't deserve you."

I opened my mouth to argue with her, and she put her finger over my lips.

"I'm not giving you up, but I don't deserve you."

I nibbled the pad of her finger.

She gasped.

"I don't deserve you, Natalie. But I'm so happy I have you. Now, let's get out of here so I can show you how much I missed you."

She nodded, dragging me toward the door as fast as we both could go.

EPILOGUE
DAISY

I PUT THE FINISHING TOUCHES ON MY DISPLAY TABLE AND looked around the camp. Mountain View Retreat was done and ready for the grand opening party. And so was I.

"This looks amazing," Natalie gushed when she stopped in front of my table. A dozen of us were set up inside the new building with all the doors and windows open wide to encourage people to wander around and check out everything there was on site.

"Thanks. It was such a great idea to have people here. And to show off the Retreat to everyone before camp starts next week."

"I wasn't sure we'd ever make it to today, so I'm happy this place is functional."

"It's so much more than functional," I told my bestie. Natalie worked her ass off to create the place she dreamed of. Nothing stopped her. Not the tree on the camper, not the minuscule budget she had, not her anxiety, and definitely not her boyfriend, even when he was being a pain at the beginning of the whole thing.

Natalie looked around, pride in her gaze. "It really came together, didn't it?"

"Yes, it did. And you got Omar out of the whole deal."

Natalie chuckled. "I almost screwed all of that up."

I shook my head. "No. He understood. You know that. And the trailer he got for you is better than the crushed one, anyway."

"Yeah, it is," Natalie agreed reluctantly. "All of this is better than I imagined it would be."

"Today is a day for fun. What time are people coming?"

Natalie looked at her phone. "Soon. We officially start in twenty minutes, so probably any time. Do you need anything?"

"Nope, I'm all good."

Natalie hugged me. "Thank you for being here. And your table looks amazing. I need one of these tattoos." She grabbed one from the front of the table.

"Take whatever you'd like," I told her. I had temporary tattoos made with my store logo and a cute animal picture. The same designs were also made into stickers. And I bought some mini beach balls and footballs with my store name on them. Kids could grab an item and parents would remember where it came from, and hopefully come in to the store next time they were shopping for toys.

"Thank you. I'll be back soon." Natalie waved and moved on to the next table.

I kept messing with things and debating if it was all perfect until the first vehicles rolled down the driveway and parked. Excited kids got out with wide eyes and even wider smiles.

That was my favorite thing ever. Seeing happy kids.

I was busy for the next two hours as a steady stream of families came through the camp. Kids played basketball and volleyball on the newly refurbished courts. Families jumped into the pool. Laughter followed everyone around.

And through it all, Natalie beamed with pride and joy. Omar was never far from her side, a hand on her hip when she faltered and a whisper in her ear when no one was talking to them.

I was so damn happy for them. I wasn't so sure about Omar at first, but he was a good man. Exactly who Natalie needed in her life. She was happier than I'd ever seen her, and she was more herself than I ever thought she'd be with a man. She was the person I knew, not the person she showed others.

I was not looking forward to the day she would move out and I wouldn't see her every day, but I was looking forward to watching all her dreams come true.

Cars drifted out of the parking lot and the other vendors packed up their things to head out. I only had a few swag items left, and I decided to leave them with Natalie for any families who didn't make it out to the grand opening.

Omar and Natalie were near the office trailer when I walked out of the building. Their heads were together, reading something on his phone. Natalie's mouth dropped open.

I rushed to them. "What's wrong? What happened? Is everything okay?"

Natalie looked up at me and exhaled a laugh. "You're never going to believe who was behind the articles about Omar."

"I thought there was no way of knowing." Omar searched for months, asking the reporter and putting pressure on the editor of the paper. No one would tell him anything about who was giving them the information.

"Casey White, the woman who interviewed Omar?"

"I remember. Melody's friend. She's behind it?"

"No, no. But she wanted to know, too. She didn't stop looking, even though after her article, no more came out. She just texted Omar. It was Mayor Levine."

"What?" I screeched. Mayor Levine resigned two years ago, and Omar took over as the interim mayor. I didn't know a lot of the details, but the little I did know sounded like it was not Mayor Levine's choice to leave.

Natalie chuckled. "That's what Casey said. The reporter who wrote the articles about Omar got the picture of us from a family friend of Levine's, someone who wanted him back in office. Once he had the picture, all they had to do was concoct a story about Omar and the article was done. The reporter fell for it, even though most of it was not true."

"Most of it?"

"The picture was real, but it was taken out of context. Omar did fire someone, but not the person the reporter interviewed. Everything that was in those articles had a hint of truth, but only if you didn't know the real truth."

"Wow. That's horrible. Why would Levine want to come back here?"

"That's what I've been wondering," Omar said. "When he left, Patrick made it clear everything he did would be exposed if he tried. I'm guessing he thought enough time had passed and everyone would have forgotten about him. If he made me look bad, then he looked good by comparison."

"Not even close," I said. "No one wants to see him in charge again."

"Well, Casey is going to run a story about him and all the things that happened, so he's not going to get a chance. It'll bury him," Omar said.

"Is that really necessary? Why destroy him when he's gone?" I asked.

Natalie shook her head. "He's not gone. Just because she found out he's the one behind all of it doesn't mean he's gone. She said it sounds like he's planning to announce his campaign next week."

I shook my head. I didn't like seeing people ruined, but the man had done it to himself. I wasn't going to be a fan of someone who opposed people in positions of power based on gender, or any other trait that had nothing to do with their skills, but a part of me felt for the man. He should have just stayed away.

"He can run, but I'm not going to hide what he did from the town if he's going to try to lead again. I was willing to let it go before because he couldn't do anymore damage, but I won't let people choose him without knowing who he really is," Omar said.

"That makes sense. Too bad he didn't move on." I shook my head, wondering what would have made him take the risk.

"At least now I know why I was being attacked. And I know Natalie is safe from the same." Omar turned to Natalie and kissed her softly.

My heart twisted with jealousy. I hated the emotion. I wasn't jealous of Omar, or Natalie, more that I wanted the same thing they had. A person who would do anything for me. Someone who supported me and was there for me. I'd never had that. Ever.

"We're going to head out," Natalie said. "Are you coming over for dinner later?"

I shook my head, knowing they needed time alone after their discovery and the day. Natalie would never tell me she was exhausted and wanted time alone, but I could see it in her eyes. "I'm going to check on the store and then have a quiet night. I'll see you tomorrow at book club."

"Are you sure?" Natalie asked.

I hugged her. "I'm sure." I hugged Omar. "Have a good night."

"You, too," they said together.

I walked to my car and pulled out of the lot ahead of them. I watched them kiss and talk next to his SUV in my mirror.

I was happy for them. I really was. I wanted Natalie to have everything she ever dreamed of. And it was so good to see her getting it.

The store was quiet, so I went home after checking in with my staff. They could handle the weekend traffic, and I wasn't needed.

I turned on some music and changed into shorts and a tank top. I started dinner, dancing around the living room. It had been a good day.

My phone dinged from the kitchen, drawing me back to my food. It was almost ready. I grabbed my phone and smiled when I saw I had a new match on Book Boyfriends Wanted.

"DrGrumpy? Who would call himself that?" I chuckled and checked out his profile. "What's the best that could happen?" I asked myself, smiling as I sent him a message. Maybe he would be the one I'd been hoping for.

THANK you for reading Natalie and Omar's story! I always wanted to find someone for Omar, and Natalie was just right. Their story took a little while to come together, but I hope you loved it as much as I did!

The next book in the series is Daisy and Kingsley's story. When they're matched on Book Boyfriends Wanted, Daisy is intrigued. He's different than anyone she's ever known, but she finds herself wanting to know more about him. Until they meet in person, and she finds out he's not who she expected. At all. Preorder His Curvy Sunshine now and start reading on January 14!

WANT MORE from Omar and Natalie? The election is over, but did Omar win? Bonus epilogue is only available to subscribers. Sign up now!

LOVE MEN in charge and women who bring them to their knees? She's a superstar hiding her true identity. He's a CEO who thinks everyone wants something from him. All they want from each other is one night, but when she turns up on his doorstep the next day, neither of them can resist. Read Walk Of Fame today!

ABOUT THE AUTHOR

USA TODAY Bestselling Author Mary E Thompson spent most of her childhood wishing she had a few less curves. She hid in the pages of books because her favorite characters never cared what size her clothes were. Now, neither does Mary, and she writes stories that celebrate women like her. Real women who have curves, chase dreams, and find love, because we should all be happy, no matter our dress size.

Mary spends her non-writing time with her husband and two kids, watching too much TV, cheering for her hometown football team (Go Bills!), and hiding chocolate from her family.

Visit https://MaryEThompson.com/ to sign up for Mary's newsletter, **Romancing the Curves**. Subscribers get free ebooks and other fun stuff, like exclusive, members only content and giveaways, plus are the first to know about new releases and sales!